# SOMETHING SO PERFECT

NATASHA MADISON

Cover Design: Melissa Gill with MG Book Covers & Designs

Book formatting: CP Smith

Editor: Emily A. Lawrence from Lawrence Editing

Proofing Author Services by Julie Deaton

Proof Reader: Virginia Tesi Carey

To the readers, each and every one of you who bought *Something So Right* and made my dreams come true. I'm forever in your debt!

Matthew Grant
Karrie Cooney

# PROLOGUE

Walking down the rubber mat to the ice, the smell gets you right away. Dry. It's a smell you can't describe. I've been skating before I could walk, according to my mom. I live and breathe for this sport. Even at the age of twenty-five, I still crave getting on the ice. When I'm almost near the door leading to the rink, I take off running, my skates sliding over the clean surface.

Game day is a mix of different things for different players. For me, I get up early, get a workout in, and then relax till I have to make it to the rink, usually five hours before the game, to eat and get in the zone.

The second I put my skate on the ice, the crowd goes wild.

Little kids all line the boards, watching us skate around, shooting the puck doing drills. I stop in the corner and look up at the crowd as they take their seats while Ozzy Osborne's "Crazy Train" fills the arena.

"Big game," my line mate, Phil, says right when he stops next to me. "We need this win if we want to qualify for the playoffs."

I handle the puck that's ready on my blade for me to shoot at the person skating from the other side. I look down at the ice, and the

Beavers are coming out strong, their goalie stopping every single puck that comes at him.

"I want to fucking smash those assholes," is the last thing I say before I take off to the center ice. The puck passed to me by Phil lands directly in the middle of the blade. I snipe it in as soon as it hits. Top corner, right over the goalie's shoulder. My goalie, Luka, tells me to "fuck off" when I skate by him. I salute him while making my way to the bench where a reporter is standing interviewing our assistant coach.

The coach walks away from the reporter, putting papers away in his coat pocket. The reporter looks at me. "You want to be interviewed, Grant?" he asks while checking his phone.

I look him up and down. "Now you want to interview me?" I ask him, grabbing the water bottle on the ledge, squirting some in my mouth. "Weren't you the one who started this fucking dumb campaign?" I smirk at him while checking the tape on my stick. "I believe the correct words were 'time to hang up the skates, he's done.'"

His head snaps up and he tries to say something, but I ignore him and skate back to center ice.

Chuck Harris, a Boston Beaver, is there watching me. "His highness is back." He stands there looking at me. "Word is that your babysitter is a walking sex doll. Is that true?"

He's trying to bait me, trying to make me snap. I smirk at him, keeping my cool. That isn't me anymore. I'm calm. I'm in a good place, and it's all because of Karrie. I look up at where I know she will be sitting, but her seat is empty.

I tilt my head to the side, wondering where she could be. The game is about to start. She is usually in her seat when we warm up, so I look around the arena to see if she is anywhere else.

"Whatcha looking for?" Chuck smiles while he takes a drink from the green Gatorade bottle. I don't bother answering him because the bell signals that it's time for the Zamboni, so instead, I skate to the bench and head for the dressing room.

I sit down, taking off the tape from my stick and throwing it in the garbage, then getting my roll of tape that's right next to my cell phone. As I reach for the tape, I see my phone light up with my mother's number. She knows I'm on the ice, so it might be an emergency.

"Hello," I answer the phone, looking around.

"Matthew, thank God. I want you to listen and say nothing. I have you on speaker. Cooper is here, too," she says, and then Cooper's voice sounds out. "Listen to us before you talk. Got me, son?" His voice is clipped.

"What the fuck is going on?" My heart starts pounding, and my neck gets hot, while I hear a commotion coming from outside the locker room. Voices rise behind me.

"There's a warrant out for your arrest. Someone is accusing you of beating and raping her yesterday," Cooper hisses out while I look at the door that's being slammed open. "I have the lawyer already on his way to you. You say nothing, son, nothing."

Two suit-wearing detectives come into the room. "Matthew Grant"—they flash their badges—"we have a couple of questions we need to ask," one of them says while I hear Cooper still on the line. "Don't say a fucking word, Matthew. We are coming to you."

"Now?" I hear Coach behind me yelling. "You do this to him now, two seconds before he's supposed to go on the ice?" He glares at them. They obviously couldn't care less.

"You need to come down to the station with us," the man continues, but I'm standing here with my mouth open, my ear drums pounding, and the phone to my ear. "We can walk out of here civilized or we can strap the cuffs on you. One way or another, you aren't getting on that ice."

My teammates are standing up to see what's going on and shaking their heads.

"This is bullshit." I hear Coach say while the guys nod.

Phil comes up to me and whispers, "Don't say a fucking word."

I don't have time to process things before I'm being ushered out of the locker room. The only thing I take off is my skates.

I walk out of the building and I'm led into an unmarked car. When I look out the side window, I see the owner of the team is now standing with Karrie by his side. His hands are around her shoulders, her face streaked with tears. "Karrie!" I yell from inside the car. "Karrie!"

Nothing. She turns around and walks back into the arena, leaving me alone with the silence that now fills the car.

# CHAPTER ONE

## MATTHEW

*Cooper Stone is my stepfather, the Cooper Stone who's the best person to ever skate. He holds every single record that's out there because he's just that fucking good.*

*"What the fuck are you doing?" I didn't even have a chance to say hello before Cooper's voice filled the room. I groaned and turned over to see that he was on speakerphone. My finger must have touched it by accident. "Matthew, seriously, I'm one second from flying out there and yanking you off the fucking ice."*

*I was twenty-one and already being benched and scratched.*

*I was no chump. I was drafted first over all. The day still played in my mind. "The Los Angeles Royals choose Matthew Grant." The minute my name was said, I sat there in shock while my little sister was yelling and my mother, Parker, had tears running down her cheeks while her face lit up with happiness and pride. Cooper was the first to grab me and stand me up.*

*"Go get that fucking jersey." His voice was loud in my ear.*

*My mother was next. "I'm so proud of you, Matthew, so, so proud."*

*I kissed her cheek and walked down the stairs toward the stage from where the general manager, the owner, and the coach all looked at me. When I walked on stage, I tried to hold my tears in.*

*Taking the owner's hand in mine, I shook it and thanked him. Putting that jersey on was surreal. Posing for pictures was a blur. I got so drunk that night I don't remember much, except Cooper having to carry me inside while I pledged my love to my mother, my sister, and the trees around us.*

*Usually, once you get drafted, you start off on their farm team, but not me. I was on the starting line. I was up to my ears in silicone. There would be a different girl every night, everyone wanting to get a piece of me. The star of the team. Then my game started to slip. The late nights took a toll on me and my body. Three years later, I was sent down to the farm team. You'd think I would wake up, but no, not me. I just partied harder. I was on the front page of almost every single tabloid magazine that you could think of.*

*Every single summer I went back home, spending the time training hard with Cooper riding my ass, promising him that I was out of the party phase, but the minute my feet landed back in L.A., it was back to the booze and the puck bunnies. Another three years later, I was put on wavers. When no one picked me up, I packed up and went back home. For two years, I played hockey at home in charity games, till the GM from the New York Stingers came knocking at my door. Robert Western.*

*Cooper, Mom, and I sat down with him. My hands shook with nerves, my legs bouncing with happiness that someone actually wanted me.*

*"We want to offer him a one-year contract, with certain rules." He eyed me and then Cooper. I knew Cooper had called in a favor.*

*"What is it?" I asked, holding my breath.*

*"Chaperone."*

*I was about to get up and say fuck that when Cooper put his hand on mine and blurted out, "He'll do it."*

*I looked at him while he glared at me. My mother put a hand on top of her husband's. United. Always.*

*Robert slapped his hands together. "Matthew, you, my friend, are going to bring another cup to New York." He got up to shake my hand*

*and then Cooper's, slapping him on the arm. "Who knows, you may also knock this asshole off a throne or two."*

*Cooper laughed out loud, but I knew he would be the one egging me on, the one daring me to push him off. He would also be the first one coming to congratulate me if I ever did it.*

*He had come into my life when I'd needed a male figure the most. I just hadn't known it. He showed me that you can fall in love with your whole heart and everything will fall into place. He showed me that you fight for what you want. But most of all, he showed me that love is a gift and once it's given, you cherish it.*

So now here I am on the plane getting ready to land in New York. I have to meet the owner of the team and the PR people tomorrow at noon. I scroll through my social media sites while I wait for the doors to open. My sister is tagging me in old photos of us from Mom and Cooper's wedding. Feels like it was just yesterday. When you see the way Cooper looks at my mother, you know he loves her with all his heart. He would walk to the ends of the earth for her.

I press the heart emoji on the picture and then hear the ping of the seat belt sign telling us we can stand up. I grab my leather jacket and slide it on, put on my aviators, and grab my leather duffel bag. Walking out of the plane, I nod at the two flight attendants, who both slipped me their numbers. Numbers I left in the side of the seat.

Fresh start. It's time to make my parents proud of me. Time to show the world that Matthew Grant is here for good this time.

On my way to my hotel in Times Square, I look out the window of the yellow cab zigzagging its way through traffic. Nothing in the world beats the cab drivers in New York City. You sit back and hold your breath while you pray to not end up being slammed forward. We reach the W hotel. I swipe my card through the card holder in the back, thanking him. I don't even have time to close the door before he races off from the curb.

I enter and check in without having anything to say. The woman at reception starts going through her routine talk. I cut in. "What floor is the gym on?"

She smiles at me, telling me the information while giving me her private number in case I have any other questions.

I nod at her and then walk up to my room. It's the size of a closet. Welcome to New York. I take my phone out to send a text to Cooper.

**Landed. Going to work out.**

**Be good.**

**I'm always good.**

**Okay, then behave.**

I laugh and throw the phone on the bed, and then get my workout clothes out of the bag. I grab my headphones and make my way to the gym.

I have texts from Allison, my sister, and Tom, who is married to my aunt Meghan and is an ex-NHLer, wishing me luck. But the one that makes me laugh out loud is from my Aunt Meghan, telling me that my dick won't fall off if I don't use it. I'm about to answer her when the elevator beeps, signaling I have arrived at the gym floor.

I walk to the gym and scan my card so I can get in. Usually, these hotel gyms are almost empty, but not this time. A girl is jogging on the treadmill, but I don't make eye contact with her.

Grabbing a towel from the basket in the corner, I walk over to the other treadmill, look down at the buttons, and turn it on.

I start off slow while Drake fills my ears, but that doesn't last long before I crank it up and push myself hard. I'm in the best shape of my life, thanks to my mom, Cooper, and Tim. They didn't let me sit down and drown my sorrows in bonbons and booze. They had my ass skating at the crack of dawn. In the gym pushing and pulling. Meaning I'm the biggest I've ever been. My shoulders are wider, my waist leaner, my arms bigger.

I'm sweating up a storm, so I look over to see if the girl is still running on the treadmill, which is my first mistake. Not only is she next to me running as fast as me, but she's in a sports bra holding up a perfect set of tits, her stomach bare, her abs defined but looking soft, and her little booty shorts not keeping anything back. She isn't tall. Her blond hair swings in the air while she's looking at the iPad she has in front of her. Is she watching the Kardashians? Jesus. She must sense me watching her because she looks over, which is when I feel the earth move under my feet. Her eyes are crystal blue, so blue it's like I'm looking into the ocean. I almost trip over my own two feet, but I recover and smile at her. I turn my head forward and continue running till my legs feel like they're going to snap in two.

Getting off the treadmill, I whip my soaking shirt off and throw it over my shoulder before I grab a water bottle and drain it all. I notice she's slowing her speed. She shuts off the treadmill, dabbing her face with the towel that she has near her. She takes the water bottle, drinking in a good amount.

I start to walk out of the room when she gets off the treadmill. I stop right before we collide with each other, then put out my hand, giving her the right of way.

"Thanks," she says, her voice soft, sweet, pure.

Following her out, I watch her ass swing in front of me. I don't even notice she stops and I crash into her, grabbing her shoulders and making sure she doesn't fall on her face because I was staring at her ass. "I'm sorry, I was…" I'm sure I don't have to say anything to her because my cock is nestled in her back.

She shrugs my hands off her shoulders while she presses the elevator button. We stand here not saying anything while we wait. What can you say? Sorry my dick poked your back? Sorry I was watching your sweet ass instead of watching where I was going? Silence is golden right now.

When the elevator arrives, I wait for her to walk in before entering and see that we are on the same floor. Great. The ride lasts no longer than a second before the door opens and she sprints out, away from the crazy pervert who poked his dick into her back. I head to my door and see she's in the room right next to mine. I want to say something, anything, but by the time I look up, she's already in the safety of her own room.

# CHAPTER TWO

## KARRIE

I wait for the door to click before collapsing on it and letting out the breath I've been holding in. Jesus, I didn't think the first time I'd meet Matthew Grant would be when I was running on a treadmill in the middle of a gym watching the Kardashians. I slowly slide down to the floor, thinking about how I got here.

*I rushed into the building my father owned, running past security while I waved hello. I was a few minutes late and I knew my father was a stickler for that. 'Karrie, the early bird gets the worm.' It was stuck in my brain. He summoned me to his office early that morning, not giving me a chance to say no. As soon as I reached the floor to Cooney Communication, I walked to the corner office I'd been visiting since before I could walk. My great great-grandfather started this company. Over the years we'd branched out to entertainment. We owned the Cooney SportsCenter where our hockey and basketball teams played as well as all the sold-out concerts.*

*My mother and I would visit every single Thursday, our standing lunch date until she passed away from breast cancer at forty-two. Then it was only me. He would send the car for me and we continued on the tradition. I think this was why I came today. The calendar showed that it was Wednesday. Once I got to my father's office, his assistant, who had also been there for longer than I could remember, smiled at me as she took her glasses off.*

*"Look at you." Alice got up and came around the desk to hug me.*

*"Hey, Alice." I hugged her back. "I was asked if I could come in. I thought it would be for lunch, but," I said while I let her go, "I guess it's not."*

*"You look just like your mother." She smiled at me while she took my face into her hands.*

*"She does, she really does." I heard from behind me.*

*I turned and came face to face with my father. My father, I had to say was my hero. He stood at six foot four, blond hair, and blue eyes, eyes that still had the sadness from losing Mom, even though he tried to mask it. I walked up to my father and wrapped my arms around his waist.*

*"Dad." I lay my head on his chest. He leaned down to kiss the top of my head.*

*"Did you eat?" He let me go as I entered his office. "Alice, can you please get us something to eat?"*

*I knew she'd already picked up the phone and ordered our favorite food. My father's office hadn't changed in forever. Family pictures were hung on the wall. Pictures of my mother were still on his desk. Their love was that of a love story.*

*Rich boy met a poor girl from the wrong side of the tracks. Fell in love against the odds. Not only had they run off and got married, they lasted longer than anyone thought they would. They did it with love, honor, and respect.*

*I threw my purse on the low coffee table in the center of the office and took a seat on the couch. My father came over and sat just across from me.*

*"So are you settling in well?" he asked since I moved into a Brooklyn brownstone he bought for me without my consent or knowledge.*

*"Dad, you bought me a brownstone," I told him, "not a small apartment like you said. It's a flipping brownstone." I had never lacked*

*for anything. I had about four trust funds set up for me, yet I still attended a public school and hung around with 'normal' people, as they put it.*

*"It was an investment." He smiled at me. "Besides, I'm still not talking to you for paying your tuition all through school, so call it even." Not only had I paid for it myself, I actually got a job. My father was so proud of me, even if it was just at the coffee shop. "Now, I asked you to come here for a reason." His voice got very formal, which made my eyebrows pinch together. "I have a job offer for you."*

*"Dad," I huffed out, about to get off the couch. "We discussed this. I'm going to get my own job. I have a master's in communication and public relations. Surely that will get me somewhere." I had been a nerd in high school, so much so I graduated a year ahead of everyone my age and I was no different having completed my master's degree in just under two years.*

*"Listen to me before you start, Karrie." He got up, going to his desk where he took a folder in his hands. "We've just acquired Matthew Grant," he started, and I looked at him, not sure if I should have known who this was or not.*

*He placed the file down in front of me, and I opened it up and came face to face with the most handsome man I had ever seen in my life. His hair looked like he'd just run his hands through it. His face had a well-trimmed beard, his eyes chestnut brown, the same color as his hair. But what got me was the dimple on one side of his face. His smirk had melted many hearts as well as panties for sure. He was dressed in a suit with his hands in his pockets.*

*"He had been drafted number one over all when he was seventeen."*

*I started to go through the file he had given me, taking in all his stats.*

*"He's got a bad rep." My father started, but I put my hand up.*

*"Bad rep. He got sent down after a couple of years for partying too much. It says"—I looked back—"and I quote, that he slept through a whole game before he realized he missed it." I threw the file on the table. "How could you have actually signed him? He has trouble stamped all over him in big bold letters." I waited for his answer.*

*"His stepfather is Cooper Stone."*

*My eyebrows shot up. You couldn't be a hockey fan and not know*

*Cooper Stone.*

*"Plus, the new coach wanted him"—he looked down and blew out a breath—"and I agreed, but only if he would have a chaperone."*

*All the pieces started clicking into play. "You are not serious!" I asked, "You want me to babysit him?"*

*"No," he replied, "I want you to make sure he doesn't get into trouble, and all his publicity will be handled by you. I want you to feed stories to the press. I want to make sure by the end this guy looks like a reformed monk."*

*"Dad"—I shook my head—"you can spin this however you want to spin it. You want me to make sure he doesn't get in trouble. You want me to watch him and hold his hand. It's a babysitter."*

*"You are the perfect person for the job. Besides, it's an entry-level position, so no one is giving you anything. You would also have to travel with him to every single game, as well as let him have a room in the brownstone." His eyes moved to the floor while he said the last part.*

*I flew off the couch. "Are you insane? You want me to live with a menace to society? What if he's a serial killer and we don't know? What if he's a cross dresser? What if he brings home hookers, or better yet drugs, and I'm stuck in the middle?" My voice rose. "You can't honestly think this is a good idea." My hands went to my waist while I waited for him to say something, anything, that he agreed this plan was insane, but instead of agreeing with me he leaned further into the couch and smiled at me.*

*"Honey, you are over-exaggerating. I would never put you in any danger. You know this. And besides"—he hugged the back of the couch—"we do random drug screening."*

*I stood as I looked at him, my mouth open, no words coming out.*

*"Where is the little girl who wanted to save the world? Just think about it. You could make this into the best turnaround story out there."*

*I glared at him and crossed my arms over my chest. I knew what he was doing. He was baiting me. I'd never turned down a challenge, another thing I got from my father. He got me to stick to my eight thirty bedtime till I was fifteen on a dare. A fucking dare.*

*"I want a contract," I informed him. "And an out clause." I pointed*

*my finger at him. "If at any time I say 'I'm out,' then I'm out."*

*He nodded at me.*

*"No objections to that." He smiled at me. He knew full well he had won. "We can even include a signing bonus." He leaned forward as he placed his hands on his knees and smiled.*

*I rolled my eyes at him, and as I was about to tell him to hush his mouth, the knock on the door stopped me. Alice walked in followed by Robert, the general manager of the team.*

*"Karrie." He approached me as he put his hand out and shook mine. "I didn't know you'd be here."*

*Alice placed a brown deli bag down on the table, along with a couple cans of soda.*

*"I asked her to come over to discuss Grant. Robert, meet his new chaperone." My father pointed to me.*

*"Are you serious?" Robert looked shocked, to say the very least. "I thought more of a man who is eighty and has wrinkles." He placed his hands into his pockets.*

*My father shook his head. "No one's better than Karrie. Set up the meeting for tomorrow and let's get this show on the road. I have to head down to California in two days. I want everything worked out by then. I want him on the ice on Saturday when we face Pittsburgh," my father ordered.*

*It wasn't an option at this point, so Robert just nodded.*

So now here I am as I get ready for tomorrow. I've been staying at the W for the last two days while they paint the brownstone and turn his room into what they are calling a 'man cave.' As I've been told. I get up from the floor and make my way over to the shower, opening it on cold. I need to cool down. Jesus, if he was hot in pictures, it is nothing compared to what is in the flesh.

His body is definitely bigger, his chest wide, and when he took off his soaked shirt, I almost face-planted on the treadmill. His arms are muscled up and his skin smooth. The only thing he has on his body is a scripture writing on his ribs under his arm. Let's not even start with the abs. His six-pack is so defined that if you poured water down his chest, you'd have six separate pools. I close my eyes, trying to make my heart settle down. "Get out of your head, Karrie. This is a job. You have to ignore the pang of your vagina and focus on the goal."

I pick up my phone, texting my best friend Vivienne.

**I MET HIM!!!**

Three seconds later, I see the bubble appear on the bottom with the three dots in it. I know she is answering me.

Vivienne and I have been best friends since the last year of high school. She was an exchange student from Paris and we clicked right away. We bonded over trust funds, fashion, and all things *Gossip Girl*. The bubble disappears and instead a picture of her face lights up on my phone. I press the green button and collapse on the bed.

"Go for it, Ho Bag," I greet her and hear her laugh in the background.

"Very funny." She is almost whispering.

"Where are you?" I ask her while looking out my minuscule window. I've got a great view of the brick wall from the next building. Nothing says New York like your window facing a brick wall.

"I'm in court, so I can't talk too loud. Where did you meet him?"

"Why are you in court?" I ask her, confused.

"I followed a guy I met in Starbucks here. I swear he winked at me."

I'm the one who starts laughing immediately now. Vi has always been a hopeless romantic, thinking that love will happen at first sight. I'm always there to catch her when she falls, with wine and ice cream.

"You know he may be in court because he's a criminal, right?" I turn on my side.

"I don't think so. He's wearing a suit. A nice suit," she says, and I hear a case number being called in the back. "Oh, shit." I hear her muttering while she says excuse me a couple of times. "Jesus, why why why do I do that to myself?"

I'm not sure she's asking me the question or answering it herself.

"Hello?" I ask, sitting up.

"He was in court being charged with robbery," she huffs. "I swear we had a moment." She continues huffing as she walks faster. "Okay, now back to you, you met him?"

"I did, in the gym. I was on the treadmill watching the Kardashians and he came in."

"How many times did I tell you not to watch that show in public? You never listen to me. *Merde*," she curses in French.

"I missed the last three weeks and it was about Kim's robbery. You know I'm going to watch just to see her cry," I tell her, trying to find a good reason for watching that. "Plus, who goes to a hotel gym?"

"Obviously people who want to work out?" She points out.

"Whatever," I huff out. "He was in there with sweat all over him, huffing and puffing while he ran." I roll my eyes. It was actually gross. Okay, maybe not, but still.

"Did you talk to him?"

"No, although he did bump into me walking to the elevator, and I thought he stabbed me in the back, except it wasn't a dagger!" I giggle.

"He stuck his cock in your back? Like in your pucker hole?"

"Are you insane? I haven't even had sex the whole way yet. Well, like full-blown sex."

"Two pumps is not sex!" she yells out somewhere on the streets of New York. "Then he got soft and collapsed. He should have his penis taken away. Permanently."

"You know I saw him last month making out with a guy. Maybe my vagina broke his penis."

"Your vagina did no such thing. So when is this meeting?"

"Tomorrow. I'm arriving at eleven to go over the clauses in his contract. He gets there at noon."

"Okay, I want you to text me right after, and don't forget to dress sexy. If he got a boner with you in shorts, imagine you in tight stuff. He might be tenting all meeting long."

"Au revoir," I tell her, hanging up, going into the shower, and turning the water back up to hot. "It's going to be fine. It'll be good. I got this," I tell my reflection in the mirror, right before I close my eyes and picture him naked.

# CHAPTER THREE

## MATTHEW

I pick up the suit jacket, shrugging it on. I'm not putting on a tie, so the collar is open. I pull out the cuffs so my sleeves are smooth in my suit. I pick up my wallet, putting it in the pocket inside my suit jacket. I grab my phone and walk out ordering an Uber. As soon as I schedule the pick-up, my phone rings and a picture of Allison with her tongue out flashes on my screen.

"Why are you calling me at eleven? Aren't you in school?" I ask her, listening to her giggle.

"Calm down there, big boy. I'm on lunch. I was calling to wish you luck. Don't fuck this up."

"Watch your mouth." I shake my head. My little sister isn't so little anymore. In her place is a fifteen almost sixteen-year-old spitfire. She is the reason I see some extra white in Cooper's hair, and the other ones are for the twin girls, who are almost going to have to be homeschooled they are in trouble so much. The only sane one is my brother.

"Yeah, yeah. Okay, well, don't mess this up. I gotta go. The teacher is coming." And she clicks off.

I send her a text instead.

**Liar, you said you were at lunch!**

She doesn't answer. Instead, she just sends the kisses emoji. She might be adding white hair to my head, too. I make it down to the lobby and escape without anyone seeing me. My Uber app shows me that the car is waiting for me. I jump in, saying hi and nothing else.

Instead, I scroll on TSN and Hockey News. My hands are sweaty. My stomach is rumbling. We make it to the building ten minutes before my meeting, but you know what they say, the early bird gets the worm. I shake my head, thinking about the saying my grandfather used to always tell me.

Walking up to the security guy, I give him my name and he lets me in since I'm on the list.

I make my way up to the reception desk after stepping out of the elevator. I smile at the girl who sees me and then blushes. "Hi there. Matthew Grant. I have a meeting." I don't even have to say anything because she nods.

"Yes, Mr. Grant." She gets up and walks around her desk. "Follow me. I'll take you to the conference room." She walks ahead of me, swaying her hips so wide I hope she doesn't fall.

When we reach the end of the hall she opens the door, allowing me to walk next to her. I see Robert getting up, walking over to me. "Hey, Matthew, looking good." He shakes my hand while I nod at him. "This is Doug Cooney, the owner of the team. I'm just waiting for Dan, the coach, to get here. Let's have a seat." He points to the chairs.

I take a seat, putting my hands on the desk.

"I have to say thank you both for taking the chance on me." I look at both of them. "I promise I won't let you down."

Doug nods at me, leaning back in his chair. "I'm going to be honest here. I didn't want to give you that chance. But Robert here," he says, looking at Robert, who looks at me, "fought for you. Don't let him down."

I nod at him, about to answer, when there's a knock at the door and then Dan walks in wearing the team tracksuit.

"Hey there." He walks to the table before we can get up. He smacks me on the shoulder. “Fucking great to have you.” He nods to the other two.

“Okay,” Robert starts, “we have your contract here. It’s a one-year contract for two point one million, as per your agent.” He smiles at me because I don’t have an agent. I have Cooper. “We also have the stipulation clause. I know last time you weren’t happy with some of them, but it’s the only way we can both win.” He opens the folder in front of him. “You will be living in a brownstone in Brooklyn.” The page flips over while he continues to read. “Your chaperone will live with you.” He looks up, waiting to see if I’ll say something, and I almost say fuck off. “It’s a three-story brownstone. You each have your own floor to do as you please.”

I nod at him. It isn’t as bad as I thought and maybe me and my roommate will be each other’s wing man. “Your chaperone will be at your side each time you go out. Especially, game day and traveling. Of course you will each have your own room when traveling, but it will be connecting.”

“I hope this guy is up for Netflix and working out.” I smile at them, my hand itchy to sign the papers before I call it all off.

Doug gets up, going to the phone on the table, pressing a couple of buttons. “Can you come to the conference room, please?” He hangs up right after.

“If you mess up even once, your contract is null and void,” Doug says, sitting down just as the door opens and I turn my head to stare at the person who just walked in.

“You?” I stand up, looking back at the other people at the table. The chick from the gym walks in, this time wearing black tight pants and a white button-down shirt, rolled up at the wrists. “Is this a joke?”

“I can assure you I had the same reaction when I was asked,” she says sternly. “I don’t want this any more than you do, but it is what it is.”

“She tried to pick me up yesterday.” I put my hands on my hips, telling the table.

“Are you insane?” she huffs out, her voice rising. “You and your anatomy landed on me.” She looks at Doug. “Right in my back.”

I roll my eyes at her.

"Karrie," Doug says, looking at her.

"What?" She shrugs at him. "He couldn't even contain himself, and he thinks I tried to pick him up." She looks at me. "You wish."

I pfft out. "Please, one word and you would have come home with me." I look at the men in front of me. "You guys can't be serious." I then look back at Karrie. "Besides, how old is she? Twelve?"

"Pervert. I would have pulled the fire alarm and kicked you in the nuts." She crosses her arms over her chest, making her tits strain against the buttons. "Either way you would have ended up in the same place. Alone. With bruised nuts."

Robert slaps the table. "That's enough, you two." He looks at both of us. "Now, you two have a lot of catching up to do. I will forward you both the travel schedule." He stands up, grabbing the papers, and slapping me on the shoulder. "Good to have you."

Coach Dan gets up also, smirking at me while I stand here speechless that they allow a girl to chaperone me. Not just any girl, the hottest fucking girl I've ever set eyes on. I had to take care of myself three times since I stumbled on her.

"You two try not to kill each other." Dan looks at Karrie. "Be good, sweetheart." And he kisses her cheek.

"Really?" I throw my hands in the air. "Does no one think this is a ridiculous idea?" I look around the room and the only one left is Doug, who gets up.

"I think it's the best thing to ever happen to you." He walks over to squeeze my shoulder. "But if you make my little girl cry"—he leans in, whispering—"they won't find your body."

My mouth opens and closes, and then opens again, not a sound coming out.

"Sweetheart, I'll call you later." He kisses her on the same cheek that Dan just kissed her on. Why the fuck is everyone kissing her, and why the fuck am I so irritated that it bothers me?

Just Karrie and I are standing in the middle of the room. "You're the boss's daughter?" I finally get some words to come out.

"Yes," she says, turning around to walk away from me, but I grab her arm, and it's too much. Her tiny arm in my big hand almost feels like it sears me. She looks down at where I'm touching her, her eyes never coming up to meet mine. "I want to get home." She shrugs my hand off and walks ahead of me. "We can take an Uber back to the hotel and pick up our stuff and then we can get home. Finally."

I follow her out of the conference room where she goes to the reception desk, grabbing a black matching jacket and her big black purse. "Thanks, Alice." She smiles and then walks to the elevator, and I have no choice but to follow her. The only thing I can wish for is that I don't end up fucking this whole thing up.

The minute we leave the conference room I'm already taking my phone out to text Cooper.

**We have a problem. My chaperone cannot be served alcohol in a bar. Can we have it changed? To a man? Who is older? With saggy balls?**

I press send and then put the phone in my pocket while I follow Karrie all the way outside to a car and ride over to the hotel.

We are both looking out our respective window when her soft voice fills the car. "This wasn't an ideal situation for me either."

I turn to her, which is a mistake because I want to yank her over to me and kiss her. I want to make her squirm on my lap, but most of all I want to see what she looks like when she smiles. I don't have a chance to say anything because we are already back at the hotel where she has already exited the car.

My phone vibrates in my pocket, so I pull it out and see that it's from my mother.

**He's on the ice with the twins.**

I smile while I reply because I know my sisters.

**The twins hate skating!!!**

**I know, but this is a punishment. It seems the bus driver was talking smack about Cooper and him retiring too young.**

**And? Why are they punished?**

**They got kicked off the bus indefinitely because they called him a pencil dick moron. Then Zara gave him the finger.**

I start laughing out loud when I bump into Karrie again for not looking where I'm going.

"If you're finished sexting, we can meet outside in ten. I'm already packed." Her voice comes out curt.

"Jealous that I'm not sexting you?" I ask her and then smile while she glares. "Besides, I wouldn't sext my mother. Ever."

"Whatever," she says, getting out of the elevator. "Ten minutes." Then she slams the door, making me growl.

An hour later, we're sitting in bumper-to-bumper traffic while we weave our way from mid-town to Brooklyn. We finally make it to the front of the brownstone. All the houses are lined up on the street, all attached. All literally brown. Big bay windows on each side of the door. The only thing telling them apart is the different cast iron railings up to the front doors. Those also are original because no two doors are alike. I follow Karrie up the ten stairs that lead to the big brown doors. Both doors have windows on them so you can see inside. You don't see much because there's a white rounded door on the inside with stained windows, not allowing you to see inside the house.

She unlocks the two deadbolts and walks in, throwing her keys on a mirrored table with fresh white roses in the middle. She steps in, turning the brass rounded handles, making us come face to face with a white staircase. The railing is a dark chestnut brown. The flooring is a glossy green almost black marble flooring. All I can see is Zoe and Zara trying to run and then slide with their socks.

"I'll give you the tour," Karrie says to me, turning left and entering what she calls the living room.

It looks like it's been in a magazine ad. I walk into the room, taking in the bay windows. A hidden bench makes it so you can curl up with a book. All white, the room has one color, but the couch is a huge U-shaped deep brown. There are a million throw pillows placed all over, but what gets me is the fireplace right in front of the couch. It's old school, hand-carved in white marble, the old details from the past all engraved. A huge screen television sits on top of the fireplace. The table in the middle is black with nothing on it but the different remotes.

"All these remotes are for the television as well as the music system that plays throughout the house. The small gray one is for the curtains."

"I've never had a remote for curtains before. If my sisters ever visit, we must hide that." I laugh at her while she smiles and walks back out, turning left and heading down a narrow hallway. Different types of frames line the wall from top to bottom. All personal. I try to stop and take it in, but she's already at the end of the hallway that opens up to a huge kitchen.

The middle counter is all white and gray marble. A white vase with red flowers brings out the light in the house. Skylights from the ceiling let in more light. The range against the wall is black. White cabinets line up the two walls while her huge ass fridge is against the wall on the other side. One door is see-through and you can see that there isn't much inside. We are going to have to make sure it's stocked at all times. While I'm training, I hate eating unhealthy. She walks to the other side of the room into what she calls the dining room. There's a white square marble table in the center with eight brown chairs around it. A vase of green flowers sits in the middle with a couple of candles. Her mail is on the table, so she picks it up.

"Everything is so white," I tell her while she ignores me. "Can you show me where my room is?"

She puts the mail down on the table, taking off her jacket and throwing it over one of the chairs while she takes off the heels she's been wearing. "Follow me." She leads me back to the hallway where we take the stairs up to the second level. Once we get there, I see there are two doors. She points to the right. "That's my room." She ignores me, opening the door, and then walks a couple of feet into the hallway to the door on the left. "And this," she says, opening the door, "is my off—" But she stops talking. "What in the hell is going on?" she says, walking into the huge room that doesn't look like an office at all.

The big king-sized bed in the middle of the room against the wall lets me know this isn't an office. The walls are painted a nice soft gray, making the red and navy blue cover pop even more. The furniture is all dark and very masculine.

"No, no, no, no." She keeps chanting, walking to the door in the corner. She opens it and I see it's an empty walk-in closet. "I'm going to fucking kill Jose," she says while she pulls out her cell phone to call someone. "Jose, it's Karrie. What happened to my office?" she asks, one second away from snapping and throwing something across the room. I don't know what Jose tells her, but she replies, "No, the bedroom upstairs is the gray room, not my office." She nods her head and then all she says is goodbye.

"So good news," she tells me. "This is your room. Bad news, your bathroom is upstairs. But you're fit. It'll be fine." She shrugs her shoulders while I take off my jacket, tossing it on the bed. I unsnap the buttons on my wrists.

"Whatever, I'm not difficult." I walk to the window, which is facing the small covered backyard. "I noticed that the fridge is empty downstairs, so I'll make a list and you can go and pick up the things I'll need." I turn to face her.

"Um, excuse me?" She puts a hand on her hip. "Pick up the things you need? I think you're confused just a touch. I'm a chaperone, not a PA. You want someone at your beck and call, hire someone."

"They did, you," I tell her, watching her bite her teeth together so hard, I think her teeth might snap.

She charges out of the room, opening her bedroom door and slamming it. I wait at the entrance of my room, listening to the banging that's going on behind her closed door. I'm about to go knock when the door swings open.

"You listen here." She walks up to me, huffing and pointing her finger at me. "You want stuff in the fridge, go buy it yourself. You need soap or shampoo, get it on your way out. You need your cleaning picked up, I'll call you an Uber. I won't now, nor ever, be at your beck and fucking call."

I don't hear anything else that comes out of her mouth. The only thing I can focus on is her lips and how plump they are and how she licks them a lot when she's angry and the only thing running through my mind now is making them even more plump by kissing the shit out of her.

# CHAPTER FOUR

## KARRIE

I'm ranting and raving and the only thing I can think of is his two strong arms he's showing me. Well, from the elbow down. His sleeves are rolled up and the way his hands lie on his hips, I want to jump on him, wrap my legs around him, and kiss the ever loving fuck out of him. But he made me so mad. Give me a shopping list, a fucking shopping list.

"Let's get something straight, as you must not know the difference between a chaperone and a PA." I continue my rant from before. "Do you have a computer?" I ask him, watching his eyes fixate on my lips, making me self-conscious, making me lick them even more. When he doesn't answer me, I wave my hand in front of his face. "Hello, computer?"

When he just smirks at me I'm about to pull my hair out. "You need to chill, babe."

Babe? Did he just tell me to chill and then followed it with a babe? I flip my hand to the side.

"Go change. We'll go for a walk and you can show me where to get groceries and stuff." He then looks at his watch. "It's almost dinner time anyway, so maybe we can eat out?" He walks past me, going back down the stairs to grab his bag and then running up the stairs, throwing his bag down in the corner. "Babe, change, yeah."

I'm standing here with my mouth hanging open in utter disbelief that he would ignore all the huffing and puffing I just did and follow it up with babe. "Three seconds. Two—" He stops counting so I can ask him.

"What happens at one?" Shoot me, I'm curious.

"I get naked," he says, pulling his shirt out of his pants and unbuttoning them. "Two."

I turn, darting out of the room. "I'm going to change," I say, running into my room, shutting the door. I have to walk through my closet before I reach my bedroom, which is in the back of the house. Quiet, peaceful, serene, that's what I told the decorator and she didn't disappoint. My huge king-sized bed sits against the white wall. The covers are white, cushiony, and thick like a cloud. All you want to do is sink into it. The gold throw pillows light up the room. I don't have any furniture except two side tables with two lamps. I hear a knock on my door and I'm about to tell him to come in, but he's already walking in.

"Jesus, I thought my sisters had big closets. They would vacation in yours." He looks around. "Why aren't you dressed yet?"

I look back at him and he's wearing black running pants and a white T-shirt with the team's logo in the corner. A torn up baseball cap on his head.

"You can't just barge into my room," I tell him. "What if I was naked?" I put my hand to my chest to maybe hide the fact that my heart is beating so hard he might see it almost come out of my chest.

"One can only hope." Is all he says, going to the bed and sitting on it. "Babe, go change. I'm starving."

"Okay, we need to discuss a couple of things." I look at him. "Perhaps go over a couple of ground rules." I'm about to continue when he puts his hand up.

"Can we do this while we eat? My stomach is eating itself at this point."

"Unbelievable!" I yell, walking back into my closet, slamming yet another door. I grab my yoga pants off the shelf and tug them on so fast

I almost get my foot caught and fall over with my ass in the air. I grab a T-shirt, the whole time grumbling, "Such an asshole." I put my T-shirt on. "Bossing me around, hungry, hungry. I'll show him hungry." I rip my sweater off the hanger, zipping it up, opening the door to find him still sitting on my bed while he watches something on his phone.

"Ready?" he asks, getting up. He walks past me, grabbing my hand and pulling me with him. I try my best to pull my hand from his, but he refuses to budge. He stops by the stairs, looking at the stairs that go up. "I guess that's where my bathroom is?"

I nod, looking down at my hand in his. His hand is tanned compared to mine, which is pale. "See, not too far." I shake my head, too, finally pulling my hand free to walk down the stairs where I go and get my sneakers on. "Ready?"

He nods while I get the keys, putting them in my pocket after locking the door.

We walk down the street lined with trees that are slowly turning from green to yellow and orange. It's still mild outside for the beginning of October. Some houses even have Halloween decorations out. I take the phone out of my pocket and make a note to order some online.

"It's pretty here," he says from beside me, our legs moving in sync.

"It really is. I've only been here for a couple of weeks, but I've fallen in love with it." We cross a busy intersection where cars are honking and rushing away. I point down the street to a corner store that still has a couple of iron tables outside. "That's the coffee shop. They have the best almond croissants you will ever have. It feels like you're in Paris when you bite into them."

"Too sweet for me," he says, taking his hat off and flipping it backward so you can see his eyes now. "Do they have anything else?" he asks me while we wait for the light to change to green so we can walk across.

"Yes, they have lots of baked goods you could try. They even have gluten free cakes." I start walking across the street, pointing out different shops for him when he goes out by himself.

"I don't know why you're telling me all this. You're my chaperone, which FYI I looked up the meaning while you were in your closet talking to yourself." He smiles. "Do you do that often?" he asks, looking at me.

"I mean, talk to yourself?"

I stop walking in the middle of the sidewalk. "I don't talk to myself." Okay, fine, I do. I have some of the best conversations with myself. It's how I process things. I make a note to have these conversations more in my head now that he is living with me.

"Babe, you were ranting." He stops walking and comes back to me because I'm still standing in the middle of the sidewalk.

"Stop with the babe, please." I shake my head, continuing walking with him till we finally reach the supermarket. There are crates of fruit lined up outside. He stops to grab a couple of clear bags to put the fruit in, passing some empty ones to me.

"Fill it up with oranges while I get some bananas. Do you have a juicer at home?" He doesn't look up at me while he grabs apples.

"Um, I have no idea. Probably not. Don't buy too much. It might go to waste." I fill the bag with the huge oranges.

"Shit, I didn't even check the schedule. When do we leave town?" He stops packing the bag of apples.

"Saturday right after the game. We play Philly Sunday night. Back on Monday."

"Okay." Is all he says before walking inside the market, grabbing an empty cart and putting the bags of fruit in them. "Is there a butcher around here?" he asks while we walk down the meat aisle.

"I think around here somewhere. Why?" I ask him, confused. There's a whole aisle of meat right here.

"I usually just buy big slabs of meat and they cut it to make portions." He gets his phone out of his pocket where he MapQuests the nearest butcher. "Closed now, but we can swing by there sometime tomorrow. Shit, it's game day tomorrow. Okay, Monday afternoon it is."

"Why don't you grab what you want for tonight and we can work out the details later?" I ask him, grabbing myself a piece of salmon. I'm not eating out tonight. I've been living on room service for the last couple of days and I want a home-cooked meal.

"Oh, that looks good. Grab me a piece, babe." He picks up a pack of T-bone steaks.

"Karrie," I tell him, grabbing another piece of salmon. "I know you are used to one syllables, but it's Kar-Rie It's two syllables. I'm sure even you can do it." I put the salmon in the cart.

"Funny." He pushes the cart with his elbows almost bent over while we make it into the cereal aisle. He grabs the cereals filled with all the sugar in the world. "Oh, you think they have Fruity Pebbles?" His eyes scan over the rows, looking for it.

"And I'm babysitting a twelve-year-old," I say while I toss him the box of Fruity Pebbles that's right on my side next to the granola I grab for myself.

We end up filling the whole cart with way too much food. More food than I've ever bought. We load it all on the conveyor belt. The lady starts scanning our items and when I'm about to pull out my credit card, he grabs it from my hand.

"Don't even think about it, Kar-Rie." He smirks while he gives the clerk his credit card. "See, just like a big boy."

I pfft out, rolling my eyes. "This from the one who almost had a temper tantrum when I put back the Fruit Roll-Ups."

"Hey"—he points at me—"they were a surprise flavor." He looks at the clerk. "Can we have these delivered?"

After I fill in the address we walk out, making our way back to the house.

When we get back home, I bring him upstairs to finally show him his bathroom. The walk-in shower has no door, just glass. There are about fifteen shower heads aimed everywhere. A Venetian mirror above the marble basin is in front of it with the vintage dark vanity. There are built-in shelves right next to the entrance to the shower filled with white folded towels. I hear the doorbell ring.

"I'll go get that while you look around," I tell him, walking out, because the only thing I could concentrate on was him naked in the shower while the water fell off his strong shoulders cascading around him. Me in front of him while he bends over to kiss me. I let the delivery guy in and start putting the things away when I hear him coming down the stairs obviously talking to someone.

He walks into the room with the phone in front of him. "This is the kitchen," he says to whoever is on the other line and I hear a girl's voice.

My stomach rolls with a wave. "That's Karrie."

I turn to glare at him till he turns the phone around to show me a beautiful woman.

"Babe, this is my mom." The minute babe comes out of his mouth in front of his mother my eyes go as big as saucers.

"Hi"—I wave at her—"nice to meet you. I'm Karrie, not babe." I glare at him while I hear his mother laughing.

"Oh, she's beautiful," she says, and I smile at her while I hear about fifteen voices in the background all asking to see. She turns the phone where I see two twins with strawberry blond hair get into the picture.

"I'm Zoe. This is Zara. You should know that he stinks when he goes to the bathroom. Like garbage." And then the phone is ripped from my hand where I belly laugh as he calls them little shits, and their mother shoos them away.

"Let me see her. I didn't see her." I hear again from another female voice.

He hands me back the phone where I see the most beautiful girl I have ever seen, another strawberry blonde, aqua blue eyes shaped oval.

"OMG, he's so fucked." Is all she says till Matthew's mom snaps, "Watch your mouth!"

I smile back at his sister, telling her that she is beautiful. She shrugs her shoulders as if she hears it all the time.

"So you are going to be the one holding my brother's leash?" She laughs while I look over at Matthew, who is now rubbing his hands over his face, making his shirt move up a little, showing me the waist with his Calvins coming out.

"I don't know about a leash, but I'll be tied to his side." I smile at her. "I won't be at his beck and call, but..." I don't even finish and I hear laughing in the background of the phone when a man comes on.

Cooper Stone. He was hot back in the day and he's even hotter now. I stare at him, blinking, not sure what to say.

"Mr. Stone, I'm a huge fan." I don't know what I said wrong, but Matthew snatches the phone from my hand while he talks to Cooper. "Rude, asshole," I grumble to myself while I go around grabbing the stuff I want to eat for supper. I place the salmon on a baking dish and sprinkle it with salt and pepper. I place it into the oven while I get the vegetables set up and Matthew finally comes back into the room.

"They will be here before the game tomorrow. It will only be Cooper and Mom. We will head to the arena together."

I drop the knife I was holding while cutting the vegetables.

"Your parents are coming here?" I wipe my hands on a rag, running around the house. "The house isn't clean." I run from the kitchen to the living room, assessing what we need to do before tomorrow. "If we get up by six, we should be able to make the house presentable." Holy shit, his mother and stepfather are coming over to the house. Why am I so freaked out? Why does this make me want to sit down and hyperventilate?

"Karrie," he says, grabbing me and turning me around while he puts his hands on my shoulders. "Breathe. In and Out." And I listen to his voice while he calms me. My heart is getting back to beating normal. "You could eat off the floor. And besides, my parents aren't like that. Now can we go back and finish cooking? I'm starving." He squeezes my shoulders while I watch him walk away, his ass baiting me to squeeze it with either my hands or the heels of my feet. Either way it's starting to become perfectly clear why I want to make a good impression. I like him, more than I want to kill him. This could be a problem.

# CHAPTER FIVE

## MATTHEW

Game day. It's the only thing running through my mind as I stand in the shower. Well, that and the fact that I'm tempted to go downstairs, march into Karrie's room, and bury my face in her.

From the second I saw her in the gym I was attracted to her, then she walked into the conference room and she didn't let me get away with anything. Her sassy mouth had my dick harder than all the marble in this fucking house. Last night after I talked her down from her latest walk to the edge, we stood side by side getting things ready for dinner. I've never done this before. I've had women, more than I care to think about, but I've never had the comfortable silence and ease. I've never actually been myself.

These girls don't want me; they want the jock. They want the NHL star. They want the claim to fame. But Karrie, she wants none of that. She's so pissed off when I call her babe it makes me laugh, so now I do it to piss her off even more. She gets so pissed that the vein in her head tics, making me want to grab her by the back of her neck and kiss her till it stops.

Last night we sat down at supper and went over the 'rules'.

*"Okay, so we should have some ground rules since we'll be roommates." She started saying while she finished chewing. "I've never lived with a guy before, so I'm thinking we always knock when the door is closed."*

*The thought of her living with another guy made me clench my fist. Made me almost want to push off from the table and go outside and yell till my throat was raw.*

*"Okay, must knock before walking into a closed door. But," I said while taking a forkful of salmon, "what if you're yelling for me because you're naked and need my help? Do I knock first or just charge in?" I smirked while I saw the vein coming back.*

*"I doubt I'd need anything from you if I'm naked, but in that case please come charging in. There's only one television in the house, so I think we should buy another one you can put upstairs in the office."*

*"Why?" I asked her. "Can we not just watch television together? I don't really watch it that much. I'm usually gone most of the time." I smiled at her. "And now you will be, too."*

*"I have a DVR and I record all my shows, so I'll watch them when I come back home." She pointed at me with her fork. "That's another rule. No touching my DVR."*

*I laughed at her while chewing. "I promise to not cancel or delete any of your Kardashians." I smiled while I continued eating. "Are you a morning person?"*

*"Why?" she asked, tilting her head to the side.*

*"My mother can't be talked to without at least smelling coffee. I'm just making sure I don't die."*

*She laughed at that, but she had not been on the end of my mother without caffeine.*

*"I guess I'm civil, but I do like coffee in the morning." She started using her fork to push things in her plate around. "What about you?"*

*"Me?" I put my fork down. "I'm usually up by five a.m. I like to get a little cardio in before going to the rink. I usually have a protein shake after."*

*"If you wake me at five a.m., with or without coffee, I will lock you*

*out of the house." She dropped her fork also. "There's a paper list in the middle drawer in the kitchen. If you finish something in the fridge or the pantry, put it on the list. I guess we can do the shopping once a week. They have this great outside market not too far."*

*"Done." I didn't think she realized we would hardly be home with the traveling.*

*"We should talk about dating," she said, and I smiled big.*

*"Yes, let's talk about us dating," I told her, rubbing my hands together.*

*"I'll be respectful of your dates, if you're respectful to mine," she said, and my hand in midair stopped her from talking. Her dates, what fucking dates?*

*"Are you fucking dating?" My hands came down on the table. Her arms crossed over her chest.*

*"Not at the moment, but in case I meet someone and they pick me up here or"—she shook her head—"they spend the night, I just want to make sure you aren't, well, you."*

*"No fucking dating," I snapped, getting up and picking up my plate, walking into the kitchen clutching it so hard I thought it was going to snap in two, or ten.*

*"Wait a fucking second." She stormed after me. "You can't tell me not to date. Surely you'll want to date also, and I'm okay with that." When she said it, I saw her stop talking and tried to swallow, her neck moving up and down, her neck that I wanted to lean in, bite, and mark.*

*"How about we both don't date while we are together?" I cleaned off my plate before rinsing it off and putting it in the dishwasher. "How's that?" I asked her, praying she accepted this. Either that or I was going to go apeshit on her.*

*She walked back to her dish in the dining room, came back in, and handed it to me so I could put it in the dishwasher. "We aren't together, but I guess if we meet someone, we can come back and revisit this." She shrugged and leaned into the counter.*

*There would be no fucking revisiting this. The only thing we needed to discuss was if she was going to be in my bed or I would be in hers.*

*"Fine. I think we have some ground rules now. I'm going to bed," she said, walking out of the room.*

*"Want me to come tuck you in?" I asked her.*

*She didn't answer, just flipped me the bird in the air. My laugh filled the house till the sound of her slamming the door shut me up.*

Now I'm in the bathroom wiping the foggy mirror with my hand. My eyes look rested. They don't give away I was so nervous last night that I tossed and turned. Grabbing one of the white folded towels, I wrap it around my waist, making my way downstairs where I come face to face with a sleepy Karrie. Fuck me. If I thought she was hot dressed, it is nothing like seeing her in her lace booty shorts and a matching black tank top. Her breasts are sagging just a touch so you know she isn't wearing a bra.

"Morning," she says, stretching her hand over her head, making the shorts shorter and her top go up a bit so I'm faced with the little skin on her belly. She finally takes in my towel, her tongue coming out. "Why are you naked? That should be a rule. No naked in the house."

"I'm wearing a towel. I'm not naked. Maybe I should drop the towel so you can know the difference between naked and not naked." My hand goes to the side of the towel while she holds up her hand and turns her head.

"Don't you dare."

And that's all I need before my hand unfolds the towel, making it drop to my feet. My cock obviously got in on the action and is giving her an early morning wave. He's also begging for her to drop to her knees and take me deep into her throat. Her head snaps back to look at me, her nipples suddenly peaking. She puts up her hand in front, not sure what she is blocking.

"I can't believe you. Would you cover that tiny thing up? Is it cold in here?"

I laugh at her, knowing she is full of shit. I'm not trying to give my ego a boost, but I know I'm packing down there.

"Yup, someone must have left the windows open," she says while she runs downstairs.

"Wait, come back. I showed you mine. Shouldn't you show me yours? Is there a rule for that?" I lean down the stairs, bending and picking up the towel. I have no idea what she is doing down there, but all I hear is her voice ranting again while she slams what I'm assuming is the cupboard doors and some drawers. "I'll take a coffee also if you're making it." I laugh to myself, walking into my room and closing my door behind me.

I pull a pair of basketball shorts that I put away last night out of the drawer. I need to make arrangements to have my clothes shipped here. They are already packed, but I just didn't have the address when I came out here. I wait in the room a bit to make my cock go to at least half-mast before going downstairs. Once I think it's okay I make my way downstairs. Karrie is sitting on the couch, her feet folded under her, a throw blanket lying across her legs while she holds her cup of coffee in her hand and watches something on television. She must hear me because she raises her hand to flip me the bird again. I laugh at her, going into the kitchen and making myself a cup. I go back into the living room, sitting next to her, watching what is on television. I'm here for about five minutes before I have to ask what the fuck she's watching.

"It's Below Deck," she says like it's something that everyone watches. When she sees the confused look on my face she continues, "It's about a crew that works on a yacht." She takes a sip of her coffee while she fast-forwards the commercials.

"This is a reality show?" I say, leaning back on the couch. "Babe, you watch the strangest shows."

"It's not strange and it's real life." She actually thinks this isn't scripted. "The charter guests are all getting drunk and swapping partners in the hot tub." This piques my interest.

"We see them fucking?" I ask, curious.

"Pig," she sputters out just when it goes to a commercial again. "Why is it you guys always think of sex?" she asks, looking at me.

I glance at her. Her hair is piled on top of her head. I want to lean over and take her mouth, show her exactly why I always think about sex.

"You obviously haven't had sex with the right person if you're asking me why I'm always thinking about sex." I try baiting her.

"Oh, please, calm down there, Ron Jeremy." She sits up, putting her coffee cup on the table in front of her. "I may not be a 'professional' such as yourself, but I know plenty of other men who don't always think about sex."

"Number one, thank you for calling me Ron Jeremy. You know he's like the biggest porn star out there because his dick is so big, right?" I wink at her while she takes a pillow and throws it at me. I knock it away, continuing, "I can make a bet with you right now that any red-blooded male you ask, if a girl walks in front of them, the first thing they think of is sex." I shrug my shoulders. She leans back again and shrugs, too. "I'm hungry." I get up. "I'm going to make myself an omelet. You want some?"

"When aren't you hungry?" she says, putting the blanket up to her neck and returning her gaze to the television.

I look back down at her. She must feel my stare because she turns to me.

"Whenever you're around, I'm suddenly famished. Like I haven't eaten for days." I wink at her, walking out, giving her that to think about. Meanwhile I cup my cock and tell him soon, very fucking soon.

# CHAPTER SIX

## KARRIE

Holy. Fucking. Shit. I take my phone out from under the blanket and text Vivienne.

**I think Matthew just said he wanted to eat my vagina!!**

Her text comes back right away.

**What do you mean?**

**He said that 'Whenever you're around, I'm suddenly famished. Like I haven't eaten for days.' Does that mean he wants to eat my vagina?**

**I don't know. Hey, go to the kitchen table, get on it, and lie down naked and see what happens!**

**Are you insane?**

**No, I'm trying to get my best friend laid and find out if he's packing.**

**Oh, he's definitely packing. He 'dropped' his towel today. NAKED.**

**Jesus, it's not even fucking eight o'clock in the morning and you've had more action than I've had in a month. And I'm French.**

"Come and eat, your highness." I hear from the back of the house.

I drop my phone like I'm holding a hot potato. I get up, walking into the kitchen where he's standing buttering toast. "I made more coffee," he tells me, pointing to my plate that he put on the counter.

I assess the omelet on the plate. It looks mouthwatering. "What's inside?" I ask, sitting on one of the stools at the counter nook.

"Onions, spinach, asparagus, mushrooms, Swiss cheese, some ham." He sits next to me, digging in.

"I've never had a man cook for me. Well, except my dad, but that was few and far between." I cut a piece and groan the minute I chew into it. "It's so good." I don't even look over at him. I just continue eating.

"I've never cooked for a woman. Well, except my sisters and on occasion my mom." He laughs. "Mother's Day."

We continue eating in silence, both of us just enjoying the meal. When he gets up, he takes my plate and puts it in the dishwasher. He also starts cleaning up the mess he made, but I get up.

"Okay, new rule, if you cook you don't clean. So beat it, Grant." I motion with my thumb toward the door. I'm expecting him to go back to the living room, but he surprises me by sitting on the stool. "What are you doing?" I ask him while I start throwing the things in the garbage.

"I'm going to enjoy my coffee while I watch you clean." He takes a sip of coffee, then smiles and puts it down. "I might also hope you bend over."

I stop what I'm doing to glare at him.

"What?" he asks when I continue glaring at him, but all he does is shrug his shoulders.

I start mumbling under my breath. "Pig." While I wet a rag, "asshole," squeezing the water out, "like I'm a piece of meat," turning to wipe down the counter, "just going to sit there. Staring."

"You know I can hear you, right?" he asks me, but I ignore him and the laugh that comes out of him. When I finally finish everything, I start the dishwasher. "We leave at four," he says right before he gets up and walks out of the room.

I watch his retreating back.

I throw the wet rag in the laundry basket before going back to the living room to continue watching television. I open my Instagram and start scrolling through the feed. I type in Matthew's name, but since it's set to private I can't see anything. I try to zoom in on the little circle picture in the corner, but I can't see anything. It looks like he's in his equipment, but I'm not sure.

"Babe!" I hear him yell from upstairs, making me close the app in case he comes down the stairs.

I pick up the remote, flipping through the channels till I hear him yell again.

"Babe!"

I shake my head. I don't know who he's talking to, so I turn the television louder and giggle to myself when I hear him running down the stairs.

"Babe," he says once he gets in the room, walking over to me. "I'm calling you."

"Really?" I say, muting the television. "I didn't hear my name. I heard something, but I didn't know who you were talking to."

"Babe," he says again. "My parents aren't coming."

I turn off the television. "What happened?" Worry sets in.

"Nothing really. Justin, my youngest brother, fell on the ice and his cage lifted up, and he has to have stitches and Mom doesn't feel right about leaving him."

My hand flies to my chest. "Is he okay?"

"Yeah, he's fine. They are already home." He sits down, grabbing the remote from me and switching it to the sports channel. We aren't even on the channel for long before his name is brought up.

*"Today is the day to see if New York actually made a mistake by signing the washed-up Matthew Grant."*

"Oh, please," I say out loud, looking over at Matthew, watching his eyebrows pinch together while the two reporters go on and on about the pros and cons of having Matthew here. I can't stand to listen to the bullshit, so I reach over and snatch the remote from his hand, turning the television off. "Assholes." I get up, throwing the remote on the table, sitting on the table in front of Matthew. "Listen to me. Don't let them get in your head." When he doesn't say anything I continue, "If anyone is getting in that thick headed skull of yours it's me." Nothing. He just blinks. "You get me, babe?" I throw in the babe to try and get him to focus on my words. I know I reach him when he smiles. His eyes light up, the sides of his eyes crinkling. "Now we need to get ready. You need to go pack and get in the zone. Or whatever you guys do. But you won't give those two wannabes any other thought."

"You like me." Is the only thing he says.

"Seriously, after that whole speech that's what you get?" I get up, walking out of the room, turning once I get to the first step. "You better not make me look bad by sulking." I storm up the stairs to my room.

I make my bed, going over a to-do list in my head when I hear a beep alerting me of a text. Picking it up, I see it's from Vivienne.

**Salope!!!**

I laugh because it's the French word for slut. I answer her back.

**It takes one to know one.**

**Touché, mon amie. So did he get to eat his breakfast?**

**He made us omelets. I'm packing now.**

**Omelets doesn't sound like pussy. Is that an English term?** She follows with the crying emoji.

**I'm rolling my eyes. Can you hear them? When I get back, we need to have coffee.**

**Oui, madame. Don't forget to not pack undies.**

**See you soon. Stay out of trouble.**

**Moi? Jamais**! *Me never.*

I throw my phone on my bed, going to my closet, and getting my small overnight bag, throwing panties, bras, jeans, and also PJs in it. After my shower, I close up my toiletry bag and dump it into the bag. I look at the clock, wondering how much time I have. I notice it's already three, so I decide to do my hair and light makeup. This is the first time I'm traveling with the team. I'm not sure how I'm supposed to dress, so I go for business casual.

Once I set my hair in waves I walk over, grabbing my tan pencil skirt that reaches me just below my knee. I grab a black silk button-down shirt that goes up to my elbows. I pair it with a thin gold belt and my black Louboutins. I grab a black leather dressy jacket for after the game.

I finally zip up my bag and head downstairs, spotting Matthew in the living room already dressed.

He's sitting with his elbows on his knees with his hands crossed, his head down on the bench that's right in front of the window. I walk in and he doesn't even raise his head. Suddenly a knot forms in my chest. I stop in front of him and put my hand on his shoulder. He's wearing a plain black suit, his white shirt underneath. The smell of his rich cologne fills the room. "Hey," I say quietly.

He looks up, his eyes troubled, a dark brown, so dark they look black.

"What's the matter?"

"I'm fucking scared," he finally whispers out. "What if I fuck up? What if I choke? What if I go out there and I'm really not set for this game? What if this is the end for me?"

I've always gotten the strong vibe from him. He's always carried such a presence about him, a cockiness, but this vulnerability just makes him that much more amazing.

"You can't fuck up." My hand rubs his shoulder. "The only thing you can do is prove them wrong. Go out there and skate like you never skated before, all the while chanting 'fuck you' in your head."

He smiles at me, his eyes becoming lighter.

"Do you think my father would do this if he didn't believe in you? You think everyone would be taking a chance on you if you weren't that good?" I shake my head. "It's because you're that good that people want to knock you down."

"My parents are always the ones to talk me down, always there to cheer me on. I guess them not being here is bugging me more than I thought." He grabs the hand that's hanging by my side in his. "Will you be in the stands tonight?"

"There isn't any place I'd rather be." I smile at him while he squeezes my hand. "Would it help if I wore a jersey with your name on it?"

"You would do that for me, babe?" He tries to hide his laugh, and I push him away with my hand.

"Not anymore." I look out and see that the car is here to bring us in. "Now let's go show them that Matthew Grant is back. With a vengeance." I grab my jacket, putting it on and grabbing my purse.

"You look hot," he says, standing up, and I finally see all of him. His jacket is tight around his arms. His tie is a skinny black. He's perfection, complete and utter perfection.

"You're not bad yourself." I smile at him. "Now grab the bags and let's go." I point to the bags at the door, waiting for him to walk out before locking up.

The drive to the arena is quiet. We just look out and I don't move my hand when I feel his on top of mine. I let him have this because I know he needs it, and if I'm honest, the butterflies in my stomach stop me also.

When we get into the arena, there's already a camera crew waiting to capture this moment. Matthew opens his door, stepping out, the pictures snapping already. I get out from my side, hiding behind him, but he stops so I can walk by his side, his hand going to the small of my back when we make it through the doors that will lead him to the locker room. I don't have time to say anything to him because Robert is here waiting for him.

"There he is." He shakes his hand while slapping him on the shoulder. "Ready to do this?"

Matthew smiles at me. "I am now." He winks at me, making me roll my eyes, and walks down the hallway.

I lean against the wall, catching my breath. The public relations girl, Mindy, comes up to find me. She's dressed in a pant suit, an earpiece in her ear, with a clipboard in her hands.

"Karrie?" she asks, not sure till I smile. "I'm Mindy. I was sent by Matthew to make sure I show you around. Now I've emailed you all the itineraries for the next couple of months. You have a seat on the plane and the bus, you travel with the team, so please make sure you are dressed appropriately." She smiles at me. "Also I've contacted the hotels and you'll be under Matthew's name with a connecting door. Also I have your badges for the wives' box as well as a seat ticket in case—" She stops talking when her phone rings, and she picks it up and starts telling them there was a mistake. She moves the phone from her mouth. "If you need anything, my number is at the bottom of the email." With that, she nods and walks away.

I finally make my way toward the hallway where I almost run into a guy who is looking down at his phone.

He's wearing a blue suit, a navy tie, and he has a beanie on. A blond scuff on his face. "Sorry," he says, smiling. "I wasn't looking where I was going."

I shake my head. "No worries. It's okay." I smile and I'm about to walk around him when he stops me with his hand on my arm.

"I'm Jamie. I play for New York." He smiles at me, holding out his hand.

I don't want to be rude, so I grab it and shake it.

"I'm Karrie Cooney." The forced smile is still on my face.

"Shit, the boss's daughter." He laughs. "Just my luck. The only girl to pique my interest and she's off-limits."

I don't say anything because a big booming voice interrupts us,

"Totally off-limits, bud."

I look over Jamie's shoulder, finding Matthew, who has changed out of his suit and is now in his workout gear. Jamie smiles at Matthew, walking past him, slapping him on the back.

"Got it." Is all Jamie says, making me cross my arms.

"The nerve of him," I grumble, turning around while I walk toward the arena where I flash my badge. I walk into the arena, stopping at the gift shop and I'm right away shocked at all the Matthew shirts that are hanging everywhere. I grab a jersey and a couple of shirts. Once I pay for the shirts, I walk out where I bump into a couple of the wives I've met through the years at some of the fundraising activities. I follow them into the box where we sit and have something to eat and I grab a glass of white wine.

When we hear the music come on and then the roaring, we get up to go and check what is going on. I'm not even at the door when I see Matthew's picture on the jumbotron. His face is hard, his eyes ready while he skates around, making sure his skates are exactly how he wants them to be.

I hear a couple of girls in the box next to me. "Holy shit, he's hotter than I thought he would be," one of them says while another vows to find his dick size by the end of the month.

I roll my eyes while my hand itches to point the fuck you finger at them. It's the last girl that makes me lose my shit.

"I heard his cock is like a baseball bat. I know a girl who slept with him in Cali. Well, him and another teammate tag teamed her. I think she has pictures."

I walk away before I tell them to keep fucking dreaming.

I grab another glass of wine, taking my phone out to text Vivienne.

**I can't go to these games alone. I almost bitch slapped a girl for knowing someone who fucked Matthew.**

**You know it is only going to get worse. I Googled him and there are about a gazillion pictures of him but none are with any women.**

**LIAR.**

**Okay, fine, none of him with the same woman twice.**

**ASSHOLE.**

**Him or me?**

**Both. I'm going to check Google now.**

**NO. DON'T DO THAT TO YOURSELF.**

**I think it's best if I don't do it. At least not now. Maybe when we are together.**

I don't have time to think of anything else but the game because the lights go down as the singer comes out to sing the national anthem. After that it's game on. The first period, Matthew starts on shaky legs, messing up with a pass in the neutral zone, making the other team have a breakaway. Thankfully, the goalie is on fire, stopping it. He skates to the bench, his head down, his shoulders slumped, the hockey stick taking a beating when he smashes it on the boards before sitting on the bench.

The second period they come out with the same push and pull as before till Matthew intercepts a pass at the defense line. He skates up to the puck ahead of the defenseman toe dragging the puck through his skates and coming one on one with the goalie, shooting it just above his pad, hitting the net.

The building goes crazy. The fans are on their feet. I throw my hands straight over my head, yelling at the top of my lungs. Matthew celebrates by skating with one foot bent at the knee in the front while he roars with happiness.

His teammates all go to him, celebrating with him, then they skate over to the bench, high-fiving everyone on the bench. One guy puts his glove in Matthew's face. His smile lights up his whole face.

The smile that lights up the room is now looking directly at me. He spots me and winks. The camera catches it and everyone in the arena is thinking that it's for them, but deep down I know it's all for me.

# CHAPTER SEVEN

## MATTHEW

I'm a nervous fucking wreck walking into the locker room. I grab a bottle of Gatorade, opening it and taking a big gulp. The media is all over, snapping pictures, watching my every move.

I'm introduced to the team. Some I know and have played with or against. The starting goalie, Luka, gets up to greet me, shaking my hand. "Welcome to the team," he says while I nod.

Another teammate Phil gets up, coming to me. "Can't wait to see what you've got." I don't say anything because my mouth has become suddenly dry.

The star defenseman Paul comes up to me. "Hey, golden boy." He smirks at me. I've played against him many times before. I'm happy to say that I've beat him most of the time. "Glad you're on my side now," he says, turning around to tell stories of when I used to zip by him.

The star of the team, Max, comes up to me, his smirk coming out. "I don't know what the big fuss is, but let's see what you can do."

I immediately want to knock his teeth out. His smirk is more like a leer. He comes closer to my ear so only I can hear, "You don't fool me.

You're a has-been. Just a matter of time before everyone sees it." He smacks me on the shoulder and walks away.

Brendan, another star on the team, sees this and looks at me. "Don't take too much of what Max says. He hates it when someone tries to steal his thunder."

"Don't want to steal anyone's anything. I just want to play the game," I say, going to the cubby where I see my name on it. All my equipment is laid out for me. I shrug my suit jacket off taking my workout gear and heading into the room to change. Usually I would undress in front of the guys, but the press is in there and I need a second to breathe. Once I'm in my workout gear, I walk out of the room where I hear Karrie's voice.

"No worries, it's okay." She smiles and is about to walk around him when he stops her with his hand on her arm. I'm about to go and break his hand.

"I'm Jamie. I play for New York." He smiles at her, holding out his hand.

I see her looking down at it, grabbing it and shaking it.

"I'm Karrie Cooney." The forced smile is on her face. Unlike the ones she gives me at home. Well, there are also the glares. I can't decide which one I love the most.

"Shit, the boss's daughter." He laughs. "Just my luck. The only girl to pique my interest and she's off-limits."

Okay, this is enough.

"Totally off-limits, bud."

She looks over Jamie's shoulder, finding me.

Jamie smiles at me, walking past me and slapping me on the back. "Got it." Is all Jamie says, making Karrie cross her arms.

"The nerve of him," she grumbles, turning around, walking toward the arena, and I'm pretty sure she's still talking to herself. I shake my head while I watch her ass walk away. Fuck, my handprint would look great on her.

Walking back into the room, I zone everything out. I warm up my muscles and start doing my routine that I've always done. Gearing up, I look around the room as some of the teammates argue and joke with each other while some music fills the room.

Coach Dan sticks his head into the room. “Go time, boys.”

I look at the board with the lines. I’m on the third line with Jamie and Phil. Third line is better than no line. I walk to the ice, the noise of the crowd growing when everyone skates on. I’m the last one out of the door and the roar of the crowd goes nuts. I hold my stick up, saying thank you while skating in a circle.

I stop by the board while we do drills, looking around. I look up at the boxes and my eyes find her, but she’s looking over at the other box while she must be listening to the girls talking. I don’t know what they are saying, but I can see her lips mumble from here. She’s a nut.

Once the puck drops, it takes a while before I get my feet under me. A fuck up in the neutral zone has me skating to the bench, almost ready to snap my stick on the board. It doesn’t help that Max shoots his mouth off when I get to the bench right before he goes on, “Well done, rookie.” I shake my head.

“Don’t mind him. He gets pissy when someone prettier comes along,” Phil says to me. “You’ll get it back.”

By the time the end of the first period comes it’s still 0-0. We walk into the dressing room, all of us sitting down while the coach goes over plays that we fucked up on. Once he’s done he walks out, leaving us to ourselves.

“Almost made us down one with that move,” Max says to the whole room.

Luka gets up, taking his stick.

“What, Max? You never fucked up? What about the time you had a cramp and couldn’t skate and I had a three on one?” Luka shakes his head, looking at me. “Don’t do that shit again.” He points to me and walks out to get his skate fixed.

I don’t say anything nor do I try and engage in any conversations. I

go over plays in my head. Once I get on the ice I get more comfortable. I make more daring plays, more chances till one finally pays off when I stick poke at a pass, intercepting it at the blue line.

I skate up to the puck ahead of me, my speed going ahead of the puck, so I’m toe dragging the puck through my skates and coming one on one with the goalie. I’m coming in fast and the goalie goes deeper into his net, protecting nearly every single part, but he goes a little too low and I see the sweet spot right above the pads. I lift up my stick a little, snapping it into the net.

The building goes crazy. The fans are on their feet. I throw my one leg up, skating on one, fisting my hands by my sides, roaring out, "Fuck yeah."

My line mates come and celebrate with me.

"There goes that monkey off your back," Jamie says as we skate to the bench, high-fiving everyone.

Brendan puts his hands in my face when I get on the bench. I smile big and look up at the only person I care to see. Karrie. I find her and see her smiling at me. I wink at her, the camera catching it and having everyone cheering, thinking it is for them, but she knows it is all for her.

The rest of the period is rushing to keep the lead. It ends with us sealing the win with an empty net goal. While celebrating, I'm walking off the ice when I'm tapped by a reporter who wants to ask me questions, but he has to wait because I've been voted the first star of the game. I skate back onto the ice with three pucks, throwing them into the crowd while I skate around. I look up at the box, seeing her standing on her feet while she cheers for me. Or the team. I'm saying she's cheering for me.

While getting off the ice the reporter pulls me aside with questions.

"So back on the ice it started out shaky, but you got your feet back. How did it feel?"

I push the hair back from my face, smiling.

"I've been training, hoping to get back on the ice, and it feels great. The team welcomed me, so it's great to have the support."

"Getting that first goal tonight, how big was that?"

"I think it was great. I was just lucky it was me. Could have been any of my teammates. We all played our hearts out, so it was a team effort."

"Thank you for your time."

"Thank you," I say, going back into the dressing room where my team cheers as I walk in.

One person throws his gloves at me. I sit down, taking off my stuff. Our team's bags are in front of each of us.

I take my jersey off, throwing it into the big gray basket in the middle of the room. The equipment manager, Bill, will make sure they are all washed and ready for the next game. The away jerseys are already packed. I take off my gloves, throwing them into the bag as well as the rest of my equipment. Zipping up the bag, I tell Bill my bag is ready. He walks over and grabs it, putting it on the cart.

I walk to the shower where most of the guys are already. We have an hour before the bus leaves for the airport, so we all have to get ready. I'm one of the first finished, so I get dressed and grab my phone. I have texts from my mother and Cooper. As well as Allison.

They are all messages of good luck and then congratulations. I smile, knowing I made them proud.

Allison sends me a picture of the whole family wearing my New York jersey and then the house erupting the second I scored.

Cooper went just as nuts yelling, "That's my boy."

I smile at the video. Walking out, I see Karrie leaning against the wall, her legs crossed in front of her. When she sees me walking out she smiles huge at me. I'm itching to put my hands in her hair and tilt her head to the side, claiming her mouth with mine.

"There he is," she says, walking to me. "Number one star of the team." She claps her hands.

I smile at her and am about to grab her hand when Dan and Robert walk out, my hand going back to my side instead of in hers.

"There he is," Robert says to me. "Great game." They continue walking down the hall.

"I gave them our luggage, so it's already on the bus. You ready?" I ask her, walking toward the bus. Most of my teammates are starting to follow us.

She walks on the bus before me, sitting down in the front. I sit right next to her, blocking her from the guys, or at least hoping, but it doesn't work. One by one they come on the bus, introducing themselves and laying on the charm. Fuck, some of them are married. I'm about to lose my shit so much my leg is bouncing up and down.

"This wouldn't happen if you wore normal clothes." I check my phone, seeing all the tweets and hashtags about Grant is back.

"What is normal clothes? Is my ass hanging out? No, are my tits displayed out? No. I'm covered up," she hisses out at me. "By the way"—she folds her arms over her chest—"I met a couple of your friends today. They were going on and on about you and your three-way activities." She stares out the window. "Jerkface."

"Three-way?" I don't say anything else because Max comes on the bus, looking straight at Karrie.

"Hey, beautiful, so glad you'll be traveling with the team." He smiles, walking away from us.

The last person on the bus is the coach as the door closes and we make our way to the airport where we walk on the tarmac straight onto the plane. I don't stray far from Karrie's side even when she gets on the plane, putting her purse beside her.

When I get there, I look at it while she huffs and places it under her seat. "Can't you go sit somewhere else?" she mumbles.

"I can," I say, sitting next to her, putting on my seat belt, "but then who will keep you company?" I close my eyes, resting my head on the back of the chair.

She must see me with my eyes closed and chooses not to say anything. Because the next thing I know we are going down the runway on our way to Philly with our elbows fighting over the armrest. Stubborn girl.

# CHAPTER EIGHT

## KARRIE

"*This wouldn't happen if you wore normal clothes.*" The words play over and over in my head.

I look sideways at him. "Jerk," I whisper when I see him leaning his head back, his eyes closed. What the hell did he mean by that anyway, I ask myself, checking my very stylish outfit.

The plane jerks just a touch, giving me the chance to knock his elbow, waking him. "What time is it?" he asks, his voice soft, making me forget why I was mad at him in the first place.

"We should be landing in fifteen minutes. Are you tired?" I ask him while he blinks his eyes a bit to focus.

"I didn't sleep well last night," he says quietly, taking in everyone else, who is either listening to music or with their eyes closed. Some are reading, some are playing cards, others are on their phone, but no one is really talking.

"Why?" I ask, worried he might be getting sick.

"I guess I was just nervous about today. Almost like it's the first day back at school after summer break." He smiles and shrugs. "It's stupid."

I turn, reaching over and touching the same elbow I almost tried to dislocate. “It's not stupid. I get it. I still remember the day before I started high school I set out my clothes and dreamed all night that I would miss my alarm.”

“Yeah, Allison is like that.” He sits up straighter. “She also brings a change of clothes to school. Well, she did till Cooper decided that he was going to surprise her with lunch. Let’s just say she had a wardrobe check for a month. She was pissed.” He laughs softly, thinking about the memory. The ache in my heart was faint for not having that big family dynamic. Don’t get me wrong, my dad was always there for everything, I just had no one to share it with.

“Your sister sounds like my kind of person.” I smile at him while the landing wheels make sounds, letting us know it’s time for landing.

Once the plane lands, he stands up and his hand goes out to me. I grab it so I can get up, but I shouldn’t have. The simple touch has given me goose bumps all over my arms, making me shiver. It’s almost electric. I’m not sure he feels it, but one look up at him and I see his eyes fixed on our hands that are still connected. The door of the plane opens, making him drop my hand. Reaching up, he grabs his carry-on luggage and mine, carrying it off the plane for me.

They roll the steps straight to the plane, letting us get off on the tarmac. Again, a greyhound bus is waiting for us. I hold on to the railing, walking down behind Matthew. This time he is the one on the bus first. I was planning on sitting in another seat, but once I climb the bus he’s there, standing in the aisle, not moving.

“Excuse me,” I say, trying to get around him.

“Sit down, Karrie.” Three words. Three words that make me grit my teeth together. I make my way to the window, sitting and crossing my legs. He sits next to me, his feet crossed at the ankle, his hands crossed in the middle of his legs. “See how easy that was?”

I roll my eyes at him and glance out the window, not making eye contact with anyone. By the time the bus is loaded and we are on the way to the hotel, fatigue is starting to kick in. I close my eyes, listening to the little chatter that’s now going on around me.

I don’t know how long I’m asleep till I hear Matthew whisper in my ear, "Babe, we're here."

I open my eyes and see that my head has fallen on Matthew's arm. I sit up right away, looking around, making sure no one saw that.

He gets up again and reaches for my hand, but I stand up without taking it. Walking off the bus again, I see him holding my bag, so I reach out for it, but he just shoots me a look of 'don't even try it.' So I walk ahead of him into the hotel.

The hotel coordinator is there waiting for us. The guys each line up, say their name, and get their key cards. I get to the desk and say my name.

"Here is your card. Just so you know, the room is adjoining to a Matthew Grant."

I nod, taking it and walking to the elevator that has already taken some of the guys up.

There are about six of us who fill the next elevator. The guys look beat. We are all on the same floor. Slowly they each walk into their rooms saying goodnight with a see you tomorrow. Matthew stops at his door while I continue to mine, opening it and letting myself in.

It's a standard king-sized bedroom. The shades are still open, the light from the moon coming in. I approach the window, which overlooks the highway. It's almost two a.m., so few cars are on the road. I kick off my shoes and shrug my jacket off. I start pulling the shirt from the waist of my skirt when I hear a soft knock at the closed door that separates my room from Matthew's.

Walking to it, I open it up, expecting him to spit some nonsense at me, but what I see stops me from saying anything.

His jacket is off, the tie gone, two buttons at the collar open, showing his smooth chest. He's leaning against the doorframe.

"What?" I ask, trying not to take him in fully.

"Tonight was one of the best nights of my life." He starts talking while I'm still standing here holding the door handle in one hand. "After the fuck up, that is. I beat myself up. Cursed myself. I smashed my stick so hard I'm surprised it didn't break."

I look into his eyes, a light from his room making me see that his eyes are lighter than before.

"Then I had that breakaway and saw the puck hit the back of the net. I can't explain exactly what was going through my mind. It was such a big moment. It felt like maybe I deserved this second chance."

"Matthew," I whisper, going in closer to him, "you deserve this and so much more." The hand not holding the handle reaches out to touch his chest. It is a normal action, but to him it is something more. He looks down at my hand on him, making me do the same.

"I celebrated with my team, but in my head I was thinking of two people. One, I was thinking about my family, hoping like fuck I was making them proud." His hand goes on top of mine on his chest, his huge hand covering mine. His fingers lace with mine. "The second was you."

My breath intakes and I stop breathing, or at least that's what it feels like. My heart is beating, beating so loud I'm sure he can hear it. Hell, I'm sure that everyone can hear it through the walls.

"Skating back to the bench, I looked up and saw you cheering, cheering not just for the team, but deep down hoping that it was cheering for me." He comes closer to me, my chin dipping closer to my chest.

Our chests almost touch, but with my heels off I'm almost in the middle of his chest. Our hands now both at our sides, one of mine still on the doorknob. "Tell me, baby, tell me you were cheering for me."

My throat is dry, so dry it's like I'm in a desert walking all day long, running. Till his finger goes under my chin, lifting my face so I can look at him. "Tell me, did I make you proud?" His voice is almost silent.

I don't say anything. I just nod. My feet go up on my tippy toes so I can touch his face, my hand going to his cheek. The stubble pinches my hand. "I was cheering for you." My thumb rubs up his cheek and then slowly over his lips, my body moving without thinking. My body moving on need. My need to touch him, my need to tell him, "I was so proud of you." It's the last thing I say to him before he bends down and takes my lips against his.

Softly at first, so soft I don't know if I'm dreaming this or it's really happening, till his hands go to the back of my neck, into my hair, pulling my head back, his eyes meeting mine, then he kisses me and this time there's no wondering if he is or isn't. Because he's consuming me, his mouth over mine, his tongue licking my lips, making my tongue come out and meet his.

The second his tongue touches mine his hand fists my hair tighter, the groan coming out from me, vibrating from, Or in, my body. One hand goes around my waist, picking me up while my hands wrap around his neck, our lips never separating. Our tongues play a game of tug of war. Our heads move from side to side to get deeper into each other. Our chests heave, almost like we just crossed the finish line at a marathon.

"Fuck." I hear him hiss out when we finally let each other go.

I go back in to kiss his lips softly, just wanting one more touch. One more kiss.

"We," I say, sliding down his body, "um, let's just say it was a lack of judgment." I walk back into my room, ready to close the door, but he's now in my room. "I'm really tired."

"Lack of judgment?" He shakes his head. "That kiss just knocked me on my ass." He runs his hands through his hair, making him even sexier, making me even more irritated that he can look so good.

"Matthew," I say right before his hand cups my hip, squeezing.

"Go change for bed before I pick you up, throw you on that bed, and show you exactly what a lack of judgment will get you. I'll be buried so deep in you, you'll wonder how we'll ever be apart again."

Yup, panties gone. Yup, I've lost my mind, and yup, I'm really hoping he has a lack of judgment right about now.

I turn to walk away, but his hand holds me in place, his head bending to kiss me on my lips, my lips accepting his. My lips tingle when he finally leaves. I grab my bag, going into the bathroom, collapsing on the back of the door. Closing my eyes, I still feel his hands on me. Getting up and regarding myself in the mirror, I see that my lips are plumper. I rub my fingers over them, still feeling his kiss. I wash my face, taking my makeup off, and applying my night cream.

After putting on my PJs, I close the light before I open the door. The room is pitched in darkness at this point, so I'm sure he's gone to bed. Walking toward my bed, I see something under the covers—I see him under my covers.

"Matthew," I whisper, putting my knee on the bed, but he doesn't hear me. He's long gone. His soft snore fills the room. His body finally gets the rest he needs. I get into bed with him. It's a big bed, right? Wrong. The minute I turn on my side, he's in the back of me. His legs intertwine with mine, his hand resting across my waist.

"Night, babe."

I don't answer him because the soft snoring starts again.

# CHAPTER NINE

## MATTHEW

I'm walking down the corridor right after skate practice, holding two cups of coffee. It's been four hours since I've been up and gone and I'm wondering if Karrie will even be in her room.

Last night's kiss played in my mind all night long. After she walked in her bathroom, I undressed and decided I'd wait to get another goodnight kiss in her bed. I wasn't counting on crashing. My body just gave up and sleep took over. I felt her come to bed, felt the covers move, felt the bed dip, my eyes opening just for a second to get her near me. As soon as my body hugged hers, I fell back into a slumber. In fact, I hadn't slept that good in forever.

Then waking up and peeking over at her, her mouth was slightly open while soft snores came out of her. I was almost tempted to yank her into me, but I didn't know how she would react to the whole I was in your bed last night. So I slowly climbed out of bed, my cock under protest since he felt her ass wiggle right before I moved away from her. Walking into my bathroom in my room, I took a shower and also took care of business in the name of a raging hard-on. Fuck.

Getting out and drying off, I walked to my bag with the towel around my waist. A look into her room showed me she'd turned over and that she was still sleeping. I grabbed my things for the gym and made my way downstairs for breakfast with Phil and then my first team practice.

Now here I am walking into my room, my eyes automatically going to hers. I see her sitting in bed dressed in jeans and a top, a book in her hand.

"Hey, babe," I say, walking in, handing her one of the coffees.

"Um, hey." She reaches for the cup while I go to the other side of the bed and sit down.

I kick off my shoes, looking at her. She has no makeup on today. Her feet are still bare, her toenails painted a light pink.

"What time did you get up?" I ask her while she takes a sip of her coffee.

"Um, about that, I think we should discuss what happened last night," she says, putting the coffee on the side table next to her.

My eyebrows pinch together.

"I think we got out of hand with the whole kiss thing. It was an emotional night for you and we got swept away in the moment."

"Swept away in the moment?" I ask, confused. "What the fuck does that mean?"

"Listen, I have a job here and I don't want to be known as another conquest, so from now on—" I cut her off, raising my hand.

"From now on when I want to kiss you, I'll wait till we are in private." I nod at her. "I don't want them to think this thing with us is just because of who your father is."

Her body goes straight up stiff while she faces me. "Perhaps you didn't understand. There will be no more kissing." She tries to get off the bed, but my hand grabs her wrist before she can and then she turns to glare at me.

"And no more sleepovers. You get your bed. I get mine." That's the last thing she says because the next thing that happens is she is on her back and I'm on top of her. Her crystal blue eyes are a dark, cloudy blue.

"Babe, there's going to be more than sleepovers. I'm going to be in your bed. In a hotel or at home." I lean down to kiss her lips before she can argue with me, wanting to go slow, but I can't. The minute I taste her, I can't stop. Her legs open, wrapping around my waist, locking at the ankle. I rest my weight on my elbows so I don't squash her. My tongue twirls with hers. Her hands now go through my hair, then she arches her back up, rubbing her pussy against my cock, which is straining.

Once I know I've kissed her silly, I slowly peel my lips from hers, kissing the side of her mouth, to her chin, to her neck, up to nip at her ear. "Now that I've got you breathless, I want you to listen." I run soft kisses on her chin. "You listening?" I ask her.

She nods.

"This, me, you. It's happening. I'm going to kiss you," I tell her, running my tongue out while I kiss her neck. "I'm going to come home and come to your bed. Or you can come to mine, but"—I kiss her lips again—"make no mistake about it. This thing is happening." The blue in her eyes becomes clear again.

"Matthew"—her hands rub my back—"we can't do this." Her voice is soft. "Can you imagine what they would say if they found out?"

"So we keep it quiet till we decide to tell people. Tell me you get that this is happening."

"Matthew," she groans out.

"Babe." I stop her. "I need a nap," I tell her, rolling to my side and taking her with me.

"Ma—"

I put my hand to her lips. "Shh. Let's rest. Yeah." And I close my eyes, pretending I'm going to sleep, but knowing she's glaring at me with death in her eyes. Opening one eye, I spot the look I thought she had on. Yup, dead.

"You're beautiful." Is the last thing I say before I close my eyes again. We both fall into a nap.

I'm about to put my suit jacket on when my phone rings beside the sink. I'm in my bathroom because all my stuff is here, but next time, I laugh to myself, thinking she's going to throw my shit out. I'm pretty sure. When I see it's my mom I answer right away.

"Hey, Mom," I say, packing up my stuff since we are going straight home from the game.

"Hey, sweetheart, you did so good," she tells me, and I can hear the smile on her face.

"Yeah, I'm actually feeling really, really good."

"You played a really good game last night. You ready for tonight?"

I throw my stuff in my bag, zipping it up. "Yeah, I had practice with the guys today. I like the team, like the dynamic. I'm just happy to have the chance."

"That sounds so promising." I hear her voice go off.

"What's wrong?"

"I didn't want to get involved and Cooper told me to mind my business, but your father called me."

I stop what I'm doing and look up at the ceiling, closing my eyes. I haven't spoken to my father in five years. The minute Mom had Zoe and Zara, he upped himself and moved out of state. The daily phone calls went to weekly, to bi-weekly, to monthly, to just a fucking text on my birthday. I won't even go into the shit he pulled before Mom and him got divorced. He was never really there anyway. Where all my friends would go to the rink with their dads, mine would be working. Traveling. I can count on my hand the amount of times he actually got off his ass and took me to practice.

My mother, that was who raised me. That was who gave up everything for me and Allison. Till Cooper came, then he showed me what it was to actually have a family. To actually come home to a family who did things together and that didn't just co-exist.

"He said he texted you a couple of times," she says softly.

"A text, seriously?" I shake my head. "When I got sent down to the minors, he sent me a text with one word 'nice,'" I tell her, something she didn't know because I didn't want to make her go and kick his ass.

"I didn't know," she says quietly.

"Because he's a douchebag. When's the last time he actually picked up the phone and called Allison?" I ask her, my voice getting louder. "When is the last time he actually took time out of his day for his children?" I slam my suitcase shut. "I can tell you, a long fucking time ago. I think I was maybe ten. He has no right to involve you in this shit. But you know what?" I laugh to myself. "That's just the type of person he is. Notice I didn't say man, Mom, because he isn't."

"I promise to never bring it up."

I nod, knowing Cooper will be hearing about this. The minute my mother feels sad, or her mood changes, it's like he knows. It's like he senses it, which is how strong their bond is. I look up and I'm shocked that Karrie is standing there in the doorway. She stares at me with confusion in her eyes, sadness, and most of all worry. This woman who I met two days ago has embedded herself in me and I have no idea how I lived without her.

"Mom, I got to go. The bus is leaving in ten minutes. Kiss the kids for me and smack Allison upside the head. Tell her I saw her stupid Instagram post and to delete it or else." I hang up, knowing that my mother is laughing and calling Allison right away.

"Is everything okay?" she asks from the side of the door. She is standing there with her tight blue jeans, a beige jacket, some scarf thing around her neck, and brown high heel boots. I toss my phone on the bed, looking back at her.

"It's"—I look back at my bag then up at her again—"it's nothing." I shake my head. "Come give me a kiss."

She stands there, her stance going from worried about me to pissed while she crosses her arms across her chest, cocking her hip out. "No." She shakes her head.

"Babe." I start to walk to her when she holds out her hand.

"Don't come near me, Matthew Grant." She steps back. "You come all in my face"—she waves her hands in the air—"and I forget things, like how I don't like you." She closes the door to her side of the room.

I knock on the door, whispering, "Karrie, I need a kiss good luck."

"No," she says from her side of the door.

"Please," I say smiling, hoping it's winning her over.

The doorknob turns, opening the door. "No kissing," she says through the small crack.

I wait for the door to open more.

"I have lipstick, and I've just applied it. And I don't want—"

And that's all I let her say before pushing the door open and grabbing her face.

"I don't care." My lips land on hers. My tongue invades hers as her hands go to my hips. My tongue twirls with hers, her strawberry lip gloss now transferred to mine. My hands never leave her cheeks.

I let go of the kiss, leaning back while her eyes slowly blink open. "See, wasn't that easy?" I say while her nails dig into my hips, making me laugh.

She lets go, letting my hands fall to my sides. Going to her bag, she opens it up, grabbing what looks like wet ones.

"Here"—she hands me one—"clean your face so you don't have any glitter or shine."

I take it from her, wiping my face. "Do I have any more?" I ask her.

She walks up to me, taking the rag from me and cleaning me again.

"I still don't like you," she says, while I try not to smile. "Just so you know." She finishes and turns around, throwing the towelette into the garbage. "Now let's go so we don't miss the bus." She zips everything up, walking to the door. "Don't follow me." She points to the door. "Go out there so people don't suspect anything."

"No one is going to suspect anything," I tell her, going to my room, grabbing my stuff, and walking out of my room. I meet five of my teammates when I walk out. I say hello to everyone, my eyes landing on Karrie, who is standing there with an 'I told you so' look.

I can't really say anything to her because for once she's right. Okay, maybe more than once, but I won't ever tell her that.

# CHAPTER TEN

## KARRIE

I glare at him, knowing that he knows I'm right but won't say anything. The smirk says it all. I avoid standing next to him. I even avoid sitting with him on the bus, instead going to sit next to Robert, who is already on the bus. Just when I think he is going to go sit in the back, he sits in the same aisle on the other side. He puts his ear buds in and watches something on his phone and by the time I look around we are headed home, back on the plane after winning in Philly three to one. He didn't score this time, but he did have two assists. His third line is on fire. The reporters are all waiting for them to interview them after the game. Matthew stays out of most of them, choosing to let his other teammates get the spotlight.

I'm standing by the bus thinking this when a reporter comes on with the highlights of the game. While they talk about the new addition, they also point out some of the key top line players that are slacking. There's also a close shot of Max yelling something at the ref. I can't make out what he says, but I'm sure it isn't words of love. There's another shot of him telling Matthew to fuck off clear as day. Matthew just looks at him, shaking his head. Mr. Cool. That is what the reporters are dubbing him. I smile to myself while the door to the bus opens. I get on, sitting in the front again, grabbing a magazine, this time to read while I wait for the team to get on. Slowly they trickle in. When I feel someone sit next to me, I look up expecting it to be Matthew, but the snide smile of Max makes my insides flop down.

"What? Expecting Mr. Perfect?" he says a bit loud so everyone can hear.

"I'm not expecting anyone actually and if I was expecting Mr. Perfect, he's definitely not the one sitting next to me," I tell him, flipping pages on the magazine, not even reading anymore.

"That was funny," he says, picking a piece of lint off his jacket. "So what did you think of the game?" he asks me, and I'm not sure where he is going with this. I also don't want to be a bitch either.

"It was good, a great win, especially since their goalie was on a five-game winning streak." I repeat the statement that I just heard watching the highlights.

"Yeah, it was good to fuck with them." He smirks when he sees Matthew get on the bus with Phil following him. He takes in the sight of Max next to me and I see a vein in his neck tic. He takes the seat behind me while Phil sits next to him.

The conversation with Max ends the minute I feel two eyes staring through the seat. When we get off the bus at the plane I slow my steps, pretending to be searching for something in my purse, till Max walks ahead of me, walking up the stairs.

"Let's go." I hear growled beside me and feel his hand at the base of my back. I'm about to argue with him, but I feel the anger radiating off him.

"I didn't." I don't even finish saying anything before he turns almost black eyes on me.

"Not now." Is all he says while I climb the stairs to the plane.

I'm almost tempted to go and sit somewhere else, but something tells me this would not bode well for me, so I sit in the first available row. He puts his bag up in the overhead compartment and sits next to me. I look around before I say something, but there are just too many people here, so instead I grab my earphones and put them in, leaning my head against the side of the plane, closing my eyes.

By the time we are dragging our bags into the house, it is way past three a.m. I'm dead on my feet. "I'm so tired," I say, dumping my bags at the door and kicking off my shoes. I don't get past the doorway before I'm turned around and I'm in Matthew's arms. His whole body engulfs me. His smell invades me.

"Don't do that again," he hisses out before he kisses me. Actually that's not a strong enough word. He claims me, he swallows me, he invades me. And I let him. He grabs my waist, picking me up. My legs wrap around his waist while he carries me upstairs to my room. Our lips never leave the other. One of my hands is in his hair, the other around his neck, trying to get closer to him. His tongue plays me like a fiddle. He lets go of my lips to drag his tongue down my neck where he sucks a touch, making my core shiver to his touch.

"Mine." Is all he says when his legs hit my bed, and my legs come off of him, my knees going into the bed in front of him. My face meets his chest.

I look up at him. His hands push the hair behind my ear, the touch soft and lingering. His thumb then traces my cheekbone.

"Beauty," he says while his thumb rubs my bottom lip, which still tingles from his kiss. "Get ready for bed," he says, walking away from me and leaving the room.

I get up, following him to see him walk up the stairs. Well, I guess that answers that question. I close the door softly, going into my bathroom to change and wash the makeup off. I feel like a vampire these days, sleeping most of the day and up at insane times of the night.

I close the light while I rub cream on my hands, walking to bed. I stop in my tracks. There he sits. His back to the headboard, sheets at his waist.

"What are you—" I say, walking to him in my long shirt nightgown.

"Do you have a side you sleep on?" he asks while I stand here staring at his chest. His chest of perfection, I might add. His chest that I would like to sleep on. His chest I would like to put my hands on while I ride him, hard. His chest that I would bite if he were on top of me. "Babe?"

he asks me with a twinkle in his eye, like he knows I was thinking about him.

I almost want to squeeze my knees together, but I don't want to give him the satisfaction. Instead, I pull the covers up, seeing that he's in his boxers, and his cock is ready for that riding I want to do.

"See something you like?" he asks, throwing the covers off of him so I can see him. I curse the gods for making black boxers.

I shrug my shoulders. "Nope," I huff, pulling the covers on top of me to my neck, fluffing the pillow, "nothing at all." I close my eyes, trying to find slumber. Instead, I feel a hard body against my back—not just the body but a hard dick. A dick I would like to be very familiar with.

"You can pretend all you want, babe, but I bet if I slid my hand down into your shorts I'd find your pussy wet for me."

Assface, that's what he is. Two can play this game. "You probably would. I've just finished masturbating before coming to bed." I smile while I feel his body go tense.

"You didn't?" he asks.

"You'll never know either. Goodnight." I turn back around and close my eyes, his groan making me smile to myself right before I fall asleep.

The next day we wake up to the sound of his alarm at nine. "Turn it off," I mumble while I turn to face him, coming face to face with his chest that I spent the night dreaming about.

He turns the alarm off or presses snooze, I'm not sure because he turns back to face me, pulling me close to him. I snuggle into him, falling asleep again, only to be woken up to his alarm, again.

"Get out." I push him back. One eye opens, watching him get out of bed. He's in the same state as he was last night. Alert and saluting. "Go rub one off before practice or you'll be really uptight."

"You thinking about my cock?" He smiles, cupping himself.

"Not as much as my pink vibrator in the bathroom. Hey"—I lean up on my elbow—"can you close the door on the way out? You know, just in case." I smile at him.

"I'm going to find that plastic dick and I'm going to melt it," he says, walking to the bathroom.

"How do you know it's plastic? It could be glass. Or it could be a replica of my ex's." I want to continue, but I think his head is going to explode. He turns, storming out of the room, slamming the door. Leaving me to giggle to myself. I pick up my phone, texting Vivienne.

**Coffee?**

**Bien sur. Meet you there, same place, oui?**

We always meet at the French coffee shop by my house. It's almost like home according to Vivienne.

À **bientôt.** I reply I will see you later in French. I get up, going to the bathroom and then downstairs where I find Matthew sitting in the kitchen eating what looks like cereal and fruit with yogurt. He's already dressed in his workout clothes. I walk over to the coffee pot and pour myself a cup, adding milk to it.

He lifts his gaze from his bowl with a scowl on his face.

"What's up, buttercup? Did you not drain the snake?" I smile in my cup while he glares at me. "Are you one of those that can't"—I make a fist in front of me, thrusting—"you know, finish things?" I laugh at him. "It's okay if that's what you suffer from."

He drops his spoon into the bowl and gets up, carrying the bowl with him. He places it in the sink softly then turns around, coming straight to me. "It's a good thing I have to leave and Phil is picking me up, because I'd show you exactly how I finish." He leans in, whispering, "All fucking day and night I'd show you till you beg me to stop."

I stand here mouth open. I got served.

"Bye, babe." He kisses my lips before walking out to Phil, who has just honked.

"Assface, jerkoff." I slam my cup down on the counter, and then wipe down the mess I made. "It's all his fault. Comes into my life"—I rinse his plate—"bossing me around"—I swing the dishwasher open, yanking the drawer out, placing the cups from breakfast in there—"sleeping in my bed." I slam the door back closed. "Who does he think he is?" I put away the box of cereal he left out. "I'll tell you who he thinks he is, the boss of me." I slam the cupboard closed. "He isn't the boss of me." I storm upstairs, fixing the bed. "Doesn't even make the bed." I throw the pillows to the end of the bed and then continue fixing it. I pick up his pillow, bringing it to my nose, smelling him. "Ugh and he smells good.

Piss off," I tell the pillow, throwing it on the bed. Then like a lightbulb in my head I run to my closet, taking my pink rabbit vibrator out. "I'll show you fucking all day and night." I put the vibrator under the covers on his side. "Take that," I tell the covers.

After I finish, I walk up to my office where I open my computer. I go through the emails that the PR girl has sent me about the travel schedule. There's a ten-day road trip in three weeks. Then we get five days off. I check the calendar and see if maybe I could get away. I pull up some vacation to Cabo, some to California. I mess around on Facebook. I'm shocked to have a friend request from his sister Allison. I ignore it for a second, wanting to talk to Matthew about this. Noticing the time, I've spent four hours doing nothing on the computer. I have to meet Vivienne in less than twenty minutes. I put on a coat of mascara, throw on some yoga pants with a tight camisole, a jacket, and scarf. I make it to the store in record time.

I spot Vivienne right away, her hair the color of a red velvet cake, long to the waist, in bouncy curls. She sits there wearing her black tight jeans, black shirt, and a peach color jacket. Her accessories are all black. I take the seat in front of her while she looks up.

"Enfin." Finally, she says in French. I air kiss her from my side of the table.

"Please, you probably just got here." I glance around and then at my phone. "I'm one minute late."

"I've been here for four minutes. You know how I have a phobia about sitting alone in restaurants." This is true. She won't even eat in a fast food restaurant by herself. She would rather go through the drive thru and eat in the car. "So tell me"—she looks at me—"no sex yet, I can see."

I scoff at her. "How can you tell?" I say, grabbing one of the coffee cups on the table. It's our thing that whoever gets there first buys the coffee and croissants. I pick a piece off, chewing. "I could have spent all night having sex."

She leans forward on the table. "Chérie"—sweetheart in French—"you wouldn't be able to walk."

"I would so be able to walk. Maybe his penis is small." I cringe because it's the opposite of the truth.

She slams her hand on the table, drawing attention from the other people in the shop. "Lies." She pulls out her phone, typing something on it, showing me a picture that Matthew is posing for. He's in shorts and is flipping over what looks like a tractor tire. His abs are so defined you can see each muscle. His arms are huge with drops of water shining in the sun. The sweat leaking down all over him, his stare is on the camera and not on the tire that might break his nose. "This doesn't come avec une petit penis," she says small penis in French in case the French owners can't understand her.

I sit back in my chair about to answer her when my phone rings. "Hello."

"Where are you?" is barked out.

"Well, hello, sunshine." I roll my eyes.

"You aren't home?"

"Wow, aren't you Sherlock Holmes. What is the problem?"

"I'm home."

"Okay." I peer at Vivienne, who is snickering like she is drunk. "So you're home. I still don't understand. What do you want?"

"Where are you?"

"I'm out with my friend having coffee."

"Where? I'll come meet you."

I'm already shaking my head while Vivienne yells out the coffee shop's name.

"See you in five." And he disconnects.

"Great." I put the phone down. "Thanks for that!"

"De rien," she says I'm welcome.

I get up, going to the counter and ordering two more croissants. I sit down and am about to take a bite when I hear the bell over the door chime. I know right away it's him because I see Vivienne's eyes almost bulge out of her head and her mouth hangs open.

"Hey, babe," he says, kissing my lips and sitting next to me.

"We are in public." I point out to him. "Anyone can see."

He shrugs his shoulders, picking the hat off his head to scratch it and then putting it backward.

"Menteuse!"You liar, Vivienne yells next to me. "He is so hot."

I roll my eyes while Matthew puts his arm around my chair and moves his thumb against my back. "He's not that hot."

Vivienne laughs at me, leaning in. "Did you go to the optometrist again and they put that dye in your eye making you see blurry?" she asks me with a serious face.

"No. Meet my friend Vivienne."

He smiles.

"The last time she did that exam she broke her foot walking into her bedroom door." She laughs, picking up her coffee cup. "Remember you had to get that scooter for your foot?"

"Okay, so this has been fun," I say, getting up.

"Relax, sit down," Matthew says, leaning in to grab a croissant and chewing it. "These are awesome."

"They are," I agree with him, sipping my cold coffee.

"So, Matthew, tell me, we were discussing proportion," Vivienne says. Being French, they have no qualms about discussing sex in the middle of the day in a corner store.

"We were not discussing anything like that." I try to change the subject, giving Vivienne my narrowed eyes, hoping she gets it.

"Oh, okay. Sorry, we weren't discussing if you have a big penis or not. Ma faute." My bad, she ends that sentence.

"She'll tell you I'm like a horse."

I roll my eyes.

"Tell her." He points to Vivienne

"I'm not telling her anything because I don't know anything. And really, Matthew, a horse?" I watch him smirk.

"Okay, fine, not a horse, but close to it." He motions with his hands. "Big."

Vivienne can't stop laughing and for the next hour the two of them trade sex jokes while I pretend that I'm not with them. By the end of the hour, we have plans to meet up the next time we are home. Which is in about a week.

When we say goodbye Vivienne whispers in my ear, "J'espère que tu vas prendre ton pied!" She did not just tell me she hopes I get properly fucked in the middle of the store.

"I don't know what she said, but we should do it," Matthew says, holding my hand while we walk away.

"She said she hopes that the medicine you got for your crabs works." I smile up at him, then down at our hands. It feels like we've been doing this forever, yet last week I didn't even know him.

# CHAPTER ELEVEN

## MATTHEW

When I got home and saw that Karrie wasn't anywhere, my heart sped up a bit, not sure why, but I just wanted her there. Must have run up and down the stairs in two seconds flat. When she told me she was having coffee I ran down there. Literally. She was sitting with her friend Vivienne, who is a hoot. The way she switched from English to French made it look so natural and then hearing Karrie speaking French, my cock had never been harder. I made a mental note to ask her to speak French to me while I eat her.

"I don't know what she said, but we should do it," I tell her while I grab her hand in mine as we walk down the street.

"She said she hopes that the medicine you got for your crabs works." She smiles up at me and then looks down at our hands.

I stop walking, throwing my head back and laughing at this comment.

"You guys were talking about my dick?" I ask her, turning to face her, pushing the hair away from her face with my free hand. I lift our hands up together, kissing her fingers that are linked with mine.

"Seriously, after everything I just said that's the only thing you thought about?" She turns to continue walking, dragging me with her. "I'm starving," she says, smelling the aroma in the air. It smells like barbecue, making my stomach grumble also.

"You have a grill at home?" I ask her, walking across the street to where I see a butcher.

"Yes, but I…" she says, following me into the butcher shop. "I don't know if it works."

"Whatever, we can pan cook it if anything. Can I get two Rib eye steaks about eight ounces each?" I ask the butcher. "What do you want?"

"You just ordered two."

"For me. I'm training, babe, got to eat the protein. We'll take three then." My hand lets go of hers, but only for my arm to wrap around her shoulders, pulling her toward me.

She smiles at me and it lights up her eyes. Her face goes soft. I lean down and softly kiss her lips.

I pay the butcher as we walk home holding hands, not saying anything. I feel peace, which is a feeling I haven't felt, well ever.

I feel settled, almost like if something happens, it will all be okay.

"We should make some baked potatoes with those steaks," I tell her while she unlocks the door and almost stumbles into the boxes that fill up the entrance.

"What the hell is all this?" she asks, looking at about fifteen to twenty boxes that are scattered around.

"It's my stuff. My mom shipped my clothes and stuff." I assess her while she takes in the entrance. "And that box over there"—I point to the white boxes—"are T-shirts and jerseys and stuff to sign for the foundation. Grab yourself one for the next game." I walk to the kitchen.

"I already bought mine," she says from behind me, having me stop mid-step, turning to her.

"You bought my jersey?" I ask her softly, my heart beating fast, my hands becoming clammy. I don't know why it's a big deal, but it is. I've always had people cheering for me, wearing my jersey, asking for my signature. It was always just a thing, but now knowing that she bought it. She bought it, not that I gave it to her, or made her. It's something. It's everything.

"Matthew." Her voice breaks through the haze. "You okay?" she asks, coming to me, her hands landing on my chest. Her palms open right over my heart.

"You bought my jersey," I whisper while she nods her head yes. "I can't tell you how turned on I am right now." I grab her hips, pulling her to me, my cock busting to get out.

"Um, Matthew, you are pretty much always turned on." She smiles at me, getting on her tippy toes, kissing under my jaw. "Now feed me, please."

I shoot my eyebrows up at her. "I can feed you something really big right now."

She tilts her head to the side. "Can I bite it off?"

I hiss out, thinking of her teeth chopping on my rod.

"Glad you agree."

"Okay, you start the potatoes in the oven. I'll go in search of the grill." I tap her nose, turning to walk outside. I uncover the new grill, turning it on. I march back inside where I see her cutting up the making of a salad. "The grill is good to go. How do you take your steak?" I ask her, going over and prepping them with salt and pepper.

"Medium rare would be good."

We work side by side till I grab the steaks and head outside. By the time I'm done I walk into the house, going to the dining room. The lights are dimmed. Some jazz music is filling the house. Karrie is lighting some candles while swaying to the music.

I walk to her, kissing the back of her neck that is bare, since she tied her hair on top of her head. The smell of peaches fills my nose.

We sit down and fill our plates with food. She grabs a glass of wine, filling it, "You want some?"

"No. I'm good with water." I cut into my steak, taking the first bite. Not bad.

"So." I hear her voice while she takes a sip of wine. "I think we should talk about things."

I smile at her while I cut another piece of steak. "You're a talker, aren't you?" I drink some water. "Even in bed?" I wink at her.

She puts the bite of potato in her mouth and then points the fork at me. “This is why we have to talk.”

“Let’s talk,” I say, eating.

“Are we really going to be sleeping in the same bed together all the time? I think that’s a little extreme.” She cuts her own steak.

“If you are in the same house or hotel with me, we sleep in the same bed. Next,” I tell her. This isn’t an option.

“What if I want to sleep alone? What if I need alone time?” she asks me.

“You need alone time, you tell me, you don’t need alone time when you sleep,” I say, grabbing more salad.

“What about sex?” she asks, and I almost choke on the piece of steak in my mouth.

“What about sex? We are going to have it. Lots of it. I plan to have lots and lots of sex with you.”

“Why me?” she asks me, putting her fork down and drinking the rest of her wine, then filling up her glass again. “I mean, honestly, you're you.” She drinks again. “There’s a reason I was hired. I didn’t read your file.” She drinks again. “I just.” She drinks again. “I’ve never done the whole boyfriend sleeping over and stuff.”

I put my fork and knife down gently, instead of slamming them down. “Let’s tackle that one at a time, shall we?” I lean forward, “Why you?” I start, “Why not you? I was pulled to you the minute I saw you, then I saw you in the office, and you gave me that sass. You didn’t give a shit who I was. You called me out on all the bullshit I threw at you and did it with almost a smile on your face.” I smirk at her, remembering that day. “You wanted to stab me that first day.” She smiles in her glass. “And most of the times after that.”

“Pretty much.” She sips her wine again.

“You're beautiful, sexy, and sassy. You're independent and you will never cave and let me get away with shit,” I continue while she sits there with her wine glass, watching her, not sure if she should drink or not. “You also don’t give a shit who I am or that I’m a professional athlete. You look at me and see me. That makes you worth everything.” I scoot back in my chair. “Come here, Karrie.” I wait for her to look at me and see the things that must be running through her head. I don’t know why

I'm holding my breath, but I am.

She takes a second to take me in before pushing back and coming to my side. My hand goes up her legs to her ass, where I squeeze and then move up to her back. I grab her hips, turning her around so she can sit on my lap. Her ass sits directly on my cock while she crosses her legs that hang on the side of me.

"I don't know what is in that file." I start while I look straight into her eyes. "I have no doubt any of it is good. I was a young stupid kid." I close my eyes, thinking back to the way I just let loose once I was out of my house. "My whole life I pretended to be happy."

She looks at me, confused.

"Don't get me wrong, I had a great childhood. My mother made sure we were always her priority. But my father, he"—I shake my head—"he couldn't care less who he hurt or what he did. When they divorced, I used to listen to my mom cry at night." The memories are etched into my heart. "I vowed to never be the one to make her cry," I continue while Karrie puts a hand over my shoulder and comes in for a hug, her face going into the nook of my neck. She fits into my body as if she were made for me.

"I'm sorry," she whispers, another thing that draws me to her. Her heart is soft and even if she didn't want to care she does.

"So I just pretended nothing bothered me. I pretended I was happy when all I wanted to do was yell at the top of my lungs, wanted to get into his face and yell 'Why?' but I did the only thing I could. I took care of my mom and sister. It was easier than having a meltdown and seeing my mother add another thing to worry about to her shoulders. Then she met Cooper and I slowly started coming out. I was way more aggressive on the ice." Her face comes out of my nook. I move her hair off her shoulder while I kiss her neck. "My first NHL game, I dropped the gloves. It was stupid. I got benched for two games after that. I got my ass chewed by everyone that I knew. So then I took it out when we went out. I would get into fights with anyone, just for the fuck of it, because I was The Matthew Grant. There were even a couple of lawsuits that they buried. The partying took over my life also. I was just happy to not be perfect Matthew."

"You don't have to continue," she tells me.

"I don't have to, but I want to. I want to give you all of me. I don't want to hide who I am from you. That past is a piece of me, just like what we are doing is a piece of me, just like my childhood is a piece of me." I take a deep breath. "There were lots of women." The minute the words come out of my mouth her body stills, she gets stiff, and tries to get up.

"Okay, I think we have had enough talking for one night." But I block her with my arm around her waist.

"No, we are doing this because once I get in there, I'm not fucking leaving. So we do this now."

"Once you get in there?" Her head cocks to the side.

"Yeah," I say, pointing to her heart. "Once I get in there, I'm never leaving."

"Okay, I get it you had women. You weren't a boy scout. You had orgies, I get it." She starts babbling. "I don't really need to hear the details."

"I didn't have orgies," I tell her. "Seriously, I wasn't that bad."

"You have a number?" she asks, now crossing her arms, the look almost like she wants to shank me.

"I don't, do you?" I feel like throwing up. I might be sick. The steak that I just ate is sitting like a clump of coal in my stomach.

"Do I what, have a number? Um." Her head drops. "One," she whispers, "Ish."

I look at the vein in her neck moving fast. My finger goes to it so I can feel her heartbeat. "Ish?" I ask her.

"I really don't want to do this," she says to me.

"In this room, in this house, anywhere we are, when it's me and you, it's a safe place. I will never ever throw anything you tell me in your face. I will never treat you without the respect you deserve. I will never put your feelings in the back of mine. I will always make you feel safe, because that's the man I want to be, but more importantly that's the only thing you deserve."

She looks right through me, her blue eyes shining bluer than I have ever seen. "I've never really done it."

"What do you mean? You don't think you did it?" The blue eyes now glare.

"It was our first time for both," she hisses. "You happy now, Mr. My Penis is the social butterfly?" She pushes and gets up because she catches me off guard. "He finished early, okay?"

"Wait, so you're a virgin?" I ask, shocked and thanking whoever the god is that gave her to me..

"You're an asshole," she says, grabbing her plate and storming out. "Let's have a talk," she talks to herself. "It's going to be okay." She rinses off her plate. "I've been with women. I'm a manwhore." She continues while she is putting the plate in the dishwasher and throwing her hands in the air.

"Babe," I say, watching as she throws her hands up, turns, and walks back into the dining room, blowing out the candles.

She turns around. "Don't you babe me. So what? I'm not 'experienced' like you." She puts up her hands, making the quotation marks around experienced. "You know what? I should go out and have sex tonight." Is the last thing she says because I go to her and pick her up over my head, throwing her over my shoulder, making her squeal. I smack her ass with one hand. "Put me down, you baboon." She slaps my ass with her hands while I turn and walk up the stairs.

Once I get into her room, I toss her on the bed. "The only cock that will be fucking you will be mine," I tell her while she gets on her elbows, raising herself up. "You got that?" I ask her.

She rolls her eyes at me. "Yeah, yeah."

"Good. I need a shower." I point at her. "Get your ass ready. Tonight we go to second base."

I don't wait for her to answer. Instead, I run upstairs to shower in my own bathroom, only because I haven't moved my things to hers. I make a note to remedy that tomorrow.

# CHAPTER TWELVE

## KARRIE

What the hell does that mean? Second base? Is there a thing? Is that boob groping or is it oral? I get my phone and call Vivienne.

"What does it mean when he says tonight we are going to second base?" I ask as soon as she answers.

"Mon Dieu." Dear God, she says. "What are you talking about?"

I get up off my bed and tiptoe to my door, sticking my head out to hear where Matthew is.

"I had the talk with Matthew," I whisper, going into the hall.

"You mean the nonexistent sex you had?" She laughs while she says.

"Merde." Shit, I say in French when I hear the water from the upstairs bathroom shut off. "Okay, quick, what is second base? Is it nipple play or sucking dick? Matthew just said get ready for second base."

All I hear is laughing on her side of the phone. "I think you should bounce on that all night long, twice. Make your own second base."

"I don't know why we are friends," I whisper, looking up while my back is against the wall.

"Parce que tu m'aimes." Because you love me, she says. "Appelle moi plus tard. Explain what second base is." Call me later, she asks.

"D'accord." Fine, I say, hanging up, going to my bedroom. I start pacing the floor when I see Matthew walking down the stairs, towel around his waist.

He comes in the room, the water still dripping on his chest from his hair. "Babe, you didn't shower?" He takes in my appearance, noticing that I'm still dressed.

"I was"—I hold the phone in my hand—"I was on the phone. Vivienne called."

"I like her," he says, coming into the room. "We should set up drinks with her and Phil. They might hit it off."

"Why are you naked?" I shake my head. "Sorry, why aren't you dressed or in your boxers?" I ask him.

"I usually sleep naked," he says, going to the bed and sitting down, the towel cracking, showing me his legs, but covering the family jewels.

"You can't sleep naked. Second base isn't naked. It's dressed."

"Would you feel better if I was wearing boxers?" He gets up.

"Um, yes, I think I would," I tell him. "Now go get your boxers and clean up the kitchen downstairs. You left your plate on the table and it's going to stink."

"On it," he says, stopping to put his finger under my chin, kissing the side of my mouth. "Can't wait for second base," he says, walking out.

I start to panic, running to my underwear drawer, getting matching lace panties and bra. "Black or white?" I ask no one. "Not red, that's a third base color." I walk into the bathroom and take a shower in record time. Thankfully I shaved and groomed in the shower this morning. I spray my peach oil on myself, rubbing it in. I take myself in. "I can do this. I got this." I walk into the room and notice that he still isn't back upstairs, giving me time to get under the covers and wait. In anticipation, shit, I forgot deodorant. I lift my arm, smelling. All good. I lean back, watching my boobs move, not making them be perky. "Okay, sitting up."

I hear him walk into the room, shutting off the lights in the hallway. He comes in wearing his boxers that fit him like a second glove. Water actually pools in my mouth. I lean over, opening the light on the side table. It's a dim light. "All clean," he says, walking over to his side of the bed, peeling off the covers, and he stops. At first I don't know what's wrong till I look over and see the vibrator I forgot I put there. "What the fuck?"

"Oh, that." I try to grab it, but he already has it in his hand. "I finished with it this morning after you left. I forgot." I'm lying out of my teeth.

He turns the button on and all you see is the shaft move in circles, the silver pearls inside moving. He walks over to the window opens it and tosses the vibrator outside. I get up, rushing to the window.

"Are you insane?" I ask him, peering outside to see it lying in the middle of the road. "You could have hit a car, or better yet a person."

"Where are the rest? Might as well get rid of them now," he says, walking to my closet where he moves things around.

I close the window and follow him to my closet where he is tossing hangers left and right to see if maybe it's hidden in the back. "Do you mind?" I ask him.

"Nope, I don't mind at all," he says, going to my shelves with my shoes.

I get in front of him. "Okay, that's enough. You can do what you want, but the shoes, they don't get touched."

He laughs at me for a second and then he takes in my lace outfit. My breasts rise and fall while he watches. "Playtime is over," he says. "Get on the bed, legs spread."

My hand goes to my throat that has suddenly become drier than the ocean. "I," I start to stutter, "I thought we were going to second base?" My heart is beating so loud I hear the echoes in my ears. "I think legs spread is a third base kind of thing."

He walks toward me while I take a step back, my back hitting my shoe rack, his hand coming to touch my face, the light touch giving me goose bumps all over. "There's nothing I'm going to do to you that you aren't going to like." His thumb goes down to my nipple that has perked up for him. He puts his thumb into his mouth and them comes back again. The wetness against the lace makes it tingle even more. "Your body lights up for me." He continues going in a circle with his thumb, my eyes fixated on his hand. "Need a taste," he says and I blink my eyes, not sure what he means. He wants a taste of what, me? But I don't have to wait for long because he bends his head and his teeth bite my nipple right through my bra. His teeth clamp down on it. I wait for the pain, but it's the opposite of pain. It's need. The feeling goes straight to my stomach, which then goes straight to my core. My head flies back taking in the feeling. He sucks my nipple deep into his mouth, while his tongue turns around the puckered nipple. My hand flies into his hair. "Do I have your attention?" he asks the minute he lets my nipple go. My eyes slowly open, almost as if I'm in a haze. I nod my head yes because he's got my attention and so much more. "Get on the bed and spread your legs for me." He kisses my neck, my head moving to make way for him. "Please."

"Well, since you asked so nice," I say, walking to the bed. I get on it, not sure if I lie in the middle, on my side, or on his side. So I sit in the middle of the bed, my legs crossed Indian style. "So, as this is the first time I've gone to second base, I'm not sure where I should sit. I mean, I've had sex. Or maybe."

"Babe, really, not a good time to talk about you in bed with someone else while I'm about to go to third base." He gets on the bed with me and pushes me down, and pulls my legs, making my back hit the bed. "Trust me, when we have sex, you'll fucking know you had it. And I'll make damn fucking sure you feel me in there for weeks to come," he tells me while he crawls over me. My hands start in his hair, running over his broad shoulders, down his thick arms. His lips come down on mine. My lips open for his tongue, my tongue seeking his. The kiss leaves me breathless. He kisses my chin, going down to my neck. His finger drags down the bra strap from my shoulder, till he stops at my elbow. His finger traces the top of the bra cup, slipping in to tease my nipple.

"So fucking perfect," he says while he is pulling the cup down my pink peaked nipple waiting for his mouth. He sucks in so deep I wonder if you can get a nipple hickey. "I bet you're wet." He repeats the action to the other breast. My legs spread open. Without even knowing I arch up my back, pushing my breast into him. His mouth lets go of my breast, leaning back on his legs. Both his hands go to my breasts where he squeezes them, then rolls the nipples at the same time between his thumb and forefinger. "Are you wet for me?" he asks, the whole time looking into my eyes. His hands run down my sides, now making me squirm because the touch is so soft. The same thumb that was rolling my nipple is now rubbing up and down my center, the wetness soaking through the lace. "Soaked." He rubs it again. "Where did you get these?" he asks and I'm not even sure I can comprehend what he's saying. "I owe you a new pair," he says right before he rips the sides, the panties falling to the bed, leaving me open for him, glistening. "Third base." His voice is thick with need. His fingers go back on me again, this time skin on skin. Two fingers go from my clit to my opening, gathering wetness and then going back up to rub circles around it. "Pink and perfect." Is the last thing I hear before he leans down and takes my clit into his mouth, twirling his tongue around it. My legs move wider apart, my head digging deeper into the bed. "Play with your nipples while I play with your pussy."

I pull my hands from my sides and bring them to my nipples where I pinch them lightly. Matthew's tongue runs down my folds till he slides it inside me. "Oh my God." I close my eyes, feeling him all over me.

His finger joins his tongue. "Shit. So tight, you're squeezing my fingers," he says, entering me with just his fingers while he moves up to bite my clit, and I feel it all the way down to my toes. "You taste like heaven," he says to me while he licks me from bottom to top again, circling his pointy tongue around my clit. I'm on the edge, I can feel it. My tits are getting tighter, the nipples more sensitive while I pinch and roll them. His fingers slowly work their way inside me while he sucks, bites, and rubs my clit.

"I'm going to," I don't say anything else because he knows. His fingers move faster while his tongue rubs back and forth on my clit. My head goes back and I let go, leaving my tits and grabbing his head between my legs, pushing him more into me. I spasm around his fingers, and when the feeling starts to fade away I loosen my hold on his head. My hands go out to my sides. "Third base is really a good place to be." I smile at him while he watches me. My eyes roll down his chest till they land on that place I've been dreaming of going to. I sit up, slowly grabbing his waist. "You know what's the best thing about third base?" I ask him, watching his eyes as I take my finger and fit it into the elastic at his waist, his stomach sucking in as soon as I get close to his cock. I peel his underwear down over his hips, his cock springing free. His beautiful cock. Can a cock be beautiful? I have the answer. Yes, yes, it can and yes, it is. His is so perfect. "Oh. My. God," I say out loud as my eyes make contact with his cock. His shaft is so thick and wide, my fingers try to wrap around the base, but it's so big they don't touch. When I move up his shaft, I hear his hiss coming from above me.

"You're killing me, babe."

I shake my head, "Nope, not yet, but I will," I tell him, leaning in and licking the tip. "Get ready for third base."

# CHAPTER THIRTEEN

## MATTHEW

"Third base is really a good place to be." She smiles at me while I watch her. Her eyes move down my chest, landing on my cock that's straining to get out and in her. She looks like she's about to eat me. Her tongue comes out to lick her lips. She sits up slowly, grabbing my waist. "You know what's the best thing about third base?" she asks me, but I can't answer because her fingers touch me, making my mouth dry, like sand in the desert. She puts one finger and fits it into the elastic at my waist, her touch making my stomach suck in as soon as she gets close to my cock. She peels my underwear down over my hips, my cock springing free.

"Oh. My. God," she says out loud as her eyes finally make contact with my cock, her fingers trying to wrap around the base, but it's so big they don't touch. When her hand moves up my shaft, I hiss out over her.

"You're killing me, babe."

She shakes her head. "Nope, not yet, but I will." Is the last thing she says before she leans in, licking the tip. "Get ready for third base."

Her mouth covers the tip of my cock, my eyes closing while I try not to come right away. Her small hand squeezes my cock while her mouth tries to deep throat me, stopping halfway down. I open my eyes, watching her hair fall over her face, blocking the view of my cock sliding into her mouth. I take one hand, pushing her hair to the side while my hips move on their own, thrusting into her mouth. Her hand works with her mouth, coming up when her mouth comes up. Her tongue curls around me while she sucks me back down into her mouth. My other hand goes to the back of her head as my hips continue to thrust, this time going a little deeper. Her moaning shoots through my cock down to my balls.

"Fuck. I'm not going to last long." And I'm not lying either. Her mouth on me, it's almost my breaking point. She sucks me, her cheeks going hollow, and then her eyes meet mine. My balls get tight, and I know I'm about to come. "I'm going to come," I tell her while I let go of her head so she can move her head, but she doesn't. She just sucks me deeper, her eyes never leaving mine as I let go and come into her mouth, watching her swallow all that I have to offer. She doesn't let me go till I empty inside of her mouth. She continues for a minute longer till she's sure I'm done.

The minute my cock leaves her mouth, she smiles at me shyly, turning her face to the side, trying to get off the bed. I stop her by putting my hand under her chin. "Not so fast there."

She stops, facing me.

"Naked."

She looks confused.

"From now on, new rule. We sleep naked."

"I'm not sleeping naked. I don't like sleeping naked. What if there's a fire?" she asks me while my hand leaves her chin. "What if there's a fire and I have to run in the street naked?"

I smile at her, seeing that she is secretly freaking out about sleeping naked. "Babe, if there's a fire, I'll make sure you're dressed before we go out."

She crosses her arms over her chest. "What if the fire starts in my closet and I have no clothes?"

I lean down and kiss her on the lips, smiling. "Okay, leave a robe by the bed. Happy?" I get off the bed. "Problem solved. Now I'm going to make sure everything is locked. Get into bed."

She turns around to get off the bed, picking up her bra from the floor.

"Naked, babe."

I walk out of the room while she is glaring at me, going downstairs and making sure everything is locked up. I pick up my phone from the counter and go upstairs. I walk into the room that's now dark, and I see her under the covers in almost a ball.

I walk over to my side of the bed, tossing the covers over while getting underneath them. I go to the middle where I touch her bare skin. She came to bed naked, for me. Smiling, I pull her to me.

"Fuck off, Matthew," she tells me, making me laugh into her neck. "We better not be naked in the middle of the street."

My hand rests on her stomach while I kiss her neck and listen to her fall asleep. The sound of her soft breathing fills the room. I hear my phone buzz, but I don't move away from her. Whatever it is can wait for morning. Closing my eyes, I follow her into sleep.

I don't know what time it is, but all I hear are phones ringing. I open my eyes slowly, my arm dead asleep with Karrie's head on it. She must hear the ringing also because she shoots her arm out to grab the phone.

"Hello." Her voice is still sleepy. I don't know who is on the phone, but she bolts up, grabbing the sheet from falling down her chest. "What are you talking about?" she asks, throwing her legs off the bed and rushing to her closet. "Where are they saying that he was?" I get up, grabbing my phone, seeing the twenty-seven missed calls from Cooper, along with one text.

You better be fucking sleeping! IN YOUR OWN BED!!!

My eyebrows pinch together in confusion while Karrie comes out of her closet, dressed in yoga pants and a sweater that falls off a shoulder, showing her perfect skin. My cock must think it's time to play because he's ready for action.

"You need to get dressed," she says, throwing her phone on her bed. "My father is on his way here." She runs around the room, talking to herself again.

"Why does this happen to me?" She walks to the bathroom, then comes back into the bedroom. "I should have gone with my gut." She continues while she picks up my boxers that are lying on the floor the minute the doorbell rings. Her face goes whiter than white. "Oh. My. God." She throws my boxers at me while she walks to the window and looks outside. "It's my father." And she ties her hair on top of her head, pacing the room. "Oh my God, this is horrible. Get dressed. Meet me downstairs." And she runs out of the room, down the stairs, yelling, "Coming."

I run my hands over my face, grabbing my boxers and putting them on with the basketball shorts that I put on the bedside table last night. I walk down the stairs into the living room. I stop in the doorway when I take in that it isn't just Karrie's dad, but it's the coach and Robert, all sitting there, their eyes landing straight on me.

"Well, look at this," Karrie's dad, Doug, says, folding his arms over his chest, but I don't say anything because the door opens again with Mindy, the PR girl, coming in.

She stops at the doorway, looking me up and down, taking me in. "Perhaps you could put on a shirt." I hear Karrie from the side of the room sitting next to her father, her knee bouncing with nerves.

"Oh, you don't have to do that," Mindy says, walking into the room, taking the remote, and turning on the television.

*"It looks like the bad boy has come out to play in New York."*

The second I hear the broadcaster's voice on the television I look up and see that they have a picture of me sitting on top of a bar with my shirt off, a blonde straddling my lap while she pours tequila down my throat, my hands in the air.

*"These pictures were leaked from a credible source and my question is what is Doug going to do now?"*

Mindy turns off the television while everyone in the room turns to me. Robert is shooting daggers at me. Doug has steam ready to blow out of his ears, and Coach is sitting back on the couch, his leg moving in the beat of Karrie's leg also.

"This is a fucking nightmare," Doug says, then addresses Karrie. "I thought you could handle him."

"Watch it," I say before I can even think that I'm talking to my boss, and her father. His eyebrows move up, surprised while I continue, "This isn't Karrie's fault in the least. Let me see those pictures," I tell Mindy, knowing full well she has them in the bag she is carrying, and I'm not mistaken. She takes out a folder, opening it, and giving me about fifteen pictures, all of different spots. One is with me standing on the bar, my hands in the air, my hair slicked back. One is me sitting on a bar stool, picking up my shirt to show my abs. I look at the same picture that they posted on the television screen. I give the pictures back to Mindy, who smirks at me.

"We need to diffuse the situation," Mindy says. "We can say he snuck out."

"Bullshit," I say. "I was here all night long. Those pictures were taken more than three years ago, maybe even four."

They all stop talking and look at me. Robert is the first one to talk. "How can you be sure?"

"My tattoo." I point to the tattoo that I got across my ribs. "I got this the summer three years ago. In the picture you can see I don't have it. Call bullshit on their pictures. Let them get the 'credible source.' I bet they can't come up with one."

Karrie gets up and walks over to my side. "He's been nothing but on his best behavior. I can guarantee that he didn't go anywhere last night because he went up to bed before me and I slept on the couch, so if he had left I would have heard him. Now," she continues, "I need coffee." She looks up at me, making me smile. "You want one?"

"Yup, I do," I say, following her out of the room while I listen to the four of them start talking to each other. "Babe," I whisper to her when we are out of earshot, but she shakes her head and walks to the kitchen, getting the coffee going. I go to the fridge, getting the orange juice out and drinking from the container.

"Matthew, is getting a glass too much work for you?" she snaps at me while she grabs a glass and hands it to me.

I take it and put it back on the counter while I continue to finish the rest of the juice.

I throw the container into the garbage. "I didn't want to waste a glass when I knew I was going to finish what was left of it," I say, leaning against the counter. "We going to talk about this?" I ask her, watching her back stiffen while she stands there staring at the coffee pot.

"I'm sorry to interrupt you two."

I turn to the doorway where Doug stands with his hands in his pockets.

"We would like to discuss perhaps a press release."

I nod my head and turn to Karrie, who isn't making eye contact with me or her father. Instead, she is pouring coffee into two cups.

When she doesn't say anything, her father clears his throat. "Is there something else that we should be talking about?"

Karrie puts the coffee pot down and levels her gaze on her father. "There's absolutely nothing else we should discuss, unless you want to discuss how you thought I wasn't doing my job. We could discuss that. We could discuss how you didn't trust me to tell you it wasn't last night." Her tone is curt and direct.

"Honey, that isn't what we meant." He starts to say, but Karrie puts her hand up, stopping him from talking.

"I know what you meant, and to be honest I'm insulted. I take my job seriously, and if you thought I was the right person for the job, you wouldn't be second-guessing me. Now," she says, picking up one of the coffee cups on the counter and walking away, "let's go hear this statement you want to put out." She walks out of the room, leaving the second coffee on the counter.

"If you hurt her, I'll bury you so far down they won't find you." He starts to say while my spine goes straight.

"I'll give you the shovel." Is all I say, picking up the coffee that she made for me and walking out of the room. I put the cup down in the hallway, going upstairs to my bedroom to get myself a T-shirt.

I pull my phone from my pocket and dial Cooper. He answers before the first ring even finishes.

"Tell me that isn't you." He blows out a long breath.

"It's me, but from three years ago. It was before I got the tattoo on my ribs," I tell him, sitting down to take a minute.

"I didn't even notice."

"Yeah, I didn't either till I saw my hand in the air. Anyway, I just wanted to touch base with you. Everyone is here. We are going to discuss a statement."

"Yeah, Robert is going to call me in a few. So we will talk after. Text your mom, please. She has been freaking out since this morning. I would also text Allison. She started cropping you out of the family pictures!" He laughs and then hangs up.

I send a group text to both my mother and sister with one sentence.

**It's an old picture. Check my ribs. No tattoo.**

Allison answers right away.

**I knew it.**

I respond with a, **No, you didn't.**

I put the phone away when I hear a knock on my door. "Come in."

Karrie opens the door and walks in. "Hey. We are waiting for you."

"I was just calling home to give them the heads-up." I look back down at my hands. "They don't need this."

She closes the door and walks to me, her body fitting in the middle of my legs. My hands go up her legs to her ass and then finally land on her hips. "I'm sorry."

Her hands go to my hair, running them through it. "I should be apologizing. I freaked out without thinking. I was so scared that it was a picture of us walking down the street or something that I was relieved when that picture came out."

I smile at her. "You're happy a picture of me with another woman is circulating?" I shake my head, thinking of how crazy this woman is.

"No, not that part, the part where it's still just you and me without anyone knowing." She leans down and kisses my lips. "Now let's go and get this thing over with so we can go back and see if third base will slip into a home run."

"You know that I don't play baseball, right? Hockey," I tell her, thinking how I know nothing about baseball.

"Yeah, yeah, it's just easier to put sex terms in baseball instead of hockey." She drops her hands from my hair and grabs my arms, dragging me out the door, dropping our hands the minute we get to the second floor but not before she squeezes it to give me her strength.

# CHAPTER FOURTEEN

## KARRIE

I watch the city fade away till we are in the clouds. I close my eyes, blocking out all the buzz in the plane. We have been on the road for the last six days and I'm dying to climb into my bed. It's been six days of dodging the press. They are trying to get anything they can to make Matthew be the asshole.

After we put out a statement that the picture was an old one, it was one old story after another. I know it's playing on Matthew's mind and his game. He got six penalties tonight and was benched the last three shifts of the game. It didn't help that they are on a losing streak. Night after night, we would fall asleep in the same bed, him holding me, but I feel he is almost shutting down.

By the time the plane touches down, it's three a.m. I walk off the plane and head to the car waiting for us. Once we get inside and away from everyone's eyes he finally grabs my hand, bringing it to his lips. "You okay?" I ask him softly.

"Not even a bit, but I'm happy to be home. I don't have to practice tomorrow, but I think I'll go in and just skate with Phil," he says while he looks out the window. “I fucking hate this shit.”

“It’ll blow over,” I tell him, hoping to fuck it’s the truth. I don’t know if I can put up with much more. The pictures of him half naked, with girls all over him, make my stomach hurt. The only thing I think makes it better is that it’s never the same girl. Puck bunnies at their finest.

When we walk into the house we don’t even open the lights, going upstairs straight to my room that has slowly become our room. His suits now hang in my closet, his clothes are in my drawers, his shampoo in my shower. His razor on my sink. Our clothes in the laundry basket.

I wake up the next day to an empty bed but a note rests on the bedside.

*At the rink. Text you later.*

I put my phone back down and get up, grabbing my robe while I walk to the bathroom. Matthew wasn’t joking when he said naked to bed. I learned this mistake when we were in the hotel room. I went to bed with a T-shirt. When he came in and saw, he walked right back out and came back in. I didn’t really pay much attention to him till he turned me on my back, straddled my thighs, and cut my T-shirt right down the middle. Cut. It. Right. Down. The. Middle.

“Babe, naked.” Is all he said till he leaned down, taking a nipple in his mouth. After that, I went to bed naked each time for fear that my clothes would end up in shreds.

I’m washing my face when I hear my phone ringing in the other room. I run back and grab the phone to see it’s Vivienne.

“Bonjour.” Hello, I answer in French.

“Salope.” Slut, she answers back, making me laugh. “Are you finally back in New York?” I hear beeping in the background, so I know she is walking down the street somewhere in the city.

“Yes. Thank God.” I walk down to the kitchen, starting the coffee. “I’m home for a whole five days. I’m planning to watch television and make a permanent mark on the couch cushion.” I make a list in my head of all the shows I’m going to be watching for the next five days.

“Good. I’m on my way to you. We need to catch up,” she tells me the minute I hear the bell buzz.

“Are you here already?” I ask, walking to the door and seeing the UPS guy. “It’s UPS. Get your ass over here, or I’m starting *Below Deck* without you." I hang up right when she starts cursing in French again. I open the door and smile at the UPS guy when he asks if I'm Karrie Cooney. When I tell him I am, he makes me sign for the huge box. He brings it in, placing it on the floor next to the table. Once I close the door behind him I walk to the box with an Red Apple logo on the corner. I pick it up, struggling with it while I leave it on the table in the living room. I go to the kitchen to make my coffee and grab a knife to open the box. My phone beeps with an incoming message. I grab it, seeing it's from Matthew.

**On my way home! Don't open the box till I get there.**

I squeeze my eyebrows together, thinking what the hell could be in that box. I don't have time to think about it anymore because there's a knock at the door. I smile to myself, knowing it's Vivienne. She is the only one who refuses to ring. Walking to the door, I smile seeing her face plastered to the door.

"Fofolle." Crazy girl, I tell her, opening the door.

"I come with presents." She puts the bag up, showing me that she stopped to get croissants.

"Then you can come in." I walk away while she closes the door, shrugs off her coat, and throws her purse on the table.

"Are we going to watch *Below Deck* naked?" she asks, making fun of me and my new rule.

"Très drôle!" Very funny, I tell her. "Make yourself at home. I'm going to go get dressed. I wasn't expecting company today," I tell her, walking up the stairs, throwing on a pair of shorts and a team T-shirt with Matthew's name on it.

I walk downstairs right when Matthew walks in. He's in his team tracksuit, scruff on his face, baseball cap backward. He takes off the jacket, leaving him in the same shirt I'm wearing just bigger and tighter on him. His muscles fill it out. My mouth waters watching him. He tosses the keys on the table, his smile lighting up.

"There's my girl," he says softly, walking to me while I stand on the last step, "and she's wearing my name." His arms wrap around my waist, picking me up. My arms wrap around his neck, my face going into his neck. He smells of his soap, so I know he showered at the rink.

"Excuse me, I hate to interrupt first base, but," Vivienne says, leaning against the door to the living room. "Oh, presents," she says, spotting the box, clapping her hands together once she puts her cup down.

"Um," Matthew says, putting me down. "I think." He doesn't say anything else since Vivienne picks up the knife and cuts open the top of the box.

Once the box is open, she throws her hands up in the air, laughing. "Home run. It's going to be a home run." She laughs, picking up a box that's inside the box. "Look at all this," she continues while she takes box after box out of the box.

I walk over to the table. Picking up the box, my eyes go wide. It's a sex box. Not just a little sex box, it's filled with everything I think this company sells.

A vibrator, a rabbit vibrator, anal plugs, cuffs, a clit vibrator, bullets, cock rings, lubes, lotions, edible stuff, a cheerleading costume that's so small it fits into the palm of my hand.

"Oh. My. God. Are you insane? You just threw my vibrator out the window two weeks ago. Now you got me not one, but a million," I say, trying to put everything back in the box, but I'm failing since Vivienne is still pulling things out. I look back at Matthew, who comes in and throws himself on the couch, picking up the box of nipple clamps.

"I ordered a treasure chest that only I will have the key for, so I'm locking it all up when I leave. Besides, that was yours, this is ours!" he says matter-of-factly.

"Oh, this is my favorite toy," Vivienne says while she holds up what is called Eve's triple pleasure rabbit. "I could go all day with this one. I usually last maybe a minute it's so powerful. Don't go full power or you'll be done in thirty seconds flat." She hands me the box and I take it in my hand. There are three parts to this vibrator, one for my pussy, one for my ass, and another for my clit. "Don't blush, chéri," she says to me while I stand here blushing because I'm actually standing in my living room with my best friend and my, I don't even know what he is, my naked sleeping partner while we take in the box of dicks.

"I'm not blushing," I tell her while I look at Matthew, who is now holding the anal plug trainer's kit. "Is that for you?" I ask him while

Vivienne snickers, pulling up the bondage kit.

"Babe, this is all yours." He throws down another box next to him, grabbing the cheerleading outfit. Opening it, I see it's a tube top and the smallest plaid skirt ever. "I want you wearing this tonight."

"Naked, isn't that what you said?" I put my hands on my hips while he leans in and grabs me to sit on his lap.

He pulls my head to him, whispering in my ear, "I want you wearing this while you bend over in front of me and I eat your pussy while I slip a plug up your ass." He nips my earlobe. "We are doing all the bases tonight." He kisses my neck while I sit on his lap completely aroused now.

Vivienne is pretending not to watch us but is smirking. She tosses me the lube. "For you right before you bend over." She laughs, making Matthew throw his head back and laugh. It's the first time he has laughed since that whole picture leaked.

I get up, grabbing all the things that are on the table, throwing them in the box, smacking Vivienne's hands while she tries to take them back out. "Enough of this. You"—I point to Matthew—"take this upstairs to the attic. I'm not using any of this." And then I point to Vivienne. "And you, you are on my side!"

"I'm always on your side, which is why I told you to use the lube." She shakes her head, sitting down on the couch, kicking her ballerina shoes off. "Now let's watch *Below Deck*."

"Yup, I'm out," Matthew says while he grabs the box from the table. "I'm going to put this all away in your closet, babe. You just lost a shoe shelf."

"Matthew, I will snap one of your hockey sticks if you touch even one pair of shoes." I glare at him. "You want to use a shelf, put your clothes in your room."

He bends his head, kissing me on the lips, making me forget what I was saying.

"You have it so bad, you don't even know it," Vivienne says while I watch Matthew walk out of the room.

"Vas te faire foutre." Go fuck yourself, I tell her while I sit on the opposite end of the couch, grabbing the remote, and putting our show on. We sit and watch three hours of reality television before Matthew comes back downstairs.

"This was exactly what I needed today. Merci, mon amie," she says, getting up, putting her shoes on, "but I have a date tonight and I need to exfoliate." She kisses me on the cheek, looking at Matthew. "As the Americans say, 'God Speed.'"

He throws up his hand to high-five her.

"A plus tard." See you later, she says, walking out of the room, slamming the door behind her as she walks out.

"I really like your friend," Matthew says, lying down on the couch, putting his head in my lap. "We should hook her up with Phil."

I shake my head. "We have a pact. She doesn't set me up. I don't set her up."

"Fine," he says, "I'll let Phil do all the work."

I shake my head while Matthew grabs the remote, puts it on SportsCenter, and we sit here and watch all the highlights from last night. The best thing about it, not a single word about Matthew and that fucking picture.

# CHAPTER FIFTEEN

## MATTHEW

I'm standing at the sink in the bathroom, brushing my teeth while I look in the mirror. I watch Karrie lathering herself and I'm hard at the sight. The towel that's wrapped around my waist suddenly forms a tent.

We spent the afternoon lounging on the couch, the stress of the last couple of days finally leaving me. It also helped that they stopped talking about that fucking picture. A picture that had been published three years ago.

"You might faint, you know?" she says while she tilts her head back to rinse the soap out of her hair.

I spit in the sink, turning to face her while I lean on the counter. "What are you talking about now?"

"All the blood in your body is shooting straight to your dick. You might be light-headed." She laughs at her own joke.

"Maybe I'll faint and fall dick first into you!" I smile at her while she stands there watching me with an open mouth. "Hurry up. I have plans for you." I turn back around to put my toothbrush away. Tossing the towel into the laundry basket, I see her watching me. I grab my cock, stroking it a couple of times while I watch the soap suds from her hair go down her neck and over her nipples, that are already hard and probably tight, streaming down to her pussy. I lick my lips while picturing my face buried in her. "Hurry up, babe."

She turns her head and turns off the water, squeezing the water from her hair. I walk out of the bathroom, going straight to the bedroom. I dim the lights in the room and light some of the candles that she has in her bedroom. The room is a soft yellow from the glow of the candles. I blow out the last match when she walks into the room, the white towel wrapped around her, another towel twisted on top of her head.

She looks around the room, taking in the candles. I take that opportunity to walk to her. I grab the towel from her hair, twisting it off. Her hair falls down to her shoulders. I throw the towel to the floor, grabbing her hair in both my hands when I lean down and kiss her gently, softly, once, twice, and then my tongue comes out, tracing her bottom lip. Her hands go to my hips while I tilt my head to one side and my tongue invades her mouth. Our tongues join together and twirl. My hands grab her hair tighter, pulling her closer to me while her fingers dig into my hips. I let her go, moving away from her, watching her blue eyes changing color.

"I can drown in your eyes, do you know that?" I tell her while my thumbs rub her cheeks. "Will you save me, Karrie?" I smile at her, watching her nod yes.

My hands move down to the towel tied around her chest. I loosen the knot on the side, watching the towel pool around her feet. "Beautiful," I say to her while I lean down, taking a pink nipple into my mouth, sucking it deep, twirling my tongue around the tip. I copy the same thing on the other side while my hand cups her breast, rolling her nipple in between my thumb and forefinger. "You're fucking perfect," I tell her while I kiss her in the middle of her chest. The beating of her heart vibrates through me.

Grabbing her hand, I walk with her to the bed. "Get in the middle and open yourself for me."

I watch her climb onto the middle of the bed. Lying down in the middle, she holds out her hand to me. I climb on the bed with her, going to her, and lying on my side next to her. I turn her to face me, my finger moving from her leg up her side, over her breast, to her mouth where I trace her lips. Her tongue comes out to lick my finger, my cock getting harder than it was before. I lean in, kissing her neck, then kissing her chin, "So fucking beautiful." I kiss her lips. "I knew we'd end up here." I kiss her again softly, her head falling back. "I knew I wouldn't stop till I got in you." I lick her bottom lip then kiss her. "Knew you'd bring me to my knees." Her tongue comes out to meet mine, the taste of her making all my other senses wake up.

I kiss her with everything I have. Her hands come to my chest while mine goes down to her breast. The nipple is hard, making me pinch it a little. Her groan is swallowed by our tongues that are fighting with each other. My hand moves down to her center. She raises one leg for me, giving me access to her. I take my fingers, testing her wetness. She's soaked. I bring my finger up to her clit, where I go in small circles, the nub getting plumper. I leave her clit, going down, my finger slipping inside her. Now it's my moan that's swallowed by our kiss. I finger her while our kiss becomes erratic while our needs become more than we know what to do with. I feel her pussy get wetter, so I slip another finger in her. Her pussy starts to get tighter and tighter, her breathing coming harder as well. Our lips slip away from each other, her moans now filling the silence that was in the room.

"Please." She is begging me. I don't stop. I just look down at my fingers disappearing in her. My thumb goes up to put pressure on her clit while my fingers continue to fuck her. "Oh, God," she continues saying while she turns on her back, her legs opening more. "Don't stop," she says right before she finally comes all over my fingers. Her eyes close while her head goes back and her back arches up.

I watch her eyes open as soon as her pussy stops pulsing on my fingers. I pull them out, bringing them to my mouth where I lick them clean while she watches me. Her legs are still open for me. I lean over and grab a condom out of the bedside drawer. I bought them on the way home. Grabbing one, I open it with my teeth while I get on my knees in the middle of her open legs. "I promise it will be longer next time," I tell her, knowing that the minute my cock enters her I might shoot off.

She smiles at me while I roll the condom on.

I rub my cock up and down her slit, getting her wetness on my cock. Leaning in, I put my cock at her entrance, pushing in a little. “Fuck,” I say out loud, her pussy squeezing the shit out of me. My body hovers over her, my weight straight on my elbows. “Let me in, baby,” I whisper to her, leaning down to kiss her while my hips thrust in a little bit at a time, in and out, her pussy getting wetter. Her pussy squeezes me, our lips never leaving each other while her back arches, making me lose my mind, making me thrust all the way in. Her lips leave mine while she moans out. “Are you okay?” I ask her, but she doesn’t answer. Instead, her legs wrap around my hips. I take that as go ahead, so I pull out and slam back in. This time I moan out.

I pump into her twice more, till she starts thrusting her hips up to me. “You're going to come on my cock.” I thrust in hard. “Come all over me.” I thrust again once and then twice. I know she’s close, so I put my hand between us, playing with her clit, her breathing coming in huffs, and the moaning starts. “So tight.” I continue pounding away. “Babe,” I tell her while my balls start to get tight.

“I’m going to come,” she says right before she squeezes me, pulsing around my cock. I thrust in one more time till I plant myself inside her and throw my head back, coming inside her.

# CHAPTER SIXTEEN

## KARRIE

I’m having the best dream ever, or is it a dream? I open my eyes the minute his tongue slips inside me. I look down at Matthew’s face in the middle of my legs. My hand goes into his head, pulling his hair to get him to stop, yet my legs tighten around his face. “Matthew,” I say softly just as his tongue leaves me and goes to my clit, where he bites it softly then licks, and bites down harder, making me come with a moan. I haven’t even finished my orgasm and he is sliding into me. Hard.

His body hovers over me, my legs wrapping around his waist, my arms around his neck, pulling his lips down to mine. My tongue teases his lips while he grunts out with each thrust. Going harder and harder. Our breaths get heavier and heavier. Our bodies slap together. No words are needed. My legs tighten around him as soon as I know I’m going to come again. He must feel it because his thrusts come harder and shorter, till he pulls completely out and then slams into me. We don’t say anything, his body collapsing on top of me, turning me so I’m on top of him.

“Morning,” I tell him, kissing underneath his chin.

"Afternoon." He laughs out, hugging me closer on his chest. We are in another hotel room. This time in Florida. We play the Tigers tonight. We are starting on a three-day road trip. Florida first, Tampa Hurricanes, and the last stop will be Dallas Rockies.

I'm about to answer him when there's a knock on my door. I watch his eyebrows pinch together. I jump up, almost hitting him in the balls, watching him wince and roll off the bed while I grab the robe next to the bed. I wait for him to run into his room before I open the door, shocked that it's Max.

"Hey," I say, grabbing the robe at the collar, closing it tighter.

He comes in to lean on the doorjamb. "Wow, you look beautiful when you wake up." He smiles at me.

"Is there something you need, Max?" I ask him, still holding the doorknob in my hand.

"I was wondering if perhaps I can entice you to join me for breakfast and then maybe a walk on the beach." He stands up now, putting his hands in his pockets.

"Umm." I'm about to answer him when I feel heat at my back.

"What happened to the two blondes you brought back to your room? Did they run away when they saw your pencil dick?"

Max smirks at me. "So what do you say, Karrie? Have breakfast with me."

"She'll pass," Matthew says, slamming the door in his face.

I turn around to see that he has thrown on a pair of gym shorts, with them hanging on his hips.

"That was rude," I tell him, crossing my arms over my chest. "I could have handled that, I'll have you know."

"Are you really going to have a fit because I sent the douche away?" Oh. Fuck. No.

"Did you just say I'm having a fit?" I walk past him to the bathroom where I walk in and slam the door. "A fit." I laugh to myself. "A fit." I shake my head while I turn on the water and step inside the shower. "I don't have fits, jackass." I put my face into the water. "Fits, pfft." I continue talking to myself right before I feel two hands grab my breasts.

"Calm down there, I don't want to fight because of Max," he says while his fingers start rolling my nipples between his fingers. My head falls back on his chest, his cock literally poking me in the back.

"We aren't in a fight because of Max. We are having a disagreement because you're a jackass who doesn't know when to use words." I'm about to say something else, but his hands drift down to between my legs, his fingers finding my sensitive area. "This doesn't mean I'm not mad at you." My hands roam to the back where I fist his cock in my hand. Two can play this game, stroking him up and down. "You can't keep doing that." I stroke him while his fingers slip inside me, my feet going to my tippy toes. "Secret. Remember?" I open my legs a bit more. I turn around, where I lean up for him to kiss me and that he does. He kisses me deeply while I stroke his cock with one hand and he fingers me. His cock grows in my hands, so I know he's close. My eyes open and my head goes back while I come on his fingers and he comes on mine.

Now here we are five hours later on the way to the arena for the game tonight. I'm walking next to him while he has his earphones in his ears. The minute we step off the elevator he goes into game mode. The arena is one street over, so we opted to walk instead of taking a car over. I don't say anything to him when we get there because the camera crews are already there, so instead I walk to the side where Mindy is waiting for the players to come by.

"Hey there," I say to her, smiling while she hands me a Starbucks cup. "Oh, thank you so much."

"Well, I kind of need a favor, so that's to butter you up." She starts saying to me. "We have two functions going on in November and another in December and I was hoping you could drag Matthew to them. He's heating up the ice, his game is on point, and he's the big talk on the circuit."

I take a sip of the coffee. "Next time lead with wine. What functions exactly?" I ask her.

"We have the Pediatrics Dinner with a secret auction. The kids love Matthew. Then we have the team Christmas Party. So far he told me a fuck no to the second and a maybe to the first." She tilts her head.

"That sounds about right."

"I even told him he could bring a date for that night and he glared at me. I think he just needs to get laid," she says, leaning in, almost whispering, "I don't know how you deal with him."

"Yeah, it's been really hard lately." I smile to myself, thinking of the pun I just did. Her phone rings and she excuses herself.

I turn to walk away and come face to face with Max again. Jesus, what is it with him today?

"There you are," he says to me, pulling his buds out of his ears.

"Here I am," I say to him.

"Sorry about before. I should have known you would have your toddler with you." He tries to be funny. "So about dinner."

"Max, listen, I don't want to be rude, but I'm really not interested." I try to continue but more guys come in, all yelling at us saying hello. Max nods at me and walks in with his teammates, making me blow out a breath I didn't know I was holding.

I walk down the same corridor as the guys, heading to one of the boxes that our team has during the game. The television is blaring in the background.

*"Matthew Grant is on point. I have to say it's great to see this kid skating again. By seeing some of the plays he's been doing it's only going to be a matter of time before he's placed in the top line. The question is who is going to be knocked down?"*

I listen to the sport reporter talk about everyone on the team with their stats. I sit here, pride washing over me. He is killing it and I couldn't be more proud. When the puck drops three hours later, Matthew's line is the first one on the ice, where it takes them eleven seconds to find the back of the net. Their tic-tac-toe passing makes it really a team effort.

The rest of the game is even better with him scoring his first hat trick of the season, giving him the most ice time of the team. Everyone is celebrating the win except Max, who slams his stick on the boards and walks back to the dressing room.

I get a text from Matthew while I'm walking outside of the lodge.

**Will be here for a while. Interviews and stuff. Meet me back at the hotel.**

**Great game, Grant.** I send him back a response, walking out with

Mindy.

I'm in the hotel room for about an hour watching television when the phone rings with Matthew's ring tone. Something that he changed when I wasn't paying attention. Now it's set to "Sexy Bitch" when he calls.

"Hello," I say, tossing the remote back on the bed.

"Come down to the hotel bar. We are going to eat here."

I can barely hear him.

"Please?" I say into the phone.

"Please with a cherry on top." He laughs at me and hangs up.

Grabbing my jacket, I head downstairs. I have changed out of my skirt to a pair of black jeans with a white tank top and a black leather jacket to tie up the look. I put my heels on, making it classy-ish.

I make my way down to the hotel bar and I'm shocked to see it completely crammed. I see different players from the team. They all give me the chin up when I walk in. I spot Matthew at the bar with Phil. The two of them are surrounded by five girls. My heart starts to beat a bit faster when I see one of them lean in and whisper something into Matthew's ear. I'm about to leave when he notices me. He gets off his stool, pushing the girl aside, walking up to me.

"There you are," he says once he gets close enough to me.

"Here I am," I say with a forced smile on my face. Looking over his shoulder, I see two of the girls glare in my direction. "I didn't know it would be this busy."

"Come on. I ordered you a glass of wine." He pulls me by my hand to the bar, giving me the stool he was sitting on.

"There she is, the good luck charm," Phil says while he grabs his beer, bringing the bottle to his lips.

"Here I am." I pick up the glass of wine that's sitting down next to Phil's beer and Matthew's water bottle.

"Are you like his sister or something?" one of the blondes asks while twirling her hair.

"Nope, I'm his chaperone," I say, drinking another sip.

"So you babysit him," the other Bobbsey twin asks.

"I guess you can say that." I smile at them both while I see Matthew lean against the bar right next to me. One of the girls is trying to talk to him, but he turns his head to me.

"Did you watch the game tonight?" he asks me, turning his back to the girl while I turn on the stool to him.

"Oh, it was one of the best games of the year," one twin says while she tries to put herself in the middle of me and Matthew. "In fact, we should go and celebrate." She looks down like she's shy and brings her eyes back up. "In private." She smiles.

Matthew shakes his head. "Not going to happen, but see that guy over there?" He points to Max. "I heard he needs cheering up since I took all his ice time."

"But, Matthew," she whines and puts her hand on his chest, "he's blah," she says while Matthew pushes her hand away from his chest.

"Phil, we're out," Matthew says to Phil, who is in deep conversation with the other twin's breasts. Grabbing my hand, he leads me out to the elevator, pressing the button. "Fuck, what the hell was with all those people?"

I blink my eyes at him. "I don't know, Matthew, you're so big and strong and they just want to celebrate with you." I smirk at him while he throws his head back.

"Oh, I'll let you celebrate all right. I expect you on your knees the minute we make it in the door."

The door opens and he steps in. "Don't make me throw you over my shoulder, Karrie."

# CHAPTER SEVENTEEN

## MATTHEW

"Don't make me throw you over my shoulder, Karrie." I'm almost ready to carry on my threat when my phone rings, the display showing it's Cooper.

"Hey," I say into the phone while Karrie walks into the elevator and stands next to me. "Hi, Mom." The doors close and I put my hand around Karrie's shoulders, pulling her closer to me, kissing the top of her head.

"Matthew, what a fucking game, son," Cooper says, his voice booming with pride.

"Thank you. It felt"—I squeeze Karrie's arm closer to me, thinking of how happy I was when I scored that third goal. Seeing her cheering and beaming with pride made that moment so much better—"fucking fantastic."

"Watch your mouth, Matthew," my mom butts in.

The elevator dings open on our floor where we walk out, our hands intertwined with each other's. Karrie walks over to her door, inserting the key.

"Sorry, Mom." I laugh while my hands go to Karrie's waist as she walks in the room, closing the door behind me, my back to the door.

"Well, we know how crazy it gets, so we just called to say it's good to see you play," Cooper says while my mom starts to ask questions only to be shushed by Cooper. "Leave him be." Then he comes back. "Call your mother tomorrow," he says and ends the call.

I toss my phone on the bed, not moving from the door.

"Now," I tell her, "where were we?" I turn her while her eyes come up. "Oh, yes, you were going to help celebrate my goals by sucking my dick." I move her hair from her shoulder, tossing her jacket off her. The tank top hugs her tight in all the right places. "You like this top?" I ask her, already ripping it down her tits, along with the bra. "Fuck," I say, taking her peak into my mouth, biting down on it hard. Her moan comes out loud. "My girl likes that." I'm about to twirl my tongue around her nipple when we hear a soft knock at the door.

"Matthew." It's the whiney girl from downstairs.

"What the fuck?" I whisper while Karrie lifts her shirt that isn't so snug anymore, moving me out of the way.

Opening the door, I see a different side to Karrie. "Wrong room," she says to the blonde while I stand behind the door, watching Karrie's eyes turn dark blue.

"Awww, reallllyyy," she sings out, her voice making my cock shrivel, "but Max told me this is his room."

"Nope, not his room. Last I heard he was complaining about his dick being super itchy, something about crabs, or what is that other STD that causes itching?" Karrie says while I stand behind the door laughing with my hand over my mouth. "Although he was saying something about green slime."

The gasp that the blonde shrieks out makes me grab my junk just thinking about it.

"Thanks for letting me know." Is the last thing we hear before Karrie closes the door and glares at me.

"What?" I ask her.

"What? What? A puck bunny just knocked on my door looking for you. This morning Max knocked on my door and you almost beheaded him." She folds her arms over her breasts, making them push up.

"Babe," I say while she puts up her hand, but I walk up to her. "I didn't even notice who she was. I have eyes for one girl and one girl only. My girl."

"Do those lines actually work?" she asks while she takes her shirt off. "You owe me one hundred and twenty-five dollars. That was a designer." She points to the shirt lying on the floor.

"How much is the bra?" I ask her, walking her backward to the bed.

"Don't you dare, Matthew, this is one of my favorite bras and it's discontinued!"

"Are you going to be nice to me?" I ask her while she falls on the bed. "Are you going to give me a celebration surprise?" I straddle her, pushing her tits together. "Are you going to give me what I want?"

"No," she says, yet in her eyes I see it's going to be yes.

"I think you will," I tell her while I trace her nipple through the padding, her eyes almost closing.

"Get off me, you big oaf." She tries to buck me off, making her bra cup open a little just enough for me to get my two fingers in to roll her nipple. "You're really annoying. You know that, right?"

I smile at her, leaning down to whisper in her ear, "Best part of tonight, having you to come home to."

She rolls her eyes at me. "Oh, please, like you were really missing me with all your harem at the bar."

I sit up again. "Babe."

"Shut up, Matthew," she tells me, trying to push my chest back.

I grab her hands, putting them by her head while her eyes never leave mine.

"Babe, you have to know"—I kiss her cheek—"that I didn't even give them a second thought." I kiss her other cheek. "You don't go after fake when you have a diamond in your hand." I kiss her lips, softly watching her eyes. I don't let her think; I kiss her again, this time letting my lips linger on hers.

I kiss her softly, watching her eyes till her fingers close on mine, till her hands hold mine. "You," I tell her when she opens her eyes. "All I see is you."

"Okay, I get it. You can stop with the lines," she tells me, her thumb rubbing my finger.

"Not a line, babe. I will never feed you those lines. It's the truth, no matter how much it will suck. I will never ever lie to you." Her smile starts off slowly till it's full blown. "Now are you going to give me my celebration surprise?"

"I guess you earned it," she says, her head coming up so she can kiss my lips. And for the rest of the night she congratulates me more and more. So much that we almost miss the two alarms that we set.

We make it to the bus right on time. I look down at the floor while Mindy chimes in, "Seriously, how do you both sleep in?"

I'm thinking about making an excuse when Karrie leans over me. "How is it possible that I hear him snore through the walls and a door? He kept me up all night."

I smirk at her, thinking if anyone of us snores it's her.

"Oh, you poor thing," Mindy says right as the bus takes off toward the airport. The rest of the team are half-up half-sleeping. It's a travel day thankfully, so no skating till tomorrow morning.

Checking into the hotel, the rest of the team starts talking about a team dinner. It's decided that we will all be headed to the steakhouse two streets down. Once we get in our room, we both collapse on the bed and fall asleep the second our heads hit the pillow.

We get ready by taking a shower together, which only leads to me having my dessert before my meal. I grab my jeans out of my bag while I look over at Karrie, seeing her put on a black loose skirt with a jean button-down top.

"What if it's windy and your dress flies up?" I ask her, thinking that everyone will be seeing her ass, and I'm not okay with that.

"It's winter in Texas, which means no wind," she tells me while she sits down on the bed, bringing out her strappy heels and I know she will be wearing only those tonight. We walk out of the room and my hand automatically goes to grab hers, but the sound of a door opening has both of us dropping our hands and looking behind us to see who it is. Noticing an older man with his wife, we smile at them and wait for the elevator. My hand goes to her back once we get off the elevator to see most everyone waiting at the bar. I go sit with Phil and Luka while

Karrie goes toward Mindy. It doesn't take much longer before we are all on our way to the restaurant walking. I make sure I'm walking behind Karrie, just in case the wind picks up, but she is right. There's no wind in winter in Texas.

Once we get to the restaurant, I sit next to Karrie while she sits next to Mindy.

"So, Matthew, Karrie said you agreed to the Christmas Party. I can't tell you how thrilled I am. Lots of the big sponsors will be there. It will be a great time." She smiles at me and I just look over at Karrie.

"Yeah, well, she did agree to be my date, so how could I say no." I grab the water glass and take a sip.

"Agreed, really? I felt bad when I beat him at rock paper scissors and he almost cried." Karrie sits back in her chair, smiling at me.

"I don't care how she did it. I'm just glad she did," Mindy says, and then they start talking about some new reality television show.

We all have a great time eating, and the bill is picked up by Mindy.

"I can't wait for the break," Mindy says. "I'm going to close my phone for five days straight. And sleep."

"I can't wait. I'm going to hit Mexico," Karrie says while my head whips around. "I can't wait to sink my feet in the sand." She closes her eyes and exhales.

"Are you going to leave straight from the last game or are you going back to New York?" Mindy asks while I take in the conversation.

"No, I'm going to leave from New York. It's easier that way. I don't have to bring two bags of luggage. My flight is an early morning one, so I will be sipping Mai Tais by lunch."

"Okay, girls, let's go," Phil says while he pushes his chair away from the table.

I don't say much on our way back to the hotel, or that night either. Instead, I make a plan, an evil plan. A plan that will make her all mine for five days, whether she wants to be or not.

# CHAPTER EIGHTEEN

## KARRIE

I'm so tired I can hardly stand up. I don't know how Matthew does it. Being on the road is fucking hard. I miss my bed. I miss my house. I miss my routine. I have one more game to get through and then it's five days off. Five whole glorious days.

"I can't wait, Vivienne. Honestly, I think I'm going to sleep for seventy-two hours straight," I tell Vivienne while we are on FaceTime.

"What is Matthew doing?" she asks, and I have to admit I have no idea. We really never brought it up.

"Je ne comprend pas." I don't understand, she cuts in. "You sleep with him every single night, tout nu." Naked, she adds in. I roll my eyes at her while she leans back in her chair. "Chéri, you play with fire, you get anal!"

I laugh at her. "I think that's the exact saying. You play with fire you get burnt."

She waves her hand in the air. "Même chose." Same thing.

I hear the click of the hotel door and sit up, watching Matthew come in. He throws his hat on the chair before falling into bed.

"Bonjour, Vivi," he says in broken French while he leans in and kisses me on the lips while cupping my breast. He lays his head in my lap.

"Matthew."

He peers into the phone. "She's French. They do a lot worse." He winks at her while she throws her head back and laughs at him.

"You know it, Matthew. Okay, I've got to work," Vivienne says. "Text me to let me know when you land. D'accord." All right, she ends the sentence.

I click the phone off, putting it on the bedside table while I rub my hands in his damp hair. "What time are we going to the rink tonight?" I ask him while he closes his eyes.

"Four-thirty," he says to me. "Fuck, I love when you play with my hair."

"You love when I play with anything on your body, not just your hair." I laugh at him while I sink into the pillows and watch the television show that's playing in the background. "I want to be Judge Judy," I tell him, but his soft snore fills the room. My heart beats just a touch different. We've been together twenty-four/seven for two months now. The thought of not seeing him every day makes my chest hurt. Laughing with him, fighting with him, but most part being hugged by him at night. His arms holding me close. Yup, I have to go. It's going to do us both good.

The game that night is a tough one. Matthew is hit from behind, leaving the game early in the second period, but he comes back strong in the third period, getting a goal and an assist. His line is on fire, with the trio moving up to second line. The buzz around is that they are almost going to replace the top line. When we finally walk into the house we do the same thing as we have the last time, throwing everything down, except this time I just take out my toiletry bag and open it on the vanity since I'm leaving tomorrow morning. I grab the sunscreen, tossing it inside also.

I walk over to my closet, bringing down a bag that I have packed for tomorrow morning. Matthew is downstairs making sure that everything is okay. In twelve hours I'll be on a beach. I walk over to the bed, sliding inside the crisp cold sheets. I close off the lights while I wait for Matthew to come upstairs. "All good?" I ask him while I watch him go to his side of the bed and slide inside.

"All good, babe." He kisses my head, taking me in his arms. "I'm beat," he says while tucking me close to him. I fall asleep to the beating of his heart and the smell of what I can only describe as Matthew.

The phone beeping makes me open my eyes. I try to reach out and close it, but my hand is stuck. Panic fills me as I open my eyes. My hand is tied to the bed with a black strap. The cuff has fur on it. I pull harder while my eyes roam around the room. I'm by myself, but both my hands are now strapped. "Matthew!" I yell out, knowing he is somewhere in the house. "Matthew fucking Grant," I say while tugging on my cord. "This isn't funny, Matthew."

"Oh, I find this very funny," he says, walking into the room, stopping at the doorway. He is dressed in his track pants and team T-shirt. His feet bare while he sips a cup of coffee.

"Matthew, let me go." I pull again but nothing happens. "I have a flight to catch."

He throws his head back, laughing. "If you think for one minute I'm letting you go to Mexico by yourself without me, you're fucking dreaming." He walks to the bed where I'm almost thrashing to get away from the restraints. "There's no way in fucking hell you are going anywhere without me. Ever." He smiles at me, infuriating me even more than I thought was humanly possible. This, this, this big bully has me strapped to a bed.

"You know this is kidnapping, right?" I try to pick the straps, but my nails can't get to it. "I mean, you can't honestly think you can keep me strapped to the bed."

He smirks at me, his side smile making me want to take his stick and smash it over his head. "Oh, not only am I keeping you strapped to that bed the whole fucking time, you're going to beg me to *not* let you go."

"I think that bump to the head you got last night has messed you up." I try to keep calm, yet I'm so mad I think I'm the hulk, except I'm really not. "Matthew, seriously, I have a plane to catch."

"Sorry about that. I was able to cancel the flight, but I couldn't get your points back. Or your money." He sits at the end of the bed, his fingers going from my big toe all the way up the arch of my foot, to my inner ankle. "Mine," he says to himself while his fingers go to the front of my leg. "I have the same straps for your legs," he says while his finger trails my inner thigh till he gets to just under my pussy. "Those are going to come later."

"Oh, no, they aren't. Matthew, let me go. What if I have to go to the bathroom?" I ask him. Surely I can make a run for it.

"I can carry you there and back. Five days, five days of nothing but you, me, and time together," he says while his finger goes from my inner thigh to the front where my bikini line is.

I scream out in frustration, "Matthew, seriously."

He gets on all fours, crawling over me. Me and my naked body because of his stupid rule. My nipples are already peaked for him. Traitors. I'm not even going to tell you how my legs just want to open up for him.

"Did you really think I would just let you walk out?" he asks, bending down to take a nipple into his mouth. Nothing soft, it's a bite, and it's hard, the pain shooting through me, till his tongue twirls around it, the throbbing turning to pleasure now.

"Did you think I was going to let you walk out for five days without me?" He does the tsk tsk tsk with his mouth. "I don't let what's mine go, ever." He takes the other nipple in his mouth. I'm waiting for the sting. Instead, he just sucks it deep into his mouth. My back arches off the bed. My hands now hold the strap of the cuffs. "I was going slow before." He continues while I watch him kiss the center of my chest, my heart beating so fast, I'm sure I will see it come out. "Not anymore." He kisses my heart. "This shit stops now. I gave you time to get used to it. Well, your time is up." He kisses down to my stomach.

"Are you crazy?" I ask him, watching him kiss just under my belly button. "This is crazy. I agreed to sleeping naked with you. I agreed to be your girlfriend." His eyes come up to meet mine. We have never had the exclusive talk, but assuming I'm with him all the time, I figured.

He smiles at me. "Girlfriend." He shakes his head. Okay, maybe that wasn't the right word. "Girlfriend doesn't even come close to what you are to me." He kisses me again on my hip this time. "You're more than just my girlfriend." He kisses the other hip. "You're my lover." He kisses the lower part of my stomach. "You're my tomorrow." I pull my hands, hoping they snap so I can rub his face. "You're my forever." He kisses the spot right on top of my pussy, so soft I barely feel it.

"Matthew," I whisper out, "let my hands go." I try, only to see him shake his head.

"Not any time soon. I need to show you that you belong to me. Mark and claim you." That's the last thing he says before his face is planted in my pussy. Open mouthed he kisses me, his tongue coming out, making little circles. My legs fall more open only for him to put them over his shoulders. "All around you all you will feel will be me." He licks from the bottom all the way to the top, sucking my clit. "All you will see is me." He repeats the same things again. "All you will be is mine."

My eyes close at his words. They hit me right in my heart. It's a feeling I've felt only once before when I lost my mother. It's a feeling of complete and utter love. It's a feeling knowing that you will forever be linked with them. It's a feeling I will never forget, because it's so very different this time. This time I'm not grieving. This time I'm embracing it. "Matthew." It's the only word that can come out because he now has pushed my legs back, his tongue sliding into me. Curling up and coming back out, he does that five more times, releasing a leg to stick two fingers in me while his thumb presses down on my clit. His fingers slide in halfway and then come out only to be pushed in again to the knuckle. My hands are still holding the strap this time, so tight my nails are now almost white.

"Mine." He keeps saying while his fingers never stop assaulting me, never stop playing with me.

I'm about to come. My tits get tight, my stomach starts to roll, my toes start to curl, and my moan leaves my lips the same time that his fingers come out of me and stay out. I open my eyes, watching him lick me off his fingers. "You aren't going to come till you tell me you're mine."

I glare at him. "What?" I ask him, knowing what he will say next.

He sticks his fingers back in. My body wakes up again. My eyes close halfway, taking in the feeling of him surrounding me. He fingers me harder now, his fingers filling me while he bites down on my clit, which is throbbing. "Don't stop, please," I say, waiting for the crash to happen, waiting to jump off the bridge into the bliss or orgasm, only to be pushed back. His fingers slow down, his pace almost stopping.

"You going to say it, babe?" he asks while his fingers enter me so slow I can feel all his ridges. His thumb strings on my clit side to side. His body comes up while his fingers still fuck me. Taking my nipple into his mouth, he bites down. My senses are almost overloaded. I don't know what to concentrate on first. His fingers in me, his fingers on my clit, or his tongue around my nipple. He's all over me. He's everywhere. "Fuck, you're squeezing me so tight. You're there. Babe. Right there. You want to come?" he asks me, knowing the answer. My head moves from side to side while I tilt my hips up and my legs back. "Say it. Say it and I'll let you come."

"Matthew," I beg him, almost crying for it. "Please." His fingers start harder now, rubbing the G-spot inside me, the pressure so much, so good. "I'm going to come."

"No, you're not," he says, stopping all his fingers.

I groan, cursing at him.

"Say it, babe. Say it and I'll make you come and then fuck you so hard."

I open my eyes and lick my lips at the sight of his tented pants. "How hard?" I ask him, seeing him bite down tight, the vein in his jaw ticking. I'm not the only one on the edge. I push my tits up, trying to rub on him. "How hard are you going to make me come?"

"Mine." His mouth covers mine while our tongues fight with each other while we both try to kiss each other harder. His mouth leaves mine while he looks down at his hand disappearing inside me. "So wet," he says, and I know I'm wet. I can feel myself leaking all over his hand, all over the bed. "This little clit, so tight, so red. Want me to rub it, baby, rub it till you come?"

"Yes." I push up my hips now, trying to move side to side. I open my eyes to watch his while I say the words he's been waiting for. "Yours. Only yours." His fingers slam into me. "Always yours." Is the last thing

I say before I come all over his hand, and he doesn't stop. He continues pumping into me till I'm sure I'm going to come again, till I hear a Velcro strap open on my right wrist, only to be flipped to my stomach where he pulls my hips up. My hands grab the sheets while I look over my shoulder at the same time and he slips into me. Slowly to the root and then out again, only to be slammed into over and over again. The bed knocks against the wall, his hips crushing into mine, my body pushing back against his. His hand grabs my hair, pulling my head back, making my back arch, getting him deeper in me.

"Play with your clit. Get yourself there with me," he tells me while his hips never stop. My hands move under me, where I flick it with my nail, still sensitive from before, but the need to come overpowers it. My fingers rub it hard, from side to side. "You're almost there. I feel you squeezing me." His hands grip my hips. "Fuck, so good," he says while I breathe out, the orgasm coming so fast I don't even know how to tell him. Instead, my body stills, my pussy spasms, and my breath stops, my chest heaving while I close my eyes, riding the wave that has come over me. Riding till I'm almost at the shore, till he slams in me one more time and lets his head fall back and roars out his own wave.

# CHAPTER NINETEEN

## MATTHEW

It's been four days since I've tied her to this bed. Four days since I told her she's mine. Four days since she admitted she's mine. The first night I untied her and tied her to me just in case she would take off running. She did worse. She yanked me so hard while I was sleeping I thought my shoulder was dislocated. We showered together, ate together, watched television together, fucked each other like rabbits, and the whole time she was tied to me. I loved every single fucking second of it.

Now here we are in the bathroom after four days. My body has never been more relaxed in my whole life. "I have to be at the rink tomorrow morning for practice skate." I spit my toothpaste out of my mouth while she stands at her side of the sink brushing her teeth. My white big plush robe hangs on her. It's four sizes too big. "We play tomorrow night."

She spits out her toothpaste and rinses out her mouth. "I'm aware." She glares at me. "I hope you know that you ruined my vacation."

I wink at her, obviously irritating her even more. "Please, you're trying to tell me that four days home with your reality television shit playing wasn't better than Mexico?"

"No." She folds her hands, the front opening a bit more, showing me her one plump breast. She is also sporting some of what I call 'love bites' all over her. In discreet places of course. Nonetheless her breasts have them, her inner thighs, her shoulders, the back of her neck. I stopped myself short of sucking on her neck this morning while she rode me. Instead, her left tit got it. I reach out, pulling her to me. "You ruined my beach vacation."

I don't have time to say anything because her phone rings.

She walks to the side of the bed, picking it up, shooting me a surprised look. "It's my father." She looks at the phone again then at me. "Hey, Pops!" she says, sitting on the bed.

I take my cue to go downstairs and make sure everything is closed up. Walking back upstairs, I see her in bed under the covers watching television.

"Everything okay?" I ask her.

"Yes, he wanted to know how my beach vacation was. When I told him I got the flu and couldn't go, he asked me to meet him for lunch tomorrow and I'll stay in the office and head to the game with him."

I walk to my side of the bed, getting in, lying on my side. "You're beautiful. Every single time I look at you I hold my breath." I grab her hand and kiss her inner wrist. "This was the best four days I've ever had," I tell her softly. She sinks down in the bed, coming to me so now we are face to face, chest to chest. She doesn't say anything. She just kisses my lips.

"You owe me a Mexican vacation when this season is over. I'm going with or without you. FYI. And if you tie me to this bed one more time"—she leans in—"I will set your balls on fire while you sleep."

"Babe, you know all this sweet talk gets me all hot and bothered."

"I'm out of commission tonight. My vagina is closed. Besides, if we have sex one more time you might chafe," she says, cuddling in closer to me. "Save the energy for tomorrow night, big guy."

I smile at her, kissing the top of her head while we both fall asleep. When the alarm rings I roll over, getting out of bed, watching Karrie sleep. She is on her stomach, the sheet to her lower back, her hair fanning her pillow. A bite mark is on her shoulder right next to the hickey I left.

I smile to myself. She's mine. Fucking forever if I get my way. I lean down on her side of the bed, kissing her shoulder before I get dressed and leave for the rink.

Once I get to the rink, I get ready to go on the ice with Phil and Luka. We skate around, making plays and shooting the puck. Coach skates on the ice with the rest of the team, where we spend the next two hours going through all the new drills. By the time I skate off the ice I'm happy to get my skates off. Coach comes in after going to the board. "We are going to have some shifts with the lines that I'll be making tonight. Expect some changes."

With that he walks off while I rip the tape from my socks, forming it into a ball.

Max speaks up, "Fuck, I'm tired. Five days of fucking and drinking. I need another vacation."

I look down at my other sock, ignoring him while he talks about his whole five days off.

The guys around us start talking about television shows and about the beach vacation a big gang of them took. I get up going into the shower, making a note that I will be taking Karrie to that house in Mexico that Cooper bought Mom. Once I'm dressed I walk out, going to my phone and calling Cooper.

"Hey, son," he says as soon as he answers.

"Hey." I smile. He's been calling me son since almost the beginning and I love it.

"You okay? How was your time off?" he asks while I hear the twins in the background.

"Good, good, nothing crazy. We just stayed home."

"We?" he asks me.

"Yeah, Karrie and me," I say to him, looking around to make sure I'm alone. "She's the one."

"Matthew, son," he starts talking quietly, "you need to be a hundred percent sure of this. Her father is your boss. The biggest media mogul on the east coast."

"I would die for her. Remember when you met Mom and you said you want to be the one who makes her smile?"

"Yeah." His answer comes out soft as he probably remembers just that moment.

"Well, I want to do that. I've never wanted to do that before in my life, but with her I want to make sure she smiles all the time. I want to be the one who laughs with her, who wipes her tears, or who kicks the shit out of whoever makes her cry."

"Okay, son, when do we meet her?" Just like that he doesn't try to talk me down, doesn't try to tell me how stupid it sounds that after three months I'm head over heels in love with a woman who was going to go away without me.

"I want to bring her home as soon as I can." I'm almost home when I stop at the corner store and pick up a bouquet of pink tulips. "We are going to the west coast tonight, and we will be back next week."

"Oh, we are going to my college friend Austin's new restaurant opening on Saturday. Why don't you come by?"

"Yeah, we play Friday and then get three days off. Send me the details so I can set it up." I smile, thinking about finally seeing my family again. We FaceTime all the time, but it's not the same. "You guys are going to love her."

"She makes you happy, that's all we ask for, son."

I hang up as soon as I walk up the steps to the house. Opening the door walking in I see that I'm all alone. I walk to the kitchen where I put the flowers in a vase, bringing it up to the bedroom so she can see them. She fixed the bed before she left, so I just fall on the bed, grabbing her pillow so I can smell her, and just like that I nap till my alarm goes off, telling me it's time to get going.

Walking into the arena by myself is weird. I usually have Karrie with me. I go in search of her, wondering where she is. When I see her talking to Mindy and her father I walk up to them. "Hey." I nod to them and take in Karrie. I haven't seen her since I left her in her bed. She is wearing tight black pants that look like they were painted on with a peach shirt and a big scarf around her neck. Her gray jacket hangs open and loose.

"Hey, there he is," Mindy says. "We were just discussing how happy we are you are attending the kids' gala with us."

I put my hands in my pockets to stop from reaching out and yanking Karrie in my arms, even just to have her next to me.

"Now, if you excuse us, Doug, I need you to sign off on the press release." He kisses Karrie goodbye and they walk away.

I get closer to her, watching her eyes light up. "I missed you," I say low so no one can hear.

"Did you?" Her hand glazes mine. "Good. You can show me tonight just how much you missed me." I'm about to grab her and find an empty closet when the rest of the team slowly trickle in. "Go be a star, Grant. I'll see you after the game."

I nod at her, walking past her into the room. On the center board are the lines for tonight. I'm paired with Phil, which isn't a surprise, but we are put on the first line with Brendan. I don't have time to celebrate before Max comes in and sees the board.

"What the fuck is this?" He looks at the board and then around the room. The players never make eye contact with him. He comes up to me, toe to toe. "You think you can come in here and take my fucking spot, Rookie?"

I shake my head, not even giving him the time of day and planning on moving back, till he grabs the front of my jacket in both his hands. "I'll make you pay for this."

I feel some of the guys at my back, but I don't need them. "Max, on the ice I have your back because I have no choice, but in here, on the street, I don't. I'm going to give you three seconds to take your fucking hands off me before I break them both and you won't be able to hold a hockey stick for the next six weeks." I look down at his hands and then up at him. "Two." I don't even start at one when the Luka comes in and takes Max's hands off me.

"Calm down, Max," Luka says, but not before the coach, who has been watching this whole thing, finally speaks.

"You want back on that first line, earn it." He looks around the room. "No one hands anyone anything. Not in my locker room." And with that he walks out but not before Max storms out of the room.

"He's a fucking tool," Brendan says from his seat. "Ignore him."

The rest of the guys share the same opinion, but I keep my comments to myself. Instead, I get ready to show them on the ice why I belong on the first line.

# CHAPTER TWENTY

## MATTHEW

One more period till I'm off for three days. One more period till we can leave and just be us. One more step till she meets my parents. As soon as Karrie found out about the party, she tried to get out of it. She went as far as trying to call her father and asking if it was okay. That made me do one thing, confiscate her phone. She didn't talk to me for the whole night. She went as far as going into the other room to try and sleep. Well, that only ended in me carrying her back to my bed where I whispered sweet nothings to her, and she vowed to kill me in my sleep.

I look up at her now in the booth with her father next to her while she watches the play. We are winning by one, but the whole team is on shaky legs. We are down one defenseman, who got hit in the head behind the net. We keep getting penalties after penalties. Max especially takes stupid ass penalties. The coach is reaming his ass as we speak.

"Keep playing with that head up your ass, I'll fucking scratch you the next game."

He doesn't say anything because when it's his line's turn to go on, the coach yells my name. "Grant, you're on."

I don't wait to see what he says. Instead, I swing over the board, catching the puck in the neutral. I'm almost to the blue line when the defenseman behind me starts coming in on me, but I push harder, faster, and right when I'm about to shoot the puck I'm tripped straight into the goalie, my leg hitting the post.

The referee blows his whistle, pointing his arm to the middle of the rink, which means penalty shot. I get up, my knee stinging. I flex my legs back and forth to shake the pain out. Once I skate around a couple of times, the pain is gone. I skate to the middle of the ice where the captain is trying to argue with the referee about the call.

"It is what it is. He was all alone and you tripped him." He blows his whistle, skating backward so he can give the lines man the puck. He places it in the center of the ice. All the other players are already at the benches, leaning and watching.

The referee blows the whistle. I skate around the puck till I move it with my stick, the sound in the arena almost deafening with boos. I skate to the right, cutting to the left, my eyes never leaving the way the goalie comes out of his crease and then goes back in. His eyes watch the puck on the blade of my stick. I move the puck from the front of my blade to the back, his eyes still following it. I move the puck back to the front of the blade, winding up a bit, the goalie coming out of his crease a little, giving me just enough space to put it back on the back of my blade, lifting it just over his shoulder, hitting the back of the net in the top corner. The crowd gets louder with the boos as the siren sounds. I skate to my bench where I give everyone a high-five, except for Max, who stands there glaring at me instead of putting his glove out.

The rest of the game goes off smoothly, with us ending the game with an empty net goal. We skate off with a victory of 4-2. I walk into the dressing room, the reporters all waiting outside to come in. The equipment manager comes in, closing the door so Coach can speak.

We all start to undress, throwing our jerseys in the big gray container in the middle of the room. We put all our equipment in the bag in front of us, getting it ready to be shipped to the next arena. "Good game out there, boys. Good effort for the most of you," he says, looking directly at Max, who stands up and starts to walk out of the room. "I won't tolerate someone pulling a tantrum on my bench because he doesn't get his way." Coach then addresses the room. "That goes for everyone. I don't care if you are the star of the team. You don't pull your weight, I'll put someone who will." He nods at the room. "Have a great few days rest." And he walks out while I sit down to untie my skates. The door opens and the media comes in, most of them walking to where I'm sitting. I don't get up. Instead, I do this sitting down.

"Great game out there, Matthew. Can you tell us how it felt being upped from the fourth line to the first line?"

My response is almost robotic. "I just play where I'm told to play, whether it's the first line or the fifth line. I'm just happy to play."

"Matthew, your game has blown up. Is there a reason that it's sticking this time, instead of when you got drafted?"

I laugh as this guy is a fucking asshole, and always is. "Well, I was seventeen and didn't know how good I had it. Now I know what I want and I'm going to get it."

"Matthew, you got twenty-nine minutes of ice time tonight. Do you expect to stay at that pace or get cut down for the next time?"

I laugh. "Good question. I'm not the one to ask, though. Coach decides that." I get up after my skates are off. "Thanks for the questions, guys." I turn and walk out of the room while they go and interview other people. I walk out into the hallway. Karrie is leaning against the wall on her phone. She looks up.

"I scored a goal tonight," I tell her when I get close enough to her. "I need a celebration." I smile at her while she puts her phone away.

"I think I can manage to whip something together," she says while she crosses her arms over her chest. "So my father says I don't have to accompany you to the party. That Cooper will be there and there's no need for me."

My eyebrows pinch together while my hands go to my hips. "Really?" I ask her, almost taunting her.

"Really," she counters, her eyes almost gleaming with mischief.

I turn away to walk back into the room when her hand reaches out, grabbing me. "Where are you going?"

"I'm going to go call your father and ask him if he knows of a good strip club around here since I won't have a chaperone. Maybe take some of the guys."

Her hand drops. "You wouldn't."

I walk to her. "You seem to forget there's almost nothing I wouldn't do to make sure you're with me, by my side." I lean down and whisper in her ear, "I even packed the cuffs."

"You are a barbarian," she says with her teeth clenched shut.

"Meh." I shrug. "I've been called worse." I smile at her. "Give me thirty. I'll be done." I turn to walk away. "Oh, and, Karrie, don't dare me either." I walk away while she curses and starts talking about me under her breath, nothing good by the way.

We make it to the hotel where Mom and Cooper are staying. I booked us one room. The front desk greets us by Mr. and Mrs. Grant. Something about that makes me want to puff out my chest and bang on it. Karrie, on the other hand, sneers at me, waiting for me to finish. We have about two hours before we have to meet up with everyone. We walk into our suite that's all windows.

"Hmmm, I want to see you bent over in front of those windows while I fuck you."

"Seriously, that's what you think about?" she asks, putting her bag on the floor while she grabs her phone and keys. "Okay, I'm gone. See you later."

"Where are you going?" I ask her, confused.

"Shopping. I need a dress." She turns to walk away with my hand slamming the door closed right before she goes to walk out. I reach around, grabbing her cell phone and her keys. "You don't need these to shop for a dress." I also grab her purse, taking out her wallet. Once I have her wallet I walk to the wall safe, throwing everything inside and arming it with a code. "There, that's settled. Besides, I already bought you a dress. It's hanging in the closet."

"You are really going to keep me here against my will?" she asks while she leans against the door. "I don't want to go."

I walk to her, taking her face in my hands while my thumbs rub her smooth cheeks. "Baby."

"What if they don't like me? What if they think I'm not good enough for you?" she says quietly. "What if we don't get along?"

"Babe, number one, how won't they like you? If I think you're good enough for me, it's all that matters. The question is, am I good enough for you? I know I'm not, but I'd fucking die before I let someone prove me right." I kiss her lips while I squeeze her face. "How can you not get along with them? You are already on their good side. You make me happy. That's all my parents want for me." I smile. "Now go make yourself beautiful." I kiss her, walking to the closet, taking out the dress I bought online and had delivered. "Here." The only thing is I wasn't ready for the sight that was before me when she stepped out of the bathroom two hours later.

She looks amazing in her figure-skimming white dress. The top is off-the-shoulders with sexy little sleeves that cling to her biceps, and the dress hugs her in all the right places as it tapers down her thighs to stop just above her knees. Her thick hair hangs loose around her bare shoulders. "Fuck me" is the only thing I know to say because she is beautiful beyond words, beautiful beyond anything I could expect, beautiful beyond my wildest dreams.

"Don't you dare come near me, Matthew Grant. I'm not going to show up to meet your parents with you making my hair all crazy and wrinkling my dress."

I look down at her shoes, gold high heels with three bands, one at her toes, one around her middle and another at the top. "Tonight just those shoes." I wink at her. "Now come on before I lift your dress, move your panties to the side, and slide into you." My cock hardens with the picture of doing what I want to do to her.

She walks out of the room while I hold the door to let her walk out, her hips swinging to the side, my hand itching to leave my palm print on her. We get into the car that Cooper arranged for us. Sliding in next to her, she places her little purse on her lap. "Oh, Matthew"—she leans in—"I'm not wearing panties."

I don't say anything because the driver floors it, having me jolt back while she laughs at my face.

We get there and see that the press is there. "Fuck." I shake my head. "I'll get out and lead the way. Hold onto me."

She nods her head while I get out and hold out a hand for her and lead her inside while the reporters call my name. I smile and wave at them, walking into the club that's lit up and the music is pumping.

"Matthew!" Mom shouts, waving me over.

I look over my shoulder and see Mom waving. I grab Karrie's hand to guide us through the crowd to my mom and Cooper. I zig-zag through, letting go of Karrie's hand when we are almost at my mom, so I can grab her and hug her. "Hey, Mom, Coop," I greet both of them with a hug and a kiss for Mom.

"Where is Karrie?" my mom asks, so I turn around, assuming she is right behind me, but I can't see her till I spot her a couple of feet back talking to a guy with more grease in his hair than Danny Zuko. He's kissing her fucking hand and laughing with her. I knew that dress would fucking kill me.

I walk up to them, not even smiling. Instead, I grab her hand that's at her side, pulling her away from him.

Right before I get to Mom and Cooper, she pulls me to a stop. "Seriously, you need to stop that. He was just saying hello."

I walk over to her smiling, pushing the hair off her shoulder to lean in and whisper in her ear, "If you continue, I'm going to take you into the bathroom and fuck you so hard, this whole club will hear." Then I lean down and kiss her. I'm so fed up of fucking hiding everything. I don't give a shit who snaps a picture. I'm done. I finally let her go. "You get me?" I finish while she nods at me.

"Well, that settles that." I hear Cooper say under his breath as he sips the beer he is holding.

When we finally make our way to them, Mom is the first one to greet her. "Karrie, you look beautiful."

Cooper gives her a once-over and smiles at me. "Good luck, son."

I glare at him. I look back at Austin, who is Cooper's friend from college or even before that. They played hockey together. I've met him a few times over the years. He was always solo.

"Austin, this is my girlfriend, Karrie." I pull her to my side, wrapping my hand around her waist.

"I'm not his girlfriend. I'm his chaperone." She holds out a hand to

Austin and then to Lauren, who I was informed is Austin's girlfriend. Austin and Cooper both bust out laughing at me, and I'm now glaring at her.

"I'll show you a chaperone." I stare at her, and she glares back at me.

"Good luck finding me," she quips. "I don't have to be with you until next week." She tries to pry my fingers off her hip.

With that, I laugh at her and grab a beer off the tray from the waiter who is walking past us. "Try to run. I dare you," I challenge her. "Remember the last time you tried that." I take a pull of my beer.

Her cheeks turn a shade of pink while her eyes turn a dark shade of blue.

"Lauren, do you dance?" my mom asks when Rihanna's "This is What You Came For" comes on.

She nods her head and then downs the rest of the champagne, handing the empty glass to Austin.

"I love to dance," she says while the guys, including me, all groan.

"Let's go get a booth." I turn to Karrie. "The dance floor looks cramped."

"I'm going to dance. Who is coming with?" she says, heading for the dance floor, not even acknowledging my comment.

Mom follows her, and Lauren follows Mom.

"You pissed her off, and now," Cooper says, looking at me then at Karrie and the girls starting to dance in the middle of the dance floor, "we all suffer." He slaps me on the shoulder, laughing while he walks up the stairs so we can keep an eye on the women.

What the women don't realize is they are attracting attention—a lot of attention. Cooper is in the middle of Austin, his arms crossed over his chest and his eyes narrowed practically to slits. And me, I stand next to him, growling every ten seconds, and I wouldn't be surprised if steam starts pouring out of my ears. The only one calm about all this is John, Austin's business partner, who is leaning against the railing, looking at us. "Suckers."

We all turn to glare at him.

Cooper leans forward. "Um, you mind explaining what you're doing with Karrie?" he asks, turning his head to me.

"Nope. She's mine." I now sip water, having only the one beer. "She's just fighting the inevitable."

"She tried to leave you once. What makes you think she won't try it again?" Cooper asks.

"I handcuffed her to my bed for four days." I smile at the memory. "I dare her to try it again."

"You know that's kidnapping, right?" Cooper grins.

"Would you let Mom leave?" I ask him, knowing full well that he wouldn't even let my mom leave for four hours. "Just get on a plane and take off for God knows where?"

"I hope you used comfortable cuffs." Cooper laughs.

"Exactly," I state. "Now, I'm going back down there, because I've given her enough space." I walk down the stairs and onto the dance floor, going straight to her. I move in right behind her, my hand landing on her hips as I bring her close to me. She doesn't move until I whisper in her ear, "You drive me crazy," my hips moving with hers. "I can't not touch you. I can't stand here and not have you in my arms." I lick her earlobe. "Will you dance with me?"

Her arms move up my chest and around my neck.

"I want to spend the rest of the night worshipping your body. I want to spend the rest of the night buried in you. I want to spend the rest of the night loving you."

She turns in my arms.

"Want to leave?" I ask her while she nods.

I wink at the guys and wave at my mom while she continues to dance. "Let's go, baby." I grab her hand, leading her out to the sidewalk where a couple of reporters take our picture while I usher her into a waiting cab.

# CHAPTER TWENTY-ONE

## KARRIE

He has bulldozed his way into my life. He has stopped at nothing to make me stay with him. And I have to admit I have never felt as much as I have when we are together. He keeps me safe. He keeps me happy and the only other people ever to do that with me have been my parents. We walk into the hotel room, my hair already half messed up from the assault of his hands the minute we got into the cab. His lips land on mine as soon as we are out of the photographers' lenses. His mouth is on mine, his tongue mixed with mine, the need too much. I'm about to jump on his lap when we pull up to the hotel.

Once we get into the room, I see it's dim, candles lit all around the room. "What is all this?" I ask. Red rose petals scatter the whole room. There's a heart shape on the bed with a single white rose in the middle.

"I never get to do this because we are always with the team." He shrugs while I hold the white rose up to my nose. Rubbing it on my face, the petals are like a soft velvet.

I notice all the effort he put into this. Champagne and strawberries are on the table in the corner of the room with two chairs beside the table. I walk up, picking up a filled glass, the bubbles popping in my mouth. I grab a strawberry, biting into it, the sweet tart juices making the champagne come more alive. I suck the strawberry juices while I watch Matthew watch me, his lips squeezing tight, the vein in his jaw ticking. I put the champagne glass down while I lick the remaining strawberry off my fingers. I walk to the chair, turning it so it faces the floor-to-ceiling windows.

"All night I kept thinking about what you said." I reach to the side, zipping the invisible zipper down, letting the dress pool around my feet. His breath intakes as he sees that I'm not wearing anything under my white dress. "I kept picturing you here with me bent over and I couldn't wait to come back. But now," I tell him, walking to him, grabbing his hand, and bringing him to the chair, "I have something else in mind." I reach under his jacket, my hands flat on his chest while I peel his jacket off him. "But you know what I kept thinking about?" My fingers lace with his while I move him to sit in the chair. "I kept thinking about this right here." I get on my knees in the middle of his legs, my hands rubbing his thighs, moving up to his belt buckle, where I unbuckle it and open up the button. Pulling the zipper down, his cock comes out. My hand fists him from the base, going up to the tip. His head falls back while his chest expands with a heavy breath. "All night," I say, moving down, "I thought of nothing more than taking you in my mouth."

It's the last thing I say before I lick the pre-cum twirling around the tip, my mouth sucking it in. I move higher on my knees while my hair falls over me when I try to take him deep down in my throat. Matthew's hips thrust up, making me moan out, making me want to bring him to his knees. His fingers move my hair to the side so he can see me take him in my mouth.

"Beauty," he says to me while I take him more vigorously, up and down. He hits the back of my throat, and each time my hand wraps him and moves with it. "As much as I love you on your knees with my cock in your mouth, I need you to get up here and ride me."

I rise up, having his cock slide out of my mouth, a smile forming on my lips. I place one foot on each side of his legs, unbuttoning his shirt that's still buttoned. His chest smooth, my hands run up and down to his shoulders, opening it up even more. Grabbing him in one hand, I hover on him, rubbing him through my folds as I slowly lower myself on him. When he tied me up in bed, we were so caught up in each other that we forgot about the condom. After talking about it and me being on the pill, it was mutually decided we would go without. His hands hold my hips as soon as I'm on him completely. His strength lifts me up and down while I arch my back and he sucks my nipple into his mouth. The only sound in the room is from us, our breaths coming faster and faster. The moans fill the room. I'm about to come when he slams me down and grabs hold of my waist, standing up, his pants around his hips while my legs wrap around his waist. Walking over to the window, he puts my back directly on it. The cold from outside stings me, a hiss coming from between my clenched teeth, but I don't have time to think because he starts moving in me, slamming into me while the window holds me up. His face goes into my neck while my arms wrap around him. I'm like a spider monkey, wanting to crawl inside of him. "Matthew," I say because he's right there. The feel of him in me is too much. The feel of his hands on me make me lose my mind each and every single time.

"Get there, babe." Is all he says in between thrusts.

Glancing down, watching him disappear in me is more than I can take and I come hard, my head rolling side to side on the window while I feel myself leak onto him. I'm almost down when he slams forward one more time and follows me into oblivion.

We go another three rounds before falling asleep intertwined with each other. The alarm rings way too early the next day. He reaches over, turning it off.

"Baby, you need to get up." He kisses my shoulder while I press deeper into the pillow. "Babe."

"No, go away." I try to move away from him, my eyes still closed. "I'm on vacation." I hear him get off the bed and peek open one eye. He walks to the window, opening the shades, the sun from outside coming straight inside. He walks back to the bed, whipping the sheet off me. "Let's go, sleepyhead, we have to meet my parents in thirty minutes. He smacks my ass and then walks toward the bathroom where I hear him start the shower. "Babe, I would love nothing more than for you to stay in bed all day naked while I fuck you silly, but—"

"Matthew, the walls may be soundproof but the door isn't." I hear his mother's voice from outside the hallway.

I jump up, suddenly awake. I cover myself in the off chance he opens the door, but he just laughs from the bathroom.

"See you two in thirty," she says while I hope she walks away.

Matthew comes back out, looking at me.

"I hate you," I tell him, getting up and going into the bathroom. The water is set perfect as always. He gets in right behind me where he shows me that I really don't hate him. Again.

I dress in jeans and a white camisole with a see-through long-sleeved tan shirt. I pair it with brown flip-flops and Ray-Ban aviator glasses. My makeup is only mascara and lip stick. My hair is braided to the side loosely. Matthew is dressed in his dark denim jeans, a white long-sleeved shirt, and a brown V-neck sweater over it. He plays with his hair in the mirror, his brown suede boots already on.

"Let's go," he says, walking past me to the door. "Besides, you look like you're ready to drop to your knees and blow me."

I walk past him, hitting him in the stomach. "You fucking wish."

He closes the door and walks to me, draping his arm over my shoulders, pulling me close to him. Once he presses the button, he wraps both arms around me. "Give me a kiss."

"You mean, can you kiss me, please?" I reword it for him, glaring.

"Give me a kiss," he says again, my eyes glaring more. "Either you give me one or I take it." My hands are on his hips. "Okay," he says, leaning down and taking the kiss he wanted. The only time we stop is when the elevator dings. "See," he says, pulling my hand into his.

"Oaf," I say under my breath.

When we get to the lobby, I see his mother and Cooper. "Hey, you two," Parker says, going to Matthew and giving him a hug. She surprises me by coming and giving me one, too. "Karrie, you look beautiful."

I smile at her while she turns to Matthew. "Clean the shine off your lips. Cooper saw some press outside."

"Fuck," Matthew says, wiping his mouth. "Let's go before they call more."

I drop his hand and he looks at me. "I'm about done with this," he says, walking out after Cooper, who just watched the whole thing.

"Oh, ignore him, he was never very good when you told him no." She smiles at me and grabs my arm to walk out. "He also hates secrets."

I nod my head, taking it all in. I get into the truck that Cooper has rented, sitting in the back with Matthew, who is already sitting there, staring out the window at the press. His glasses block out his eyes. His hand goes to grab mine the minute I buckle in.

We don't say anything to each other as we drive to the rink. "I can't wait to get back on the ice here," Cooper says while we drive into the parking lot. "It's been forever." He parks the car, jumping out, not waiting for us.

Parker laughs in the front seat. "He's been up since six-thirty," she says, getting out of the car, following him inside.

"Hey, guys," she greets everyone as she goes to Cooper's side. "Who are these guys?" she asks Lauren, looking down at what must be her two kids.

"These are my children," Lauren says, smiling at her. "This is Gabe, who, believe or not, never stops talking." She hugs him sideways. "And this is my girl, Rachel."

"She's a beauty." Parker smiles at them.

"We need to talk tonight," Matthew tells me while his mother and Lauren exchange small talk.

Rachel leaves Lauren's side to go tap Matthew's leg. He stops talking to me and smiles at her before squatting down in front of her.

"Hey there, princess." The way his voice goes soft for her makes my heart burst and my stomach flutter. I'm sure my ovaries just exploded.

"Will you be my boyfriend?" Rachel asks him while Lauren gasps out loud and Austin, who has joined the conversation now, groans beside her.

"Um," Matthew mumbles.

"Rachel, what are you doing?" Lauren questions, going to her.

"Well, Auntie Kay has Noah as her boyfriend, and you have asshat."

Cooper bursts out laughing. She looks at Austin and smiles.

"Sorry, Asstin. So I want one, too, and I want him." Rachel points her thumb at Matthew, who is in stitches.

"I would really, really like to be your boyfriend, but Karrie is my girlfriend, and it wouldn't be fair to her." He looks up at me.

"Oh, that's totally okay. I give him to you," I tell Rachel. "No take backs, either."

Cooper and Parker are now laughing even harder.

Matthew stands up and glares at me. "I'll show you no take backs later." His tone is fierce, but I look at him and then down at my nails. "Can't. I'm busy."

"You're busy, huh?" he mocks me. "Really? With no phone, no car, no purse, no wallet?" He smiles at me. My hands go into a fist.

"Matthew," Parker whispers. "You didn't."

"He must have lost the handcuffs," Cooper chimes in. "Okay, why don't we go get ready to skate?"

"How about the girls go out for cupcakes and coffee?" Lauren asks us.

"Is Noah coming?" Cooper asks about their other friend while walking to the rooms in the back.

"I would love to go for coffee," I tell them. "You guys can be my getaway."

"You can run, but know that I'll always catch your ass and drag you back," Matthew warns with a wink, then turns, and jogs into the back.

"That man is a…" I stutter. "He's a…he's a…"

"He's an asshat," Rachel helps me out, smiling at her mom and then Parker and me, making everyone laugh.

"Okay, babe." Austin kisses Lauren. "Come back, and for the love of God, whatever you do, make sure you bring Karrie back with you."

Lauren looks at me. I'm sure I resemble those cartoon characters that are about to blow steam out of their ears. Before I actually yell out my frustration, Parker comes up to me. "Honey, I'm so, so sorry." With that, we all head out to go have chocolate cupcakes and coffee.

We walk into the little café that looks like you've died and gone to heaven. The whole room is filled with cupcakes. There are little tables in baby blue and pink all over the room. It's almost empty. We walk up to the display case, or at least one of them because there are three other display cases around the store.

"I want sprinkles," Rachel says to her mother while I look over the different ones.

"I'll take three lattes with a dozen cupcakes," Parker says to the girl behind the counter. "Karrie, honey, what flavor do you like?"

"Red velvet with the cream cheese frosting and apple pie crumble cupcake also." I hear a groan behind me and turn to Lauren.

"I hate you," she tells me and I put my hand to my chest. "Skinny, young, you can eat what you want and not gain a pound. If I ate two cupcakes, I'd have to diet for about four months before the fat was gone."

I laugh at her while she decides to get the peanut butter cupcake with banana frosting.

"I'll just double my spin classes."

Parker laughs at her and orders a chocolate cupcake with white chocolate frosting. Then she orders two sprinkle ones for Rachel and a big glass of milk.

We carry the cupcakes and the coffee to a table in the corner. I sit in the corner with Rachel sitting next to me on her knees while she claps her hands together in joy of having not one but two cupcakes.

I smile at her and turn back to Parker, who is smiling at me. We sit discussing last night and what a great turnout it was. I find out that Lauren and Austin work together, or did. She quit yesterday so they could date.

"So tell me, Karrie, how did you meet Matthew?" Lauren takes a sip of coffee and asks me.

"We actually met in a hotel gym." I fold my arms on the table in front of me, leaning in a bit. "Then I found out I was hired to be his chaperone." I think back at how it started.

"Really?" Lauren says.

"Yes, the day after I met him he moved in with me." I take a sip of the coffee. "Then proceeded to give me his shopping list." I laugh while Parker holds her forehead, hiding her eyes while she shakes her head and laughs to herself. "Then he basically bulldozed into every waking moment of my life."

"Mommy, I got to potty," Rachel says, getting up, Lauren following her.

"You love him," Parker says, leaning on the table as well. "I can see it in your eyes when you talk about him."

I open my mouth and then close it.

"Now don't get me wrong. I see that he gets on your last nerve, and he can push you to the brink of the edge and you are a second from jumping off, but," she tilts her head, "you always step back because deep inside you love him."

"I," I say, "I," stutter again.

"He took his father leaving really hard. I could see him struggling with it. He would pretend everything was okay, but deep down I knew it was brewing, it was eating at him." She wipes a tear from her cheek that slips out. "When Cooper came into the picture, he let go, and slowly, ever so slowly, the weight got lifted off his shoulders and he could be a kid again."

She takes a big breath. "Then he moved out to LA and it was like he was a kid straight out of his cage." She shakes her head. "I wanted to drive down there and ring his neck, but Cooper told me he had to fall on his own. So I listened to my husband, for once." Another tear falls. "He went to rock bottom. Came home with his tail between his legs. I wanted to kill them both. I know he's a grown man, but he's still my baby." She reaches across the table to hold my arm. "Seeing him with you, seeing you with him. Seeing the way you look at him, the way he looks at you. I know he's good now."

"I don't know if I love him," I whisper.

"Yes, you do. You wouldn't let him get away with half the shit he does if you didn't."

"He found out I was going to Mexico on our five day break and he tied me to the bed," I tell her. "He took my phone, keys, and purse so I wouldn't leave him."

She smiles at me. "You are a woman, a smart woman. If you want to get away from him, we both know that you would." She shrugs. "Well, unless you were tied to the bed, but..." She looks away then back at me. "Don't hurt him." She blinks away the tears that are pooling in her eyes.

“I love him,” I tell her, finally telling someone besides myself. “I don’t know when it happened, but he got into my heart and I can’t imagine a time without him.”

“Good. Now.” She points to Lauren and Rachel coming back. “Let’s go back to the hotel and get a massage or something. He owes me big.” She gets up, walking toward Lauren.

We walk out of the shop with her arm intertwined into mine.

# CHAPTER TWENTY-TWO

## MATTHEW

We spend three hours doing drills and practicing stick handling. We play a game of two on two, and I love every single second of it.

I show Gabe little tricks, and I have to give it to him; he soaks in every word, following up my instructions to a T and getting into it right away, hungry for more. When we call it a day, he actually groans and moans.

Craig is there when we skate off the ice. "That boy, with a little bit of coaching, could be out of this world. He's a natural." He looks at Gabe. "I got one more left in me." He looks from Gabe to Austin while I smile, thinking that this kid will be better than all of us.

"What does that mean?" Gabe asks, taking off his helmet and spitting out his mouth guard.

I walk to the dressing room, checking my phone while they continue talking. I see that Mom texted me a picture of her and Karrie at the spa. I smile when I think that she will be all relaxed for me tonight.

Gabe finishes before us and goes back to help Craig clean the ice on the Zamboni.

"Kid has the itch," Cooper says, unwrapping the tape from his legs. "Where is the father in all this?" Cooper knows all about being a stepfather.

"He's around." Austin shrugs. "He cheated on her with the kid's teacher. Found out she's Camilla the Cunt."

"Holy shit, no way!" Cooper shouts. "You think you're ready for this?" Austin has never been around kids, so his answer should be interesting.

"I know that with her comes them. They're a package deal. The kids are easy. It's the ex I'm not sure I can deal with." He suddenly looks unsure. "He broke up with Camilla, so now he's free. What's to say he won't try to get her back? They don't just have a past, they have kids. Can I even compete with that?"

Cooper throws his ball of tape in the garbage. "Oh, I know what you mean. When I met Parker, her ex was always away. The minute he spotted us together, all of a sudden he had second thoughts." He looks at me to see if I'm listening. I'm listening, and I just nod my head and agree with him. "But I knew that the minute I found out she had kids, I didn't give a shit. I wanted her, all of her."

"How do you compete, though?"

"You don't. You be you," I add from his side. "As long as Gabe sees that you treat his mom well, you make her laugh, and she isn't sad anymore, well, that's all you really need to do." I smile at Cooper, thinking back to how he drove Mom crazy at the beginning, but he wore her down.

We get dressed, each of us grabbing our bags to head out. "Okay, buddy, let's go," Austin tells Gabe as he walks out in front of him.

"Shit," I say, "they took the car."

"It's okay. I have Lauren's, and I can drive you guys back to the hotel." Austin opens the trunk. "It really is a bus." He winks at Gabe, and he just smiles and drinks the chocolate milk he got from Craig.

The minute he turns on the ignition, the sounds of "Let it Go" fill the car, and Cooper and I both groan. "I take it you guys know this song?" Austin asks us.

"Why is it playing?" I yell from the back, putting my hands over my ears.

"Because it's jammed inside the player and Mom didn't have it checked out yet," Gabe explains, his head moving to the beat of the music. "Dad used to do all that."

Cooper and Austin exchange a look before we drive off.

We get back to our hotel, and a couple of fans notice us and come up to ask us to take pictures. We sign a couple of autographs and head inside. "You want to have a beer before you go up?" Cooper asks me and I nod.

We sit side by side at the bar, both of us throwing peanuts in our mouth while we watch the SportsCenter playing. They show bits from the last game, including my penalty shot. "You are getting your legs back," Cooper says to me, taking a sip of his beer while I drink my bottle of water.

"It just feels right," I say. "It's almost like I'm centered. Like I'm comfortable in my own skin."

"You found it," he says, looking at the television then at me. "Your missing piece."

"What do you mean?" I ask him, confused.

"You were searching for your place. Looking for your place. Looking to find what was yours. You were missing the piece. You found it. Karrie, she is your piece. Your center. She is what calms you. It's what happened with your mom. I was never complete, always rushing, always pushing, always fidgeting. Till I found her. My piece. I knew from the moment she was mine that I could take on the world. That I could have the biggest mountains to climb and I would be able to do it, because she would hold my hand while I did it." He smiles thinking about Mom.

I nod, thinking about it.

"I feel peace." I play with my water bottle paper while I continue, "I was angry for so long. I was fucking pissed." I don't wait for him to answer. "But the minute I met her, it's like a calmness came over me. I mean, she does this thing, where she talks to herself, but it's the funniest thing. I can have the shittiest game ever, but the minute I touch her or even stand near her, I'm okay. I just settle." I shake my head. "She's it.

Now the next thing is finally getting her to tell people."

"Matthew," he says, "your mother fought me on this to the bitter end. Except I didn't give a shit. I was over everything, but this is your new break, this is your—"

I put my hand up to stop him.

"I know. Trust me, I know, which is why I'm not pushing it. But what if you couldn't hold Mom's hand in public? What if you want to reach over and hug her and you couldn't? What if you just want to smile at her without looking around to see if someone is watching?"

"I would go crazy. I would pull out billboards all over the fucking country declaring my love for her. I can't even stand to think about not being able to call her mine in front of anyone."

"I'm going to play it the way she wants. But I'm only going on so much longer."

He nods. "I'm here when you need me. You know that." He slaps my shoulder. "Just, son, you have to ease up a little. You tied her to a bed." He smiles.

I shrug my shoulders. "I would do it all over again." I'm about to continue when Cooper's phone starts ringing.

I don't know who is on the phone but his eyebrows pinch together. "There has to be a mistake," he says to whoever is on the phone. "I doubt the twins would actually steal the boy's clothes and bury them in the sand." He shakes his head while I look down thinking that's exactly what my sisters would do. "We can be there in about five hours," he says, checking his watch. "Okay, thank you."

"Jesus," he says out loud, "the girls just took this boy's clothes while they were in swim class and buried them in the sand."

I put my lips together to try not to laugh at him, but snickers come out.

"They wrote RIP Douche on top of the pile. Let's go tell Mom."

The laugh that I was trying to keep in comes out, my whole belly shaking while I follow him upstairs where he breaks the news to my mother, who of course blames Cooper for being too soft on them. With his hands on his hips, he argues back only for her to give him one look that shuts him up. They leave with a hug and a promise to visit soon.

I go back to my room where I find Karrie in the middle of the bed, a white robe covering her. Her head is angled to the television that's playing some kind of reality cooking show. Her soft snores fill the room. Climbing into the bed, I take her in my arms. She moves a bit but settles in. Kissing the top of her head, I follow her into abyss.

Now here I sit three weeks later. It's been a fucking crap show. Karrie caught some fucking bug last week and she is still weak from it. She throws up one more time, her ass is going to the doctor. I don't give a shit if I have to fucking drag her there. Plus, Max is being a top notch douche. Before he was just a jackass. He has since brought it up to a different level. A level that if we weren't on the same team I would smash out of him. I walk into the arena, Mindy greeting me with a tight smile.

"Matthew, so we were just thinking that perhaps it's a good idea that Karrie stays back from the next leg. It's only one day. She can head back home tonight so she can rest and get better."

"Who is we?" I ask, taking the earbuds out of my ear.

"Doug. He's in town for business and is coming to the game tonight."

"Is anyone going to be with her?" I ask, texting her.

**Feel better.**

"I think Doug said he's going to talk to her tonight about going home with him."

I nod, sending her another text.

**Your father is in town.**

I press send and see that it's been delivered but not read. When I left her fifteen minutes ago she was finally lying down before the game. I walk into the room and get ready for the early skate.

I sit down, taking off the tape from my stick, throwing it in the garbage and getting my roll of tape that's right next to my cell phone. Reaching for the tape, I see my phone light up with my mother's number. She knows I'm on the ice, so it might be an emergency.

"Hello," I answer the phone, looking around.

"Matthew, thank God. I want you to listen and say nothing. I have you on speaker. Cooper is here, too," she says and then Cooper's voice sounds out.

“Listen to us before you talk. Got me, son?” he says, his voice clipped.

“What the fuck is going on?” My heart starts pounding. My neck starts getting hot while I hear a commotion coming from outside the locker room. Voices start being raised behind me.

“There’s a warrant out for your arrest. Someone is accusing you of beating and raping her yesterday,” Cooper hisses out while the door is being slammed open. “I have the lawyer already on the way to you. You say nothing, son, nothing.”

I look up just in time to see two detectives dressed in suits coming into the room.

“Matthew Grant.” They flash their badge. “We have a couple of questions we need to ask,” one of them says while I hear Cooper still on the line.

“Don’t say a fucking word, Matthew. We are coming to you.”

“Now?” I hear Coach behind me yelling. “You do this to him now, two seconds before he’s supposed to go on the ice?” He glares at them.

They obviously couldn’t care less.

“You need to come down to the station with us,” one of them says, but I’m standing here with my mouth open, my ear drums pounding, and the phone to my ear. “We can walk out of here civilized or we can strap the cuffs on you. One way or another you aren’t getting on that ice.”

My teammates are standing up shaking their heads.

“This is bullshit.” I hear Coach say while the guys nod.

Phil comes up to me and whispers, “Don’t say a fucking word.”

I don’t have time to process before I’m being ushered out of the locker room. The only thing I take off is my skates.

I walk out of the building and I’m led into an unmarked car. The owner of the team is now standing with Karrie by his side. His hands are around her shoulders, her face streaked with tears.

“Karrie!” I yell from inside the car. “Karrie!”

Nothing. She turns around and walks back into the arena, leaving me alone with the silence that now fills the car.

# CHAPTER TWENTY-THREE

## KARRIE

*Thirty Minutes earlier*

I'm dragging my ass. I can't seem to fight this bug. I'm taking everything under the sun, extra vitamins, omega 3, extra vitamin C, but nothing is helping. I might have to admit defeat and go and see a doctor. I hate admitting that he's right!

I'm walking into the lodge the team has at the arena when I spot my father sitting in the chair with Mindy beside him and someone else I have never seen. "Hey there," I say to all of them, going over to my father, kissing his cheek.

Their faces say that something is off. "What's the matter?"

"Honey," my father starts and the way his voice is I know it's bad. What I don't expect is it to be the end of my world. "Sit down."

Mindy stares down at her feet while her hand wipes away a tear.

"I'm starting to freak out," I tell them, my heart pounding really fucking fast. I sit next to my father, who reaches out to hold my hand.

"This is Detective Horton. He's here with a warrant for Matthew's arrest." He starts to say and it's like my body is taken from me. I can hear him talk, but I don't understand what he is saying.

The only thing I can hear is the pounding in my ears. The only thing I can focus on is the little fleck of dust that has fallen on my black jacket. I'm taken out of my trance when someone knocks at the door. Our family's lawyer Ed Reynolds walk in.

"I came as soon as you called."

I look at both my father and Ed. "He didn't do this. Whatever you think he did, he didn't." The tears are now running down my face. "Dad, I swear he didn't."

My father squeezes my hand, "Honey, you don't know that. Rape." He shakes his head. "I don't want to believe it. But..."

"Wait." I shake my head. "What?"

"Karrie," Mindy says, "a woman just accused him of beating and raping her last night after the game."

My dad nods. "According to the police, she walked into the station this afternoon and said she spent the night with him or rather he went to her room at around one a.m. They spent the night having sex, rough sex." Mindy looks at the lawyer. "Where it got out of hand. She said no. He didn't stop."

I let my father's hand go. "Bullshit. He would never. Ed, I promise you he didn't do this." The tears are coming, but they are angry tears now. Why isn't anyone listening to me? Mindy's phone rings and she answers it. She nods and hangs up. "They are arresting him now."

I get up. "I have to go to him. I have to be there." I'm about to run, not walk out of the room, when my father stops me by holding my arm.

"Karrie. You did what you had to do. You can't put this on yourself. He must have sneaked out while you were sleeping."

I yank my hand out of my father's hand. "He was with me." Mindy's hand goes to her mouth. "All night, Dad." My tears run down my cheeks like a river flowing. There's nothing that will let them stop. "All night, every night."

My father puts his hands in his pockets, looking at Ed.

"I don't need you to believe me. I need you to believe that no matter what, Matthew would never do that to anyone. He has sisters and a mother that he adores. He would never ever raise his hand to anyone." I turn to Ed. "I need to know right now whose side you're on, because if you aren't on my side, which is his side, you need to leave."

"Karrie," My father starts, but I hold up my hand to stop him.

I gather whatever strength I have left.

"I love him, Dad. I love him more than I can say. I love him with every beat of my heart. I love him with every breath in my body. I love him with every single piece of me." My shoulders go square, my spine straight. "I'm in love with him. I have been from the moment he walked into the house and told me to buy his food. Now I ask you, Dad, whose side are you on? Because..." I shake my head, not ready to say the words.

"Yours, every single time it's yours," he says quietly. "Let's go be by Matthew's side."

I nod while a sob comes out of me. The thought of losing Matthew is too much. "I can't let him see me like this. I have to be strong for him."

My father takes me in his arms, where I let go, a sound of horror coming out of me, my heart broken when I think about how alone he must be.

"Get Cooper on the phone. Ed, call in the cavalry," he says over my head while he rubs my back. "Mindy, put out a statement that we stand by his side. No matter what." He rubs my back. "Okay, honey, we need to get to the police station." He guides me out while Mindy stays on my other side, her hand in mine. A form of unity.

She leans in. "No way he did this."

I nod at her, biting my lips together when we make it out of the arena at the same time they put Matthew in the car.

"Karrie!" he yells from inside the car. "Karrie!"

My first thought is to go to him, but they drive off, so I turn and my father ushers me back into the arena into a waiting car.

"The media is picking up the story. It's all over the place," Mindy says, getting in the car also. "I have Parker on the phone." She hands me her phone.

"Hello," I breathe out, my voice cracking.

"Karrie, I know what you're going through, honey, I'm on my way."

My head just nods.

"Honey, you have to be strong. For Matthew. Yes?"

I just nod, but it's like she knows.

"We should be there within the hour."

"Okay," I whisper and then give the phone back to Mindy. "I think I'm going to be sick," I say when my stomach starts to rumble and the motion of the car makes me light-headed.

"Here, drink this." Mindy hands me a bottle of water. When we get to the station, I spot five media trucks already. "Look down and don't say a word to anyone," she says, getting out of the car followed by my father, who holds out his hand to me.

I walk next to my father, who puts his hand over my shoulder and leads me inside.

Ed is already there with another man I saw once. "Ladies, this is Noah. He's Cooper's lawyer," Ed tells us as soon as we walk in.

"Where is he?" I ask, and Noah smiles at me. "I have to speak to him. I want to see him."

"You can't see him just yet," Noah says. "They are reading him his rights in a couple of minutes. He better fucking ask for a lawyer. Criminal is not my forte but everyone knows that you ask for a lawyer." He's about to say something else, but the door opens and we hear a commotion. Lights flash.

Turning, I see it's Cooper and Parker. Her face is as white as mine is. She has the same tears that have streaked her face.

One look at me and the tears come again. She rushes to me, taking me in her arms. "Sweetheart." And just like that I lose it. I cling to her because she is the closest thing to Matthew. Cling to her because I need her strength. I feel strong arms hug us, and then hear Cooper's voice.

"We are going to prove that he didn't do this." He then turns to Ed and Noah. "I don't care what it costs, private detective, find out everything."

"I don't think that will be necessary," a strange voice says from the side.

I look up to see a huge bulging guy. His eyes pierce through me.

"Off the record, her story has so many holes, you might fall in and end up in wonderland." He doesn't say anything and just goes past us to the back. Another man follows him.

"What kind of evidence do they have?" Cooper asks. "They have to have something strong to just go and arrest him."

Ed shakes his head. "Right now it's her word against his. The judge probably issued the warrant because of who he is."

"I need to sit down," I say, trying to get a handle on myself. "I think I'm going to throw up." I go to the wall that's lined with chairs.

"Someone get her something to eat, or a juice," Parker says to them and Mindy nods, going on a hunt for something.

A man walks out from the back. "Who is here for Grant? He is asking for a lawyer," one of the detectives says with a leer.

"That's me," Noah says, getting up and walking to the back. "No need to follow me. I need a word with my client. In private. And you might as well turn off the camera and the tape recording. I would hate to have this thrown out of court because you are an eager beaver." He smiles at him, walking away.

I look at Parker. "He was with me the whole night." I put my hands in my lap, playing with my fingers. "I was sick. He was a pain in my ass. Overbearing. I couldn't take it." I laugh, thinking about almost giving him a sleeping pill to shut him up from breathing. "He kept me up most of the night with his snoring." I gasp out loud. "Where is my phone? I need my phone." I rummage through my purse. "I have video." I look around the room at Cooper, Parker, Mindy, Ed, my father, and most of all the detective. I grab the phone from my purse, opening up the camera. "I took videos to show him." I look at Parker. "Only because he did it to me last week. Last night I decided I would give him payback." I turn the first video on, the room so quiet you can hear a pin drop. My voice suddenly fills the room.

"It's one a.m." I turned the phone to show the time. "Sleep, he tells me." Then I put the camera on him. He was sleeping on his back, and the snores were so loud it was really hard to say he wasn't.

I put the next one on. "It's now one-thirty and he stopped for maybe a second." I turned to see Matthew, who was now throwing his hand over his head. "Maybe he's done."

The next one was just of the clock. "It's two-thirty. I'm thinking what would happen if I put a pillow on his face?" I turned the camera to Matthew, who turned then to face me.

"What are you doing?" he asked.

"Showing you that you snore like a pig." The screen went black because he had grabbed me, bringing me into him.

"Go to sleep," he said.

The next one was an hour later. I was sitting on the couch, showing him the infomercial about snoring and a pillow that would stop it. I pointed to Matthew, who was sleeping like a starfish. His snores were so loud I'm surprised you could hear my voice.

"Well, there goes her story," the detective says, walking away from us.

Two minutes later, the two men from before come out of the room straight to me. "Hi there. My name is Mick Moro. This is my partner Jackson Fletcher. I was told that you have evidence that will close this case?" he tells me.

"Um," I answer him, "I taped him snoring." I smile finally. "He was with me the whole night."

"Do you mind if we take the phone into evidence?" Jackson asks me, his voice softer than his partner's.

"Here, take it." I give it to them. "Can I see him?" I look from Mick to Jackson. "Please."

Jackson nods. "Give us a minute," he says, going to the back and coming back out. "Okay, till this gets straightened out, he has to stay here, but you can see him for a bit."

I get up, walking toward him, following him down the white hallway, where he opens the door and the man I love sits with his head down and his eyes closed.

# CHAPTER TWENTY-FOUR

## MATTHEW

I hate this fucking room. It has a smell of stale coffee and smoke, which is weird since I didn't see anyone smoke. I'm sitting at the table, my hands on top, my foot moving a million miles a minute.

"So tell us where you were last night," the detective who calls himself Martinez asks while he leans back in his chair.

"I told you I was in my room as soon as I got back from the game."

"Were you alone?" the other detective, who goes by Mabie, asks, leaning on the table. "The whole night?"

"Yes, the whole night, alone." I'm not bringing Karrie into this. I don't give a shit what happens to me and my name, but they aren't fucking touching her.

Martinez snickers while he leans back, the button on his gut about to pop open. "You want me to believe the player of all players just finished the game and went back to his room?" He laughs.

Mabie, who is balding on top, leans forward. "The woman says you called her from a private number at about one a.m. Then you went to her hotel room. You guys had sex, but then you flipped."

"I'm telling you it wasn't me." I shake my head. "I was in my bed all night."

There's a knock at the door and a huge detective comes in. "You read him his rights?"

"They haven't and I want a lawyer," I say out loud, making Martinez and Mabie get up, glaring at the guy who came in. They shut the door behind them. I breathe out a sigh, wondering if this is actually happening to me. This is a fucking nightmare. My thoughts go straight to Karrie. The need to go to her. I don't think long because the door opens and Noah comes in, closing the door behind him.

"Noah," I say with hope.

"Hey there," he says, sitting down. "So this is the story. This woman claims you called her, went to her apartment or hotel, had sex with her, then you wanted rough sex, and when she said no you didn't listen. You beat her. From the pictures I just saw, if you did this your knuckles would be bruised. She can barely see. One side of her cheek is swollen so much you can't see her eye. Her lip is cut open. She looks like she went twelve rounds with Tyson."

"I was with Karrie the whole night." I shake my head. "But there's no way in fuck I'm dragging her into this mess."

"Oh, you don't need to drag her into this. She is here willingly," Noah says while he leans back in the chair. "Your girl just about laid out her father, or at least that's what I'm told."

"What?" I ask, my mouth dry, my tongue thick. "Where is she?"

Noah smiles at me. "She's outside in the room with your mother, Cooper, her father, and some chick who looks like she drank way too much fucking coffee."

There's a knock on the door again. The one who came in before asking if I was read my rights comes back in. "Hey there, sorry to interrupt. I'm Mick Moro. There has been a development in the case," he says, sitting next to Noah.

"What development?" Noah asks, sitting up now.

"We have a video putting you not at the scene of the crime. In fact, the video shows that you snore like a fucking hog." He smiles at us. "You owe your woman more than you know. She just saved your ass.

Although I will say there's no way this was going to stick. She couldn't identify you in a line-up. Plus, her description of you didn't even add up." He shakes his head. "I'm sorry that you got dragged into this," he says, rapping his fingers on the table. "Hang tight, we should be able to let you out of here soon."

He closes the door.

"Well, my work here is done. I'll be billing Cooper more than I'm worth." Noah slaps the table, walking out.

I sit here, looking at my hands that are still shaking with fear and anger. My head is down as I think of the mess this is going to make for me, but most of all for Karrie. A tear escapes as the door opens again. This time when I look up it's into the eyes of the woman who saved me without even knowing it.

"Baby," I say, getting up while she runs to me and buries her face into my chest. Her body shakes with the sobs that are coming out of her while her hands claw into my back as she bunches the shirt in her fingers. "It's okay."

"I'm so sorry it took so long," she says in between sobs. "I forgot about the video."

I bring her so close to me I want it to be like she is in my skin. "Baby, I didn't want you to drag yourself into this mess."

"Drag me into this mess?" she says, letting me go, leaning back. "What the fuck did you think I would do, Matthew?"

"Obviously nothing is what I thought you would do." I shake my head. "You think I wanted your name to be linked to this garbage? Never."

"You know, I don't know how it is that I can go from loving you to hating you in a split second."

"You love me?" I ask her. I've told her a bunch of times. Okay, yes, she's been asleep, but...

"She loves you so much she went toe-to-toe with me and told me that if I didn't choose you to basically fuck off."

I look at the door where Doug stands with Noah.

"Did she now?"

She rolls her eyes at me.

"He's exaggerating a bit," she says while she relaxes in my arms.

"I love you," I tell her quietly. "I love you so much that my heart hurts when you're not there. I love you so much that every breath I take is for you." I kiss her lips. "Thank you for saving me and loving me enough to want to stand by and hold my hand. And especially thank you for taping me while I snored." I grab her while Jackson comes in.

"Okay, you are free to go." He nods at me. "We fixed it up that you can leave out the back since the front has now become a media nightmare. They are saying that the mayor has to come down and make a statement." He shakes his head. "This is one time I'll be glad to rub it in Martinez's and Mabie's faces."

I thank him and walk toward the door where we make a quick getaway, the press oblivious to anything that's going on. We go straight to the airfield where a private plane is waiting.

"Your parents will be coming with us," Doug says from the front seat.

I nod to him, looking out the window while Karrie sleeps on my shoulder. When we get to the tarmac I wake her up so she can get out of the car. When I hold out my hand to her, she takes it, coming down from the SUV.

"I don't feel so well," she says while her father closes his door. "I think—" It's the last thing she says before her legs give out on her and she collapses in my arms.

# CHAPTER TWENTY-FIVE

## KARRIE

"I don't give a shit who you call. I want her to be checked by someone as soon as we get home." I open my eyes slowly, taking in Matthew's face almost turning red. I'm lying down on the plane.

"Matthew, you need to calm down." Parker is beside him, trying to calm him down. Cooper stands behind Parker on his phone.

"What is going on?" I say, my throat dry. Matthew rushes to the couch that I'm lying on, getting on his knees in front of me. My father, who is sitting in a chair beside it, comes to me also.

"You fainted," Matthew says while the team doctor pushes him out of his way. Matthew just glares at him while he takes my arm to check my pulse.

"She is probably just tired and hungry. Today was a big emotional day. She just needs rest and a good meal." Parker tries to say from behind Matthew now that he is hovering.

"I want an ambulance waiting for us in New York when we land." He looks at my father, who only nods and feeds into his craziness.

I try to sit up, but my head spins, so I lie back down. "That's crazy.

Your mother is right. I'm exhausted and hungry. How long till we leave?"

"We are ten minutes from taking off. We should be home in about forty-five minutes," my father says from his chair, his face also pale. I reach my hand for him and he takes it, so I squeeze his, offering him a little bit of I'm okay. "Patrick, the team doctor, is going to travel with us."

The flight attendant comes to tell us we are cleared for takeoff so to buckle in. I try to sit up in order to buckle up, but Matthew's voice stops me. "Don't you dare move a muscle." He comes to the couch, picking up my feet and buckling himself in, holding on to my feet. "You aren't going anywhere," he says, looking at my father, who gives him another nod.

Parker and Cooper sit on the two chairs by the table with Patrick.

"I'm okay, Matthew," I say quietly. He doesn't say anything to me, only looks at me with his eyes almost glossy.

"Just don't, okay," he says to me then averts his gaze.

I just nod at him.

Within fifteen minutes, the flight attendant comes out and has some soup for me. I sit up and eat it, my stomach feeling so much better.

"I feel so much better," I say loudly, hoping someone will be listening.

Parker looks up from her phone and smiles at me.

The wheels touch down and we are coming to a stop. I turn to put my feet on the floor to get up only to be stopped by my father, who puts his hand on my shoulder.

"Honey." He smiles at me, putting my face in the palm of his hand.

"Do me a favor. Just let him take care of you."

I turn to Matthew, who is bending over to carry me out of the airplane.

"You know this is ridiculous and I'm perfectly okay. Patrick, tell them my vitals are normal," I say over Matthew's shoulder.

Walking down the steps of the airplane, I take in the two blacked out SUVs with an ambulance waiting for us. "Are you for real? This is so pushing the limit, Matthew, even for you." I don't say anything else because I hear squealing and see Vivienne running from one of the

SUVs.

"Oh, Mon Dieu," she says, coming to me, her face shielded with worry. "I was so worried when Matthew texted me."

I glare at Matthew and then back at Vivienne. "I'm fine. I fainted."

He walks us to the ambulance where he places me on the gurney they have waiting.

"In all my life I've never wanted to kill you more than I do right in this minute, Matthew Grant. Parker!" I yell, turning my head to her. "Please tell him."

But she walks up to me, grabbing my hand. "Honey, just do as he says and then we can scold him after."

Matthew is smiling next to Cooper, who has his arms crossed over his chest.

"I have never," I say under my breath. "I can't even tell you." I look at my father. "And you." I point to him. "I quit." Then I look back at Matthew. "You move out of the house." I don't have time to say anything else. Instead, I'm loaded in the ambulance with Matthew getting in with me. I see Vivienne standing next to my father, who has a hand around her shoulders, and Parker is being hugged by Cooper, all of them waving at me. "After this I'm not talking to you, FYI." I almost pout.

The technician is now taking my blood pressure. "It's a touch high, but that's to be expectant after a trauma."

"A trauma? I fainted. There was no trauma." I can't say anything else because he slaps the back of the box, giving the driver the signal to start driving. The sirens go on and I glare at Matthew. "Ridiculous."

We get to the hospital with a nurse opening the back of the cab while Matthew steps out and she waits for the EMT to pull out the gurney. "Female fainted, sick for the last couple of weeks, might be dehydrated. Blood pressure was a tad high."

"If you check me now I might be skyrocketing," I mumble to the nurse, who just smiles at me. They place me in a room right away, where she takes my blood pressure and smiles.

"Just a tad high. You can wait outside while I take her blood," she tells Matthew.

Matthew stands in the corner, his legs open, his arms crossing over his chest. "I don't leave her side."

She smiles at me while I roll my eyes. "Can I call security on him?" I ask her while she flashes a light in my eyes. "I fainted, because I was hungry."

"The doctor will be right in. I'm going to need a sample of urine." She puts the cup in my hand. "Let me get a wheelchair."

"Oh, for God's sake. I can walk." I throw my legs over the bed, blocked by Matthew. "Ugh, fine, he can carry me. But I swear to God, Matthew, if you don't leave me alone in that bathroom while I pee I will cut you in your sleep."

I go to the bathroom where he places me on the floor and steps out. I finish peeing and stand up, my legs a little shaky, so I hold on to the wall, but I don't say anything. The door opens as soon as I flush.

"You done?" he asks, picking me up and grabbing the container in my hand.

"Matthew, I didn't even wash it off. I peed on that."

His grunt is infuriating.

The next person through the doors is the doctor, who is tall, with blue eyes and black hair. He is in scrubs and come a couple of months ago he would be my type of person. "Hi there. I'm Dr. Founder." He smiles while he looks over the chart. "So you've had fainting spells?" he asks, coming to me.

"No. I fainted. Once. I've been feeling a little under the weather. I think I caught a bug and it's just taken a couple of days to get over it. Plus, I had a busy day today and I didn't eat. Now that I have eaten, I feel fine."

"How long did you faint for?" he asks while he flashes a light in my eye also.

"A couple minutes," Matthew says to him.

"Did you hit your head?" he asks.

"No, I caught her while she was going down," he says while the doctor writes into the pad.

"Everything looks okay. I'm going to wait for the blood and urine results. I'll let you know as soon as I get them," he says, walking out.

I put my head back, closing my eyes. "I could be home right now on the couch." I open one eye while there's a knock at the door. Parker and Vivienne walk in.

"Hey," Parker says, going to Matthew's side to squeeze his arm then coming to the bed. "How are you feeling, sweetheart?" she asks with such worry.

"I'm fine." I try to reassure her.

Vivienne sits on the bed next to me. "You really know how to steal someone's thunder." She smacks my arm, laughing. "You couldn't let some attention go to Matthew and his felony!" She turns to wink at Matthew. "Je savais que c'était une connerie." I knew it was bullshit, she says to us.

The door opens now and Cooper walks in with I think every snack that the vending machine sells in his arms. Walking to the bed, he puts it all where my feet are. "That's from the vending machines in the waiting room. Your father went to the vending machines in the cafeteria."

"How?" I ask Parker. "How do you survive?"

She just shrugs. "You get used to it a bit, then you just reel them in a bit." She hugs Cooper around his waist. "If it gives him peace of mind, I just do it."

My father walks in with the same state as Cooper did. "Here, I could only get these. The machine ran out of change, so I have my assistant coming down with more snacks."

I groan out loud while Vivienne laughs and starts going through the food. "C'est come L'Halloween." It's like Halloween, she says.

I lean forward, grabbing a pack of chips and a Gatorade. "There, happy?" I ask the room when another knock on the door makes us stop. The doctor walks in with the nurse following him.

"We have the results," he says, looking at his feet and then back up.

Parker inhales deeply while tears come out of her eyes. Matthew pushes his way past everyone to get to me.

"If you will excuse us while we have a private conversation with Karrie. You can wait outside and she will call you in as soon as she is ready," he says as I look around the room.

Parker has tears pouring over her lids, as well as my father, who looks paler than Casper the Ghost. Vivienne is wiping away a tear from the corner of her eye.

"It's okay. They already think I'm dying. You have my permission to continue and give me the news." As I say that my stomach starts to turn. I don't know why I'm expecting him to tell me I'm going to die in six months. My palms get sweaty as Matthew grabs one and kisses it.

"I love you," he says to me.

"Well," Dr. Founder starts, "we have your results and you're pregnant." The second the words come out of his mouth, my ears start to ring. My neck starts to get hot again.

Parker is smiling and has her hands together. Vivienne gets up off the bed to high-five Matthew. Cooper is standing there, holding on to his wife with the biggest smile I've seen him make. My father walks over to Matthew, slapping him on the shoulder, then leaning over the bed, he kisses me.

"Your mother would be so proud of you," he says, making tears start to fall. My hand goes automatically to my stomach.

"There has to be a mistake," I say out loud. "I'm on the pill. Tell them, Matthew."

The nurse chimes in, "The pill is not accident proof."

I shake my head in shock. Matthew comes to sit by my side on the bed. He takes my face in his hands. "I love you so, so much." He kisses me. My hands go on his. "We are going to have a baby," he says, letting go of my face, his hand going straight to my stomach. Leaning down, he talks to my stomach. "I love you so, so much." Then he addresses the doctor. "So does she stay in here for nine months or do we get moved?"

Cooper laughs out loud while my father puts his hand on his mouth. "No, we will be doing an ultrasound in a bit and then she is free to go home."

Matthew gets up, his stance bigger than before. "But she fainted. She can't be home. She needs care."

"Matthew, love." Parker walks to his side. "It's normal. Now I'm going to go to the house and take care of everything and make sure you have food in the fridge. What is your favorite food?" she asks me and turns to Cooper. "We should get decaf coffee while we are out." She leans down and kisses my cheek. “I couldn’t pick someone better for him.” She walks to Matthew and grabs his face and drags him down, “I’m so proud of you.” She kisses his cheek while Cooper goes to him and grabs him around his neck, bringing him in for a hug.

“You're going to be such a great dad,” he says, and it’s then that I see Matthew blink away tears.

“Je serai la marraine.” I’m going to be a godmother, Vivienne says while she kisses me on the cheek. “Now that I know you're not dying. We shop, oui?” She hugs me. “Je t’aime fort.” I love you so much, she says while walking out and hugging Matthew.

My father is the next one to leave. “I will make all the arrangements for the next couple of weeks,” he says to me, and I’m too shocked to ask him what arrangements. He hugs Matthew and then walks out of the room, leaving Matthew and I alone finally.

“What just happened?” I ask him, wondering if he’s in shock as much as I am.

He walks to me, sliding into bed with me, turning me to face him. “You’ve just made me the happiest man in the world. Well, for now. You still have to become my wife, but...” He kisses my lips. “We are going to be parents. We made a baby.” He smiles at me, his smile radiating. “I promise you that I will never let you or him down,” he says to me.

“Him or her,” I correct him, but knowing my luck and his sperm, all I’m going to have are penises running around the house.

“I promise you that I will always put your needs and their needs before mine.”

“Theirs? One Matthew at a time, please.” I cuddle closer to him.

“I love you,” he says. “I never thought I would find my piece till you.”

My hand goes to his face.

“You, Karrie, you’re my missing piece, the piece I need to live, the piece I need to breathe, the piece I need to go on.”

“I love you, too.” I lean forward to kiss him, his hands pushing me close to him. “We are going to have a baby,” I finally say out loud.

“Knock, knock, knock,” someone says, walking in backward, bringing in a big white machine.

"Karrie Cooney?" she asks and I nod.

Matthew gets off the bed to stand next to me while the technician sits on the stool she has brought from the corner of the room.

"So I hear we are going to see a baby today?" She smiles, sitting down and turning on some buttons. "When was the last day of your menstrual cycle?" she asks, and I start counting in my head.

"Oh my God, it's been six weeks. How did I not know?" I smack my head. "It must have been all the traveling. I didn't even notice."

"So we are going to try to get a heartbeat, but it would be easier if we did internally." She reaches down to grab a hospital gown. "Why don't you change into that and we can do an internal?"

I turn to get off the bed, but Matthew is there.

"Please don't do this now," I beg him. He holds out his hands for me to grab.

"Thank you." I change in the bathroom, coming out holding the back closed. I smile up at Matthew. "Let's go see our baby!"

# CHAPTER TWENTY-SIX

## MATTHEW

"Let's go see our baby!"

Words that will forever change my life. When she collapsed in my arms, my lungs burned with fear. Fear that she was sick, fear that she wouldn't open her eyes, fear that I would have to live without her.

I walk up to the bed, seeing her get into it. The technician takes what looks like a wand in her hand, putting a condom on it. She squeezes a blue gel on it. "Okay, open your legs."

"Hold on a minute," I say out loud right before she goes to move up Karrie's gown.

"Matthew," Karrie says with clenched teeth.

"Will that hurt the baby?" I push her legs closed.

The lady laughs. "Oh, no, honey. The baby is so protected there isn't a lot that will hurt it." She smiles and waits for me to open her legs. "It's going to be cold, but it'll get warm in a second." But I stop listening to her because the room is filled with what sounds like horses racing. Galloping. "That, you two, is your child's heartbeat."

I grab Karrie's hand, bringing it to my lips. The tears are now rolling down my cheeks. My child. Mine.

"Now, you see this?" She points to a small blob that looks like it's a pea. "That's your baby." She starts clicking on things.

My eyes zoom in to what is the smallest pea I've ever seen, but it's mine. Mine to love, mine to protect, mine to teach. The smallest thing and I would give my life for him or her. I would give everything I have just to make sure this baby is okay. Not only that, I would give them everything, I would move heaven and earth for their mother. The woman who loves me, the woman who stood in a room and fought for me, the woman who held my hand with her shoulders square and her spine straight. The woman who will carry my child, the woman who will be the best mother to our child.

"So I'll give you a paper for you to bring to your ob-gyn. You should make an appointment as soon as possible," The lady says something and a couple of pictures come out of the machine. "Here you go, this is the first picture of your child." She smiles while giving Karrie a towel.

"You can go and change. The doctor signed off, so you are good to go," she says while she closes the machine and leaves the room.

I stand here looking at the black and white paper in my hand. "I'm going to change. I'm exhausted and I want to go to bed." One glance at my watch says it's almost four a.m.

I text the driver that Doug said is waiting for us outside, letting him know we are being discharged. Karrie comes out of the bathroom, throwing the hospital gown on the bed. "Ready?" she asks me, turning to walk out.

"Where are you going?" My head tilts to the side.

"I'm leaving. She said I was discharged."

"We need the nurse to come with a wheelchair. You can't walk downstairs." I walk to the bed to press the button for the nurse.

"I don't need a wheelchair."

"Can you please get a wheelchair?" I smile at the nurse.

She blushes at me. "Of course."

"What would you like me to tell your child about you?" She crosses her arms over her chest.

My eyebrows pinch together.

"Because I'm about to kill you if you continue this way. You need to relax. I'm fine. I'm pregnant. People get pregnant all the time. It is just the way it is."

"Babe." I walk to her, wrapping my arms around her. "I just want you and the baby to be okay. It's not too much to ask, now is it?" I kiss her neck while she hums.

"Here we are." The nurse comes into the room with the wheelchair.

I grab it from the nurse. "Your chariot awaits, my lady." She tries to hide her smile but sits down in the wheelchair. "See, was that so hard?" I ask her, wheeling her downstairs to the awaiting car.

By the time we get home, the sun is almost coming up. I carry Karrie inside because she fell asleep as soon as we started driving. Walking upstairs to our room, my mom is waiting on the stairs from where my room was.

"Honey, are you okay?" she asks with Cooper walking down the stairs. From as far back as I can remember, the minute they became a couple, where she went he was right behind her no matter what. When the twins were born, he did every single feeding with her. If she was up in the house, he wasn't too far away.

"Yeah, all good. We got a picture of squirt." I smile to myself. "I'll show you when we get up." I smile to my mom and Cooper. "I'm going to have a baby. I'm going to be a dad." I smile so big it is hurting my cheeks.

She smiles at me, brushing a tear away. "I know. I'm going to be a grandmother."

"You're a GILF," Cooper says, kissing her cheek. "Now let's go to bed, please. I'm exhausted and I swear to God if the twins get into any trouble I'm sending them to military school." He looks at my mother who nods at him.

"You know military school is where they sleep there, right? You can't just see them when you want. It's almost like boarding school," my mother tells him as I watch his eyebrows pinch together and the vein in his forehead comes out. "That's what I thought. Let's go sleep, granddad."

I undress Karrie and slide into bed right next to her, and it's only a matter of seconds before I'm snoring.

The smell of bacon and coffee fills my nose. Raising my head, the bedside clock says it's almost two p.m. Karrie's side of the bed is empty. I rush out of bed, going to the bathroom, and then rushing downstairs to the kitchen. She's sitting on the stool at the island wearing her white bathrobe while Cooper sits on the stool next to her and my mother is at the stove cooking.

"Why didn't you wake me?" I ask her, rubbing the sleep out of my eyes, letting them adjust to the light.

"Um, because you were sleeping." She takes a sip of what looks like coffee.

"Is that decaf?" I look from her to my mom to Cooper. "You shouldn't be drinking caffeine. It's not good for the baby."

"You should worry about standing here in the kitchen in your underwear instead of what's in my cup, thank you very much."

My mother sees that I might have steam coming out of my ears. "It's decaf. Cooper went out this morning and got it. Now please go put something on so you guys can eat."

"Okay." I lean down and kiss Karrie's lips. "Love you," I whisper to her. I turn around and by the time I get back downstairs there's a buffet of food on the dining room table. "Is this brupper?" I ask my mom, looking at everything she set up.

"Brupper?" Karrie asks, putting a couple of pancakes on her plate, with some scrambled eggs, bacon, and sausage.

"When we were younger Allison was obsessed with pancakes, so much so Mom used to make them for supper and we would call it brupper." I sit next to Karrie, filling my own plate. "Is bacon okay for the baby? Is it not too greasy, Mom?"

"You know what's not good for the baby?" Karrie says while pouring a heaping portion of syrup on her pancake. "YOU." She cuts into a pancake, moaning as she eats. "Now if you want to live here while I'm pregnant you need to chill out. Jesus," she says, stabbing a piece of sausage and dipping it in syrup. With her mouth half full she says, "Parker, this is so good. I didn't realize how hungry I was."

"So when do you want to start interviewing nurses?" I ask when I finally finish my plate. Cooper's eyes bug out while my mother's mouth opens wide and doesn't shut.

"Pardon."

"Well, we need to have around the clock care in case you get sick or you're tired. We need to have someone here to watch you." I don't continue because Karrie's hands shoot up.

"I'm going to be sick," she says out loud, her chair shooting back, scraping against the floor while she runs to the bathroom. The sound of her throwing up has me rushing down the hall, throwing the door open. I open the water to cold, grabbing a small towel from under the sink. Wetting it, I hand it to Karrie. "Thank you," she says, grabbing the towel and putting it on her face. I squat down next to her, pushing the hair away from her face. "I was fine and then in one second I wasn't."

"I know, babe." I get up to grab a glass and fill it with water. "Here."

She takes little sips of water while she waits for her stomach to stop being queasy.

The doorbell rings. Mom goes to open it. "Hey," she says to whoever is at the door. "Guys, Doug is here."

"Hey, guys," he yells. "I brought Karrie her favorite burger from Shake Shack."

"Oh, God," Karrie groans beside me, leaning over and emptying whatever was left in her stomach.

I grimace and decide this is fucking love. What feels like an eternity later, but is more or less twenty minutes, Karrie sneaks off to go upstairs to shower and brush her teeth. I go into the living room where Cooper is eating Karrie's burger.

Raising my eyebrow at him, he says, "What? I'm getting rid of it so it doesn't make her sick."

I sit down on the couch and reach out to see the white frame in the middle of the table. Inside is a picture of the ultrasound. I smile, passing it to Doug. "So how bad is it?" I ask him, looking back at him and then at Cooper. My mother comes into the room with a tray of coffee, juice, soda, water, and cookies. I smile up at her, grabbing a water bottle. "Just come out and tell me."

"I think we should wait for Karrie," Doug says, still looking at the picture.

"Wait for Karrie for what?" I turn my head to watch Karrie walk in the room. Her hair is tied on top of her head. She's wearing plaid PJ bottoms with one of my team T-shirts that fits her almost like a dress.

"Hey, Dad." She walks over to kiss his cheek.

"Hey, honey, I brought you some ginger ale and some saltines to help the queasiness." My mom leans forward.

"Thank you." She smiles at my mom while I open my arms to her and she sits next to me, cuddling into my side. "Vivienne is on her way here. She should be here soon."

I pull her to me, kissing the top of her head.

The knock at the door comes a couple of minutes later with Vivienne coming in and saying hello to everyone, sitting next to Karrie, and holding her hand.

"Okay," Doug says, "Matthew is off for the next two games. The press release went out the second we left the jail. I have to say those detectives didn't waste time in clearing Matthew's name. The investigation is still ongoing and now there are charges pending on the woman who started all this."

"Bitch," Vivienne says under her breath.

"Okay, that settles that." Doug continues, "The news stations have stopped talking about it for now. Now the only thing we have to talk about is what we will tell the team when Karrie is no longer your chaperone."

Karrie sits up straight. "Wait a second. Why am I not his chaperone anymore?"

Doug looks at me and then at Cooper. "Honey, the traveling alone will tire you out. You need to stay put."

Karrie's eyes open wide as saucers. "You know this is discrimination, right? You're firing me because I'm pregnant."

Vivienne smiles at Karrie. "Not exactly, cheri." She rubs her back.

"I don't want to tell anyone about the baby till I'm at least three months along," she says, looking at me. I nod at her, agreeing with this. "But I will not be giving up my job of watching Matthew."

"Well," Vivienne says, laughing. "You were really watching him pretty fucking close to get that baby in there."

Cooper throws his head back and laughs and I try to hide a laugh when I see Karrie turn and look at her with her eyes into slits.

"Oh, vraiment." Really, she says. "C'est une blague." It's a joke, she says.

"Babe, your father is right. You need to be home and off your feet," I speak up, trying to not piss her off.

She gets up to her feet. "No, I will not cop out just because this one"—she points at me—"shot and scored on my goalie."

"Oh, dear," Mom says while Cooper covers his mouth. "Honey, don't get upset. It's not good for the baby. Matthew, you need to not get on her nerves and stress isn't good."

"Great, then take him home with you," Karrie says. "I'm not giving up this job, and you"—she points at me—"you will support me and my decision." And then at her father. "And you, you hold my hand and tell me that everything is okay." She storms out of the room, going to the kitchen. Mom and Vivienne get up, following her, leaving the guys to look at each other.

"What just happened?" I ask the two guys left with me.

"She just got her way," Doug says. "What do we tell the team about you two?"

"No fucking way am I hiding this bullshit anymore. I didn't want to hide it in the beginning, but she wouldn't let me tell you. Man to man, I'm sorry that you found out this way."

"Wasn't exactly the best way to find out your little girl is not only in love finally, but that she is going to have a baby. With that said, you hurt her." He moves his head from side to side and looks at Cooper. "I'll make sure they never find you."

"My boy will never do anything to hurt her on purpose. He's going to make a great dad and an even better husband," Cooper says while I nod.

"Can we just slow down and get used to us being parents and then do the whole marriage thing?" Karrie says from the doorway with my mother and Vivienne, who stand behind her with two thumbs up.

# CHAPTER TWENTY-SEVEN

## KARRIE

It’s been two days since I last threw up. To some that might not mean anything, but to someone who spent the last seven weeks throwing up every single time I finished eating this is huge. Monumental.

I’m sitting in the hotel room, waiting for Matthew to come back from the morning skate while I check my emails. My inbox is full of emails that Matthew forwarded me. They come from every single parenting website on the web. They send him daily tidbits, and let's not talk about the twenty-five parenting books that got delivered to the house the night after we got home. He is actually reading them and highlighting certain things. He’s also become the biggest pain in my ass I have ever encountered.

I love him as many times during the day as I want to kill him. He acts like I’m the first woman to ever have a baby. When we got back on the road, there was no one asking if we were together since he held my hand to the plane, walked in holding it, and then kissed me. The guys did what guys did, high-fived each other and then someone won twelve thousand dollars on a bet. Gone were the two rooms. In their place was one room.

I look down at my belly that's starting to get a little bit of a pouch. The biggest change in my body is my breasts. They are swollen and my nipples hurt so much. That's another thing I had to do—talk him into sex. I still can't believe he wasn't going to have sex with me for the rest of my pregnancy.

*Getting into bed, I slid in naked. We just dropped Parker and Cooper off at the airport with promises to visit soon. I waited for Matthew to come into the room, pulling the sheet up over my breasts, hissing out when the sheet touched my nipples. I saw him walk out of the bathroom and go around the bed getting into bed with his boxers.*

*"What are you doing?" I asked him. "What happened to naked, babe?" I mimicked him from before.*

*"Babe, we aren't having sex," he said, getting in and tucking himself in, putting his hands over the covers.*

*"Hold on a second. Why are we not having sex?"*

*"Because you're pregnant," he said as if I didn't know. "I don't want to hurt the baby."*

*I laughed at him. "Honey, I know you think your dick is huge, and it is, but unless you grew a foot I think the baby is safe." I leaned in, the sheet falling off my breasts. "Besides, I need you," I whispered, hoping I wouldn't throw up on him.*

*"Karrie, what if I hurt you? Or what if, I don't know, I shake the baby?" He turned to me.*

*"Matthew, do you think everyone who is pregnant stops having sex? I know a friend of mine who turned into a sex machine when she was pregnant. It's the extra hormones." I couldn't believe I was trying to fucking convince him to have sex with me.*

*"Karrie, let's just go to bed." He turned over, shutting off the light.*

*"Fine," I said, huffing and puffing, getting out of bed. "I'll go find that treasure chest you bought and find something in there that will help me 'take the edge off'." I walked to my closet.*

*"Babe," he said, and I turned around.*

*"NO!" I yelled at him, almost about to cry. "You don't want to have sex with me, fine, I'll take my box and go sleep upstairs." I turned to*

*walk in the closet where I tossed my clothes around, looking for where he had hidden the box. Turning, I saw that he was standing in front of me naked, leaning on the doorjamb, his arms and legs crossed.*

*"Are you done?" he asked me.*

*"No, no, I'm not. It's not enough I'm going to get fat, and my boobs"—I pointed to them—"are going to be so big that I may suffocate myself if I lie on my back. But now you don't want to have sex with me." A tear slipped out.*

*"Baby," he said softly, coming to me. "I don't care how big you get or how big your boobs get." He pressed them together lightly. "I'm especially excited to have these babies so big that, hmmm." He leaned in, taking a nipple gently, but the feeling went straight to my core. He repeated with the other breast. He scooped me into his arms. My arms wrapped around his neck while my lips kissed his neck.*

*It was the sweetest sex we ever had. He was soft, gentle, and he drove me absolutely crazy.*

I smile at the memory of that and every single time since then, but I'm fucking over it. I need it hard, I need it dirty, I need it like he wants to give it to me and not treat me like I'm glass and going to break. The door clicks and Matthew walks in with two strawberry milkshakes in his hand. Something that I can't seem to get enough of. I could live on just this. Oh, and French fries. The other day I dipped them in my shake.

"Morning, beautiful." He hands me the shakes. I take them both, sipping from one and then the other. "Why don't you drink one at a time?" he asks, lying down next to me, his hand going to my stomach.

"So they melt at the same time," I tell him, obviously. "What time is the game tonight?" I continue on the one sip out of each.

"Game starts at seven," he says while kissing my stomach. "What time is the appointment tomorrow?"

It's my first big appointment with my ob-gyn. I'm excited and nervous. So far I haven't had any symptoms except for throwing up, but I haven't fainted.

"Two p.m. I had to draw the line at everyone showing up, you know that, right?" I look at him. My father, Parker, Vivienne all thought they had to be there, till I drew the line.

"Since we are home all weekend, Allison wants to know if it's okay if she comes down." He looks up at me.

"Of course, she's your sister, you never ever have to ask me if it's okay that people come over."

"That's what I told her, but you know Allison, she made sure I asked you."

I put the milkshakes on the side table and slide down so I'm face to face with him. I run my hands through his damp hair. I kiss his nose, his lips, his cheek, and then his neck. His hands pull me closer to him.

"I need a nap, babe," he says, and I put my head under his chin and fall asleep to the smell of him and the beat of his heart.

• • •

My watch says it's almost eleven-thirty. Matthew has been off the ice for over an hour. It was a crazy game with us losing with four seconds to go. When you travel with a team, you know that the plane ride will be a quiet one, whereas if they win it's a sigh of relief. A couple of players walk out all giving me a nod. I nod and then look down at my phone. Max comes out next all alone, shrugging his arms into his jacket.

"Hey there, beautiful." He smiles at me, making my stomach queasy. "Looks like you're still slumming. If you ever decide to upgrade, give me a call," he says, tipping his head down and walking away.

"Upgrade," I say out loud while he stops walking. "You don't upgrade from a Rolls Royce to a Ford." I smile at him. "Besides, word from the puck bunnies is that it's always cold around you." I smirk at him while he walks back to me.

His stance hard, his eyes vicious, his teeth together. "You think he gives a shit about you?" he throws back, laughing. "You're just another bitch on the road." He leans in. "Maybe high and mighty, but at the end of the day, you're just a pussy."

I don't even bother answering because he is yanked away from me, Matthew turning him and pinning him to the wall with his arm at his throat. "You so much as breathe in her direction one more time and I'll fucking bury you. I don't give a fuck what the consequences will be."

It takes Phil and Luka to get him off of Max, who coughs, getting some air into his lungs.

"You're a fucking maniac, Grant. I'll be bringing this up with all the necessary people," he says, tying his jacket.

"You do that, fucktard," Matthew says, shrugging the guys off of him and walking to me. "Are you okay?" he asks me, his one hand palming my face.

"I'm fine, are you?" I ask him, looking around to see that the equipment managers saw the whole thing along with some of the press. "You know this is going to make it to SportsCenter."

"Don't give a shit," he says, grabbing my hand and walking out of the arena following Luka and Phil. We make our way on the bus where Max is running his mouth.

"He's fucking lucky I didn't wipe the floor with him."

Luka starts laughing. "I thought he was going to piss himself he was so scared of Matthew."

He gets into a seat followed by Phil, who says, "Piss, I thought for sure he would shit himself." He looks at Max. "Don't bullshit anyone. The only reason you got to walk out of there tonight is because he held back."

I don't say anything. I just hold onto Matthew's hand, pulling him down into the seat next to me. "Just ignore him."

"He's a fucking piece of shit. Who the hell goes after a woman? I tell you who. A penciled dick asshole, that's who."

I turn in my seat. "You feel better?" I ask, shaking my head.

"Why, you got something to make me feel better when we get home?" he asks. His eyebrows wiggle.

I lean in. "Tomorrow I'm going to ask the doctor something really important and if her answer is what I'm expecting I'm going to get something really hard!" I turn and stare out the window. "Keep that in mind, Grant."

The coaches come in and look at Max and then at Matthew. "Fucking SportsCenter is running a fucking brawl," he says. I don't say anything and neither does Matthew. "Next practice I want you in my office before the skate," he says, sitting down.

I open my phone, searching SportsCenter and there front and center is Matthew pinning Max to a wall. The headline makes me shake my head.

"Frustration off the ice."

I turn my phone so Matthew can see it, but he just turns it off. The rest of the trip is done in silence, no one daring to say anything. By the time I get home, I'm dead on my feet. We wake the next day, rushing to the doctor's, both of us nervous and a little scared.

Matthew sits in the waiting room, shaking his legs while I fill out a paper about my health. Once I give it back to the nurse she calls me in. She tells me to undress and that the doctor will be right in.

Matthew walks to the wall that shows you the different stages of the baby in the stomach. "Oh my, this baby is huge. You think our baby will be this big?" he asks me.

I shake my head while taking off my clothes and sitting on top of the table. "I hope it isn't too big."

"I think I was nine pounds when I was born." Matthew starts talking while he flips through the magazine. "I think the twins were huge for twins." He laughs while my mouth starts to get dry. "I think one was six pounds and the other was eight. They were abnormally large." He drops the magazine, getting another one. "I really want the baby to have your eyes." He looks over, smiling at me. "We should be doing a birthing plan. I read in the book the other day that it should be done and given to the hospital. Did you want to do this natural?"

I'm almost about to tell him how fucking dumb are you, do you think I want a human coming out of me with no drugs? What part is appealing to any of that? But the doctor comes in.

"Good afternoon," she says. "Karrie, how are you feeling?"

"I'm feeling much better. The nausea and vomiting are fading out. Thankfully. I'm also feeling a lot less tired." I try not to tell her and Matthew about how hard the last six weeks have been. The traveling has kicked my ass.

"So I see here you have lost ten pounds since you were last in. The vomiting may have to do with that. It's important to start eating smaller meals during the day. It's suggested that it is normal to gain between twenty-five to thirty-five pounds during the whole pregnancy."

"Will the baby be okay if she doesn't gain that weight?" Matthew asks while his hands go to his hips.

"It's perfectly fine, depending on the child. It's also normal for the mother to lose up to ten pounds in the first trimester due to vomiting." She smiles at him.

"Have there been any more fainting spells since the hospital?" she asks, looking at my chart.

"Nope, nothing. It's been all good." I put my hands on my naked knees.

"Okay, so if you lie back, I will do an internal exam first and then we can get an ultrasound down."

I lie back on the table.

"Matthew, get over here." I motion him with my hand, waiting for him to walk to my head before putting my feet up in the stirrups that the doctor put up. "Don't you dare look at what she is doing!" I tell him while the doctor continues to do her test.

"This might be cold," she says while putting in the tools in order to do a pap smear. I close my eyes while this happens. Matthew starts to ask the doctor what exactly she's doing. "It's all normal at this stage that we get a pap smear." She smiles at him, taking out the tool that looks like a duck and slipping off her gloves. "Now comes the part that everyone is waiting for. You ready to see your baby?" She smiles at both of us while Matthew takes my hand, kissing it.

This time she lifts my gown, covering me with a towel just stopping above my pelvic area. She picks up the white bottle from the side. "This might be cold for a bit," she says, squeezing it on my stomach. The liquid coming out almost looks like hair gel.

"That's cold," I tell her while she turns on the machine, picking up something else that she holds down on the gel, spreading it around. The heartbeat fills the room. The galloping starts. I look at the screen, not sure what I'm going to see, but what I do has tears coming down my face. We have a baby, a baby who's moving, almost doing cartwheels. The hands and feet are moving slowly. I love Matthew, I love my father, my family, my friends, but this love is so hard to explain. It's an all-consuming love, a love that fills your heart to the brim, makes you want to go out there and sing in the rain, skip down the hallway for no reason. It's a love that you know will never ever fade. Matthew has his own tears while he watches her move around on my stomach, starting to press more buttons.

"Do you feel the baby moving?" Matthew asks while the baby looks like he's kicking me. I nod my head no.

I bring his hand to my lips, kissing him.

"So everything looks great. Your due date is July fourth. I'm going to want to see you in a month from now, unless there's something that comes up before." She presses a couple of buttons. Three pictures come out. She grabs the edge of my towel, wiping the gel off the machine pieces. She wipes my stomach with the same towel. "Get dressed and you can meet me in my office."

I nod to her while she walks out.

Matthew is staring at the picture. "Holy shit, it's real." He rubs his fingers on the picture. "It's the most beautiful baby in the world," he tells the picture and looks at me. "I love you." He kisses my lips.

"I love you, too." I kiss his lips again, getting up to get dressed so we can go into the doctor's office. I walk in first with Matthew following me.

"Here is a prescription for pills to help with the nausea when it comes. Do you have any questions?" She leans back in her chair.

"Yes," I say, looking at Matthew. "Can we have hard sex?" I blurt out, Matthew's head whipping around to me with his mouth open.

"What do you mean?" the doctor asks.

"Well, he's very gentle when we have sex. Too gentle, so if he were to do it harder, would that hurt the baby?"

The doctor tries not to laugh at Matthew, who is sitting there with his mouth opening and closing but no sound coming out. "It should be fine. The baby is very well protected."

"Yes, but," Matthew stutters out, "my dick is huge." Now it's my turn to look at him with an open mouth. "I just don't want to, you know, poke him."

I put my hand over my mouth, stopping the laugh that's coming out.

"I can say that in all my twenty years of being a doctor I've never had a penis poke the baby." She tries not to laugh, but she can't stop herself. "No matter how huge it is." She does the motion with her hands. "Any more questions?"

We both shake our heads, getting up and walking out of the room and the office. While waiting for the elevator, Matthew asks me, "What do you want to do?"

"I want to go home and have hot sweaty hard sex." I emphasize hard.

"You want it hard, baby?" he says, coming to me, my mouth going dry by the look in his eyes. "I'm going to fuck you so hard they will hear you on the fucking moon!" And with that, I almost come in my panties.

# CHAPTER TWENTY-EIGHT

## MATTHEW

"Is this what you meant?" I ask Karrie right as I slam into her. She's on her knees in front of me, her head on the bed, her hands outstretched while she grabs the sheets. My hands grab her heart-shaped ass as I continue pounding into her. My hands move to her hips to grip her better while I continue.

As soon as we got home, I ripped her shirt off, literally in half. Going to my knees in front of her, I bit her nipple harder than I have before, her head thrashing back while she held my hair in her hands. I pushed her back on the step, taking off her jeans, and I buried my face in her pussy, making her drip all over the stairs.

Now here we are on round four, a thick layer of sweat covering us both while her pussy grips my cock so hard I can't even go in and out.

"I'm coming," she moans out while one of her hands slides between her legs, her fingers rubbing her clit. I plant myself in her one more time, roaring out my own release. Our pants fill the room. "That's what I'm talking about," she says, hitting my stomach after I fall beside her and turn on my side. "Knew you had it in you." She rolls off the bed right before I'm about to catch her and bring her back to show her exactly what I have in me. I don't have time because the doorbell rings.

"Shit," I say, getting up to get my shorts on. "I forgot about Arnold." I run out of the room while I hear the shower go on.

Opening the door, I see Arnold in his green uniform. "Hey, buddy."

I reach out to shake his hand. "Thank you for coming out at night. With me traveling it's hard to do this in the day." I make him come in, bringing him to the stairs. "So this is what I was talking about." I point to the wall leading upstairs. "If we need to expand the stairs I don't have a problem doing that."

Arnold takes out his measuring tape and starts measuring the steps, the width, and then from the top to the bottom. He takes out his pad and is writing down something when I see Karrie come downstairs in shorts and a tank top. When she sees Arnold her eyebrows pinch together, wondering who he is.

"Babe, this is Arnold. He will be installing the stair lift."

She walks to me while I tell her.

"A stair lift?" she asks, looking between Arnold and me.

"It's a chair that you sit on and it brings you upstairs so you won't trip on the stairs." I smile, thinking this is the best fucking thing I have ever done. I'm so proud of myself.

Arnold then starts talking, "What we are going to do is install it against the wall so we won't have to touch the railing. We install it in one day, so we are out of your hair." He smiles and then continues writing on the pad. "When is a good day for you?"

"Um, tomorrow would be good," I say at the same time as Karrie says, "Never."

I look at her and then back at Arnold, smiling.

"Matthew, can I have a word with you in the kitchen?" She walks to the fridge, taking out the orange juice. I can now see her little baby bump. "I'm going to say this once and only one time. If you install that fucking chair, I'm going to have you thrown out of this house and banned. I will call your mother, Cooper, and Allison if I have to for them to come and pack your stuff. You are getting me a senior citizen chair." Her voice rises. "A SENIOR CITIZEN CHAIR, MATTHEW!"

she yells out, my hands going to my hips.

"Babe, it's dangerous going up and down the stairs. What if you slip walking up or down and I'm not here?" I ask her.

"What if I walk out of the house and a tree falls on me?" she counters. "What if I walk into the shower and slip?"

"We should get those non slip shower decals we saw on that infomercial." I make a metal note to check online later.

She pours herself a glass of orange juice. "Matthew, thin ice. Get rid of that man, so help me God."

"I can't just get rid of him. He came on his day off," I tell her, trying to convince her.

"I don't care. That's because you're an idiot." She turns to put her glass in the sink and then starts talking to herself. "Did he actually think I would be okay with that?" Her hands start going in the air. "He thinks I'm going to sit down and take a lift to get upstairs." She puts the orange juice container in the fridge. "Your father is insane." She grabs a bunch of grapes, bringing them to the sink, rinsing them off. "Why are you still here and not telling Arnold to leave?" she asks me and I'm almost tempted to ask another question, but she stands straight, daring me to so she can throw something at me.

"Okay, I'll tell him we will discuss this and get back to him." Her eyes glare at me, her lids half-mast. "Or that we changed our minds." I don't bother waiting for her answer. Instead, I go find Arnold, who is shaking his head trying not to laugh. "So change of plans."

He nods, shaking my hand and telling me good luck.

When I walk back into the kitchen, I hear my mother's voice fill the room. She FaceTimed my mother. Now it's my turn to glare at her. "And then he had this man come over to put those senior chairs in the house."

My mother shrieks while I hear Cooper in the background. "There's nothing wrong with those chairs. It's about safety."

"See," I tell her while I go to her, grabbing her shoulders in my hands, and looking into my mother's face. "I knew Cooper would understand me. I didn't want her to fall down the stairs. Shoot me for caring."

I see Cooper come into the frame. "Karrie, I think you should give it some thought considering there are a lot of stairs to get to your bedroom."

He points out. "What if there was a power outage?" He continues while my mother shakes her head. "You have no windows going up the stairs. It's a hazard."

"See," I tell Karrie, who looks at Cooper and then back at me. "He gets it."

"It's electric, so it won't work if there's no power," she tells us both.

"It has a seven hour battery life," Cooper and I say at the same time.

"He gets it because he's a neurotic like you," my mother says. "Karrie, when I was pregnant with the twins, he had a camera system installed in the house and he got live feeds on his phone every single time I would move."

I laugh, thinking of the time he raced into the house because he thought she fell in the room, but she was in her closet looking for her other shoe and it was more comfortable lying down. "You also had the ambulance, fire department, and two police cars escorting you home."

Mom looks up at Cooper. "You were over the top! He also tried to get the supermarket to only mop at night in case I walked in and slipped. He got contractors to come in and give an estimate to install an elevator."

She stands there with her mouth open while Allison comes to the phone. "You're so lucky she loves you!!!" She smiles, then shrugs her shoulders. "I mean, I would wait till you got in the shower and turn off the hot water, but hey, that's just me."

"Yeah, yeah, don't give her any ideas. You excited for tomorrow, squirt?" I ask her, hoping she is excited.

"So excited. I want to go to the Empire State Building, Times Square, Rockefeller Center, Central Park, oh, and Lego Land." She is all excited while Mom frowns and Cooper groans.

"We will do all that," Karrie says with a smile.

"With reason. She's pregnant and shouldn't be on her feet for so long." I put in my two cents while Karrie gives me the finger.

"Okay, I've got to get my girl fed. Talk to you later. Mom, text me when she takes off." We blow kisses and hang up.

The next day Karrie and I are waiting at the bottom of the escalator for Allison, who runs to me, hugging me and then Karrie.

The weekend goes by so fast I don't even see the time till she is packing on Sunday to go back home. We had to stop and buy her another piece of luggage to take back all the shit she bought. We hit up every single thing she had on her list and then some.

She comes downstairs after packing, finding me lying on the couch. "Hey, where is Karrie?" she asks, coming to sit down on the other side.

"In the shower," I say while she leans over and picks up the second frame that we have with the new picture of the baby.

"I can't believe you are going to be a dad." Her finger touches the picture. "I mean, you've been practicing since I was born."

I look over at her, seeing a tear coming out of the corner. She wipes it so fast it's almost like it wasn't there. I sit up, going to sit next to her, putting a hand around her shoulder.

"I can't wait." I look at the picture with her. "I was scared, you know." I start off telling her, "The minute they said she was pregnant, my heart swelled. I got scared. Could I do this since I technically didn't really have that great of a role model?"

"Did you tell Dad?" she asks me. It's something we don't bring up. I know she talks to him from time to time. I shake my head.

"He tried to call me after that whole bullshit with the rape charge, but I didn't answer. He wasn't there when I needed him or at least when I really needed him. You think he showed me how to shave? That was Cooper. You think he showed me what it was to be a real man? Again, that was Cooper. You think he showed me that when it gets tough you fight for it? Cooper taught me that also. You think he showed me to put your kids before your own selfish needs? Again, no. I was fucking terrified, but then guess what I did see when I looked up? Cooper stood there wiping away Mom's tears. It was in that moment I knew I could not only do this dad thing, but I could do it like a motherfucking boss." I look over at her. "Besides, if I wasn't the best that I could be, Mom would kick my ass."

"She totally would," Allison agrees with me.

"Hey, you two," Karrie says from the doorway while she holds a carton of strawberry ice cream with three spoons in it. "Wanna watch *Naked Dating*?"

Allison throws her head back, laughing. "You know that's considered double dipping even if it's ice cream." She points to the carton that Karrie is eating from, who just shrugs her shoulders, coming to sit on the other side of me.

She turns on the television, flipping channels. She stops when she comes onto *90 Day Fiancé*. "It's my favorite show." She shakes her spoon in the air. She scoops some more ice cream, offering us a spoon. I shake my head while Allison grimaces, refusing, too. "More for me," she says, smiling.

I lean over to kiss her lips. The taste of ice cream on her lips is divine. I lick my lips, going in for another kiss.

"Hmmm," she says, putting her hand around my neck, still holding the spoon.

"You guys are aware I'm right here, right?" Allison speaks up, making Karrie laugh. "Okay, love birds, before I throw up my dinner, I'll go up to my room."

"You don't have to leave. We'll stop kissing," Karrie says, straining her neck to see Allison.

"Goodnight," I tell her, going back to kissing Karrie. "We will never stop kissing," I tell her, letting my tongue slide into her mouth, her tongue cold from the ice cream. "Ever." I finish that with another kiss.

# CHAPTER TWENTY-NINE

## KARRIE

I walk up the front steps, the grocery bag hitting my knees. Turning the knob and having it closed makes my arm ache. "Fuck," I say out loud, dropping the bag on the ground while I reach into my purse, pulling out my keys. "Where the hell is Matthew?" I ask myself. He was here when I left. It's Valentine's Day and for some reason we are not playing or traveling tonight. Unlocking the door, I pick the bag up, walking in. The lights are off in the whole house, except the glow from tea candles that are lining a path of red roses. I drop the bag and my purse with my keys on the floor, walking to the living room, which is where the roses lead to.

Walking into the room, my breath hitches, my hand going to my mouth. Candles are lit all over the room. The couches and table are pushed to one side of the room. In the middle of the room, kneeling on one knee is Matthew. Candles in the shape of a heart are lit, and the room is filled with rose petals.

"From the first moment I saw you, you took my breath away. I kicked myself for letting you go into your hotel room without asking you for your name. The next day I called your room, but there was no answer." He surprises me with that information. "But then I walked into that room and there you were. It was a sign that you were mine."

"Matthew," I whisper, walking into the room and right into the middle of the heart straight to him.

"My whole life I was afraid to let my guard down, afraid to give love and not get it back. But with you I didn't even stand a chance. The day you put your hand in mine, my heart just knew you were the one." He reaches out to grab my hand. "I promise to love you till my last dying breath, or at least as long as you let me live. I promise to be the best father I can be. I want to walk holding your hand today, tomorrow, and always. I want to go to bed with you and kiss you goodnight. I want to watch our kids take their first step. I want to watch our kids drive us crazy. I want to walk our daughter down the aisle, watch you dance with our son on his wedding day. But most of all I want to be the reason you smile, the one who wipes your tears away, and the one who holds you up when you need me to. Let me be that man. Let me give you all that, but more importantly, I want you to say yes and give me the world."

The tears are streaming down my face while he opens the black box that he pulled from his pocket. When he shows it to me, my tears come even more. "I couldn't do this without asking your father's permission. So when I did he asked me for one thing and that was to be able to give you your mother's ring. It was her wish for you to wear it when you finally found someone who merited it."

No matter how many diamond rings my father bought for my mother, she never ever took off the one he gave her the night he proposed. It was a one-carat round diamond, back then the only thing he could afford. They ate ramen noodles for a year after that, but she didn't care because she had my father. When he made his first million, he took her ring and replaced it. She had a fit and refused to let him in the house till he brought her back her ring. Till the bitter end it's the only jewelry she wore. I asked her once while I held her hand at the end why she just didn't get another ring. Her answer was simple.

"He promised to love me forever with this ring. He looked me in the eye while he slipped this ring on my finger and promised to give me the life I deserved to always put me before him. And he did that every single day since then. When you find love, Karrie, you hold on to it, you cherish it, and then you love with your whole heart because loving and being loved is something you can't buy no matter how many diamonds come your way."

"I love you," I finally tell him. "I love you with my whole heart. I love when you are kind, I love when you are soft, I even love you, although a little less, when you're neurotic. So my answer is yes, yes to everything. Yes to being your wife, yes to being the mother of your children, yes to being your partner in crime. Yes to growing old with you." I lean down, grabbing his face in my hands, while my thumbs wipe away the tears that are falling on his face.

His smile lights up the room. He takes the ring out of the box, grabbing my hand from his face and sliding it on my finger. The minute he does that I feel a shiver wash over me. It's the weirdest thing, but what's more is that I feel something in my stomach. I think it's indigestion when it happens again.

"I think the baby just kicked." I look at him with wide eyes while my hand moves to my stomach that I can't hide anymore. Grabbing his hand, I place it on my stomach to exactly where I felt it before, the little flutters.

"Maybe you should sit down," Matthew says to me, but the movement makes him stop talking because he looks up at me, his eyes wide with excitement. "Holy shit." He places his other hand on my stomach, covering it now. Leaning in, he puts his lips close to my stomach. "She said yes." He kisses my stomach, but his child must get it because he kicks me again. "He really likes the sound of my voice."

I roll my eyes at Matthew. He leans in, continuing to talk to the baby while the baby continues to kick, my hand going on top of his head and my ring getting a glimmer of light. Yup, hold onto it, forever.

"You're my perfect," he says to me. I smile at him, kissing his lips. "Something so perfect."

# EPILOGUE

## MATTHEW

*July 17 (Two weeks overdue.)*

"I think this is it," Karrie says from the couch.

At this point, it's almost like crying wolf. We are sitting in our house that I just bought. That's right, our house. We went on to win the Stanley Cup, a feeling that's beyond words. While we were in the playoffs, the house next to Mom and Cooper happened to go on the market. I did the only thing I could. I put in an offer without even seeing the house, without even telling her. That didn't go off well for a couple of reasons. One, she was pregnant and hormonal and honestly she hated everything about me at that point. Well, except for my dick. That she took full advantage of. It seems those hormones were in full effect when it came to sex.

Once we finished, we packed up our stuff and came down to what she is calling our weekend cottage. Except it comes with ten bedrooms, fifteen bathrooms, a movie theater, game room, and a home gym. We got here with just three weeks to spare till her due date. She brought her file with her and luckily she fell in love with the ob-gyn here. What I wasn't counting on was for my house to be a revolving door. My sisters are always here. Allison comes over for coffee every single morning, regardless of if we are up. My brother even comes over, which is huge for him since he is deep into hockey training. Vivienne came down and is now here till the baby comes out, along with Doug, who bought a house around the corner.

"I'm serious, Matthew, I think this is it."

I look over at my wife—oh yeah, that, too. We didn't have the big wedding everyone wanted. That's going to come later, and I couldn't give a shit. I just wanted her with my name and ring before she gave birth to my child. She might have fought me a tad. Thankfully, I never threw out those cuffs.

"Babe, the doctor said she's inducing you tomorrow." I turn back to the television while she gasps. I look back to see her looking down at the water that is now seeping into the couch. I jump up, my hands going to my head. "Holy shit, this is it." I start to jog upstairs to get the bags out of our closet. I run to the nursery that my mother set up for us as her present to us, grabbing the bag that Karrie packed for the baby. I'm about to run back downstairs when she waddles up the stairs. I love her to death, but this baby is huge. She looks like she has five babies in there. "Where are you going?" I ask her, yelling while I'm watching her walk to our bedroom.

"I'm taking a shower. We had sex tonight. I need to clean up."

"Karrie, you can't be serious right now. Your water broke. It's leaking all into our couch, which we will need a new one now. Vivienne!" I yell down the hall toward her wing.

"Matthew, it will take me five min—" She stops talking while she holds her stomach.

My heart beats fast. "Oh my God, do you need to push?" I ask her, dumping the bags on the floor, getting my phone out, about to call 9-1-1 when she opens her eyes and looks at me. "We should time the contractions. I'll be back." She walks away, taking off the big shirt she is wearing. "I can't wait to be able to see my vagina again. And toes."

"Vivienne!" I yell again, louder this time.

"Mon Dieu, qu'est-ce qui se passe?" My gosh, what is going on, she says in French.

"The baby is coming." I pick up the bags. "Her water broke."

Vivienne starts jumping up and down and running back to her room.

"What is wrong with everyone? We need to get to the hospital." I pull out my phone, calling Cooper. He answers after one ring. "Her water broke."

"Where are you?" he asks right away, telling Mom that Karrie's water broke. I hear rustling and yelling from his side of the phone.

"I'm home. I'm still fucking home. She had to take a fucking shower."

"A shower?" he asks me. "But her water broke. Should we call an ambulance?" he asks while Karrie yells from the shower.

"I'm having another one."

"She's having a contraction in the shower," I say, hanging up the phone, running into the bathroom while she is getting out. "Should I call someone?" I ask her.

"I think I'm okay. I just have to get dressed," she says while Vivienne knocks on the door and comes in. I stand in front of Karrie to block her nakedness from her. They both laugh. "We're women. We see each other naked all the time. Stand down," she says while she throws on a summer dress. "You think I should put panties on?"

"You're leaking all over the fucking place, Karrie, you need Depends," Vivienne says, walking around the wet on the floor. "Oh, you look really pretty in that dress," she continues.

"Can we just please get in the car and go to the hospital?" I beg, running my hands through my hair. My palms are now all sweaty.

"Matthew, Karrie." I hear Mom's voice while she comes up the stairs, knocking on the door before walking in.

"Oh, Karrie, you're glowing," my mother starts and soon has tears streaming down her face. "Are you okay?" She walks to her.

"Can we all just get in the car?" I say with my teeth clenched together.

"I swear one of these days that vein in his head will have eyes." Vivienne laughs at me. "He might give himself an aneurism standing there right now." She walks past me out of the room, picking up one of the bags.

"I'm having another one," she says while Mom holds her hands and starts breathing with her. "How far apart are they?" she finally asks when she can talk.

"I have no idea. I keep forgetting to check."

Mom looks at me while Karrie glares. "Matthew, you have one job," Mom says to me, walking past me, holding Karrie's hand. "Now can we go?" she asks me.

I've been trying to get these people in the car the whole time. By the time we get downstairs, she has another contraction.

"I think they are a couple of minutes apart," Mom says as we walk out of the house to what looks like a parade in our driveway.

There's Vivienne sitting in our truck, with Cooper in back of our truck, Allison is behind Cooper, Doug is behind Allison, my aunt Meghan in behind them all.

Mom helps Karrie get into the car that now has white garbage bags all over the seats. "It's to catch the water," Vivienne says from the front seat.

"Here comes another one," Karrie says while she breathes, this time huffing more. "That one really hurt." She looks at me with tears in her eyes. "Matthew."

"I'm here, baby, I'm right here." I pick her up, setting her in the back. "Vivienne, you need to drive so I can sit in the back with Karrie."

Vivienne climbs into the driver's side. "Allons-y," Let's go, she says, waiting for my mother to close the door and jog back to Cooper's car.

"The address is already saved in the GPS," I tell her while I put my arm around Karrie's shoulders. My heart is beating so fast I can't seem to slow it down. I'm a nervous wreck. I'm a sweaty nervous wreck. My leg starts to move and my thumb starts drumming my leg.

"I think another one is coming," she says, sitting up panting. "Hehehe hooo hooo, hehehe hooo hooo," she chants out just like the class we took.

"Vivienne, step on it," I say from the back.

We make it to the hospital, pulling up to the curb. I don't even have my door open before I see Cooper running from inside with a wheelchair, with a security guy following him. I get out, walking around the car, grabbing Karrie, and carrying her to the chair. Cooper lets go of the back of the wheelchair, giving me the reins.

"Proud of you, son." He slaps me on the shoulder, going back to the car to park it.

I push her into the hospital, all the way up to delivery. The second I step out of the elevator a nurse is here to greet us. She tells us to follow her, bringing us into a room with a bed, a couch, and a rocking chair.

"Okay, folks, I need Mommy to get undressed and put on the gown. I need your insurance papers as well."

I grab my wallet and open it, giving her my papers and Karrie's.

"Perfect. I'll go put this in and will be back in a couple of minutes. When did her water break?"

"During *Top Chef*," I answer her, watching her eyebrow shoot up.

"Okay, and what time was that?"

"I have no idea. It's on our DVR." I shrug, looking over at Karrie, who is now moaning. I rush over to her. She is bent over, rocking from side to side.

"She's in active labor," the nurse says, pressing the button at the door. Another nurse comes in. "This is Karrie Cooney."

"Grant," I say from beside Karrie. "Her last name is Grant. We just haven't gotten the paper yet." I rub her back while she moves from side to side.

"Okay, my name is Sherry. Mr. and Mrs. Grant, how about we get her on the bed and see how we are doing?" the second nurse who came in says, walking to the other side of Karrie, helping her stand up.

Karrie sits on the bed and throws her legs up. "I need drugs," she says to Sherry. "It's on my birth plan. I want drugs about now."

"Babe," I say quietly beside her, "you said you didn't want it."

"Really, Matthew, my vagina feels like it's being lit on fire with a blow torch, because of you and that big ass head of yours." She looks at the nurse. "Drugs?"

"Okay," she says, putting on gloves. "I'm going to go in and see how far along you are, okay?"

Karrie opens her legs while the nurse checks her.

"Five centimeters, almost six."

"So when do the drugs get here?" Karrie asks, stopping when a contraction rips through her. Out is the sweet girl who was taking a shower. In is someone I have never seen. I'm pretty sure her voice has been replaced by the woman from the *Exorcist*. "I hate you," she hisses out. "You and that big head of yours."

Sherry comes over to me. "Just remember she loves you, just not right now." She smiles, looking back at Karrie. "I'm going to attach you to the monitor to make sure the baby is okay."

That makes Karrie sit up. "What do you mean make sure the baby is okay? What's wrong with the baby, Matthew?" She starts crying. "The baby."

I walk to the side of her bed. "Nothing, they just want to check and see if the baby is doing okay." I rub her head while the nurse asks her to lift up to put the elastic thing around her waist while she squeezes the gel on it, tying it around her waist. The sound of our baby fills the room.

"Now this machine will tell us exactly when you have a contraction as well as your baby's heart rate while you have the contraction. Okay?" Sherry asks while Karrie nods her head, watching the numbers on the machine.

"Another one is coming," she says, this time her moan louder and longer than before. "Are the drugs on their way?" she asks when she can finally breathe normal again.

"We just have to monitor you for a bit to see how fast you are dilating."

"I don't want to do that. I want drugs," she hisses out but doesn't say anything else because her moaning starts again. This time she grabs my hand, squeezing it. For a small girl, I'm pretty sure some fingers will be out of place when she's done.

"That wasn't even a minute apart," Sherry says. "Okay, you know what, honey, I'm going to check you again." She puts on another pair of gloves, checking her. "Okay, Karrie, I need to call the doctor. You're about nine centimeters. We are having this baby any second."

"Wait, I didn't get drugs yet," Karrie keeps saying.

Sherry presses a button behind Karrie while Karrie has another contraction.

"I have so much pressure," she says when she can finally talk.

"Totally normal." We hear from the door when Karrie's Dr. Noelle finally comes in. "Hey there, Karrie, how are you doing?"

"How am I doing? I need drugs, Dr. Noelle. Please."

She smiles at Karrie, holding out her hands to put the gown on that Sherry is holding out for her. She puts gloves on, sitting on a stool in front of Karrie's bed. A baby bed comes in while she puts the stirrups up, telling Karrie to put her feet in them.

She lifts the gown and I try not to gasp out loud, but I can't help it. I see hair. "Okay, Karrie. This little one really wants to meet his mom. I'm going to have you push a bit, okay? When the next contraction comes, I want you to bear down and push out."

"I can't do this," she says, shaking her head. "I want a cesarean. I changed my mind."

I grab her hand, scooting down beside her. "Babe, look at me." Her head turns to me, tears in her eyes. "You can do this." One arm goes over her head. "You can do this. I know you can." Her head shakes from side to side. "Come on, baby, push."

Sherry stands on her other side, counting to ten.

"That was great," Dr. Noelle says. "Let's do it again, okay?"

"It burns. It burns so much," Karrie cries out. "It hurts."

"I know it does, baby, and I'm so sorry," I tell her. "You have to do this for the baby." Because if I say for me I will probably never have another child.

"Okay, now push," Sherry says, grabbing one of Karrie's legs, bringing it back. She puts her chin to her chest and pushes with all her force while Sherry and I count to ten. I look down and see that the baby has half his head out.

"The head is almost out," I tell her with tears running down my face. I will never forget this moment.

"I'm tired, Matthew, so tired," she says in a whisper.

"Okay, how about we give one more push," Sherry says, looking at the doctor, who nods. "Big push, Karrie."

"I don't think I can." She closes her eyes. "It's too much. It hurts."

"You are the strongest person I know. You can do anything," I tell her right before Sherry yells out.

"Push, we need her to push."

My head snaps up at her urgency. I think Karrie heard it also, so she grabs her legs and pushes hard.

"Stop pushing," Dr. Noelle says. "Okay, the shoulders next and it'll just slide out. Push." And she does, she pushes till the doctor says, "Meet your baby." She places the baby directly on the towel that Sherry placed there.

Karrie lets go of my hand, holding onto our child. Her sobs fill the room. "My baby," she says while I bring her head to my lips, kissing her and looking down at my child.

"We have a boy," Dr. Noelle says. "If you will do the honors," she hands me the scissors, "in between the two white clamps."

I cut my son's umbilical cord.

Sherry takes my son from Karrie's chest, bringing him to the crib while she takes his heartbeat and his cries fill the room. Loud, angry cries.

"Go see him," Karrie says from my side, the doctor still between her legs. Walking over to the crib, I see his arms moving around while the nurse is putting a diaper on him and putting his name tag on his ankle.

I grab his small hand with my finger. He wraps it around the top. "He's so beautiful." He stops crying the minute he hears my voice. His eyes blink open slowly. "Hey there." His feet start to move now.

"We have a big boy, almost ten pounds. Good job, Mom," Sherry says while she puts a hat on him. "I'm going to wrap him up now so we can take him to go feed," she tells me while she wraps my son up like a burrito.

The nurse that met us at the elevator comes in. "Okay, I hate to crash the party, but I have a waiting room full of people pacing back and forth. Someone needs to go and tell them that this is a hospital and not a reception party."

I smile, thinking about the amount of people that must be outside. "Do you want me to stay or go and tell them?"

"You better go before they get some drones to fly in here," she says while the doctor finishes, taking off her gloves.

I walk to kiss her right when the doctor hands her the baby. "Here's your son."

Karrie grabs the baby, kissing his face. "He looks exactly like you." The baby's hands poke out from his blanket. "I love you," she tells him, "so, so much." She kisses his face, and he starts to fuss again.

"How about you try to nurse him and see if he's hungry?" Sherry says while Karrie presses the button on the bed to sit upright. "Now make sure that he latches on properly or you'll be getting cracked nipples."

"Are you hungry?" Karrie asks him while she takes her breast out, placing him the way Sherry tells her to. In a matter of seconds, my boy is latching on. "He's definitely his father's son." Her tired eyes meet mine. "Go tell the family."

I kiss her lips before walking out of the room.

Walking into the room, it goes dead silent. My mom sits down next to Cooper, who has his feet crossed at the ankles and his head down. Doug sits in the corner of the room, watching the golf game that's playing. Allison and Vivienne are sitting side by side. My Aunt Meghan and Uncle Tom sit up.

"I have a son." My voice cracks as I say it.

My mother gets up and walks to me, wrapping her arms around my waist. Allison is the next one who comes to me. The last one is Cooper, who grabs me by my neck, bringing me to him. The four of us hug with Zoe and Zara standing by Cooper's side.

"Okay, enough," Vivienne says. "Let me see a picture," she asks while I let go and grab my phone, showing her the pictures I took while he was getting weighed. "What's his name?"

"Karrie and I decided that we would name him Cooper Douglas Grant," I say, looking at Cooper. "Two of the strongest men we know."

Doug asks to see Karrie. I nod and tell him where she is.

"So what do you think, Grandpa, good name?" He doesn't have to say anything at all because I know in that moment that everything is something so perfect!

# EPILOGUE TWO

## KARRIE

*Six years later.*

"Cooper Douglas, you better get back here before I get your father!" I yell from the kitchen, looking back at the flour mess all over the brown floor, three little prints showing exactly where they went.

"I no do it," he yells from behind the couch in the family room. "Is Franny and Vivi." Franny aka Francis Parker, both our mothers' names combined. Our daughter came out one year later. They were almost what you call Irish Twins. I found out I was pregnant again when Cooper turned three months. It was a shock to both of us, especially since we literally only had sex the one time. Okay, maybe not one time, but we weren't going at it like rabbits. Okay, fine, it was daily, but it wasn't like twice or three times a day. He did travel with the team.

We decided to move out of the brownstone as soon as Cooper was born. Instead, we got a house in Long Island. The commute to the city isn't that bad, if the kids are sleeping. Plus, we had the summer house near Cooper and Parker. What I wanted was a nice and cozy house. Well, step in my husband and my father and then throw my father-in-law in there and here I am in an almost fifteen-bedroom home. I pretended to be pissed about it for months, especially when we found out that our parents had bought it for us. Cooper couldn't stand the fact that Dad put in half, so he put in the other half, and let's not talk about the gifts that arrive daily from them. All that aside, my kids are showered with so much love, it's what makes me look away most times.

Vivienne Allison came into the world two years after Francis. Again, no trying was needed. I was finally sleeping through the nights, teething was done, toilet training was almost done, and boom he shoots he scores.

I walk to the back of the couch where I see my three culprits. Cooper, with his black hair and blue eyes, starts talking first. "Franny want to make pancakes, Momma."

"No, I don't," my curly blond hair blue-eyed girl says with flour all over her face and hands. "Is Vivi."

My other blond child looks at me. All she's dressed in is a diaper.

"Where are your clothes and where is your father?" I stand with my hands on my hips.

Vivi answers first, "Shh, he's sleeping."

I shake my head and turn around, going into the game room or what was the game room and is now a princess shrine. Most of it vintage from Allison. There in the middle of the room lying on his back with blue eye shadow, pink lips, and orange cheeks is my husband sound asleep.

"See, Momma," Vivi answers, "he's so tired." She puts a finger to her lips, telling me to be quiet, but her whisper is her normal voice.

He is back home from his two-week long road trip. When I had only Cooper we would accompany him, but then when Francis came it was too tough, so he did it without us. Pouting the whole time.

*"I miss so much when I'm on the road." He started saying while he threw his bag on the bed. "I missed Francis rolling over." He turned back to get his stuff from our closet.*

*"Matthew, we all missed it. She woke up on her back." I pointed out, looking at the monitor beside my bed. Cooper was not kidding when he said he had someone to hook us up. The whole house had cameras in it and you could watch them on all the televisions. Beside our bed was a*

*monitor of all three kids' rooms, all three kids passed out.*

*"Still it's not fair." He almost sounded like Cooper. I was expecting him to stomp his foot.*

"Matthew," I say in a soft voice while he grumbles. "Matthew, you need to get up and come clean the kitchen."

He blinks his eyes open.

"Daddy, Franny and Vivi made a mess." Cooper comes forward.

"Oh, you are not going to get away with it this time," I tell him, knowing full well that Cooper has Matthew wrapped around his finger, along with the girls, who can never do any wrong.

"How did you guys make a mess when you were supposed to be resting with me?" Matthew sits up and grabs my hand, yanking me down onto his lap where he buries his face into my neck, biting it. A giggle escapes my lips.

"Is gross," Cooper says while the girls mimic their brother.

"Yeah, gross."

"What time is it?" Matthew asks me while planting butterfly kisses on my neck.

"It's clean up time," I answer while I place a hand around his shoulder, bringing him closer to me.

"Is anyone home?" I hear my father yell from the front door.

"Poppy!" all my kids say, running out of the room.

"So I was thinking we could have some alone time, so I called your father, who is taking them for the night." Matthew pulls his face from my neck. "What do you think, babe? Me, you, bubble bath?"

"The last time you had that plan we almost flooded the bathroom."

I smile when I think of all the towels it took to clean up the mess.

"That was actually your fault." His hands come up from my waist to cup my breasts. "You rode me so hard you splashed all the water out of the tub."

I don't have time to answer him since my father comes in carrying both girls in his arms. "Okay, I'm going to get this one dressed," he says to Vivi. "And then we are going to go to Chuck E Cheese's," he says and the kids lose their shit.

"Dad, please don't bring home any more knick-knacks. Seriously."

I try to get up, but Matthew holds me on his lap. When I feel his hard cock under me, I understand why.

"Honey, you can't tell a grandparent not to spoil your children." He looks at us both. "Now excuse us while we go and have fun without you two."

"Dad, please don't make them eat ice cream too late!" I yell at his retreating back while he walks away, saying ice cream for everyone. I shake my head, looking back at my husband.

"Your father almost saw my huge dick," Matthew says while I put my head on his shoulder. "That's awkward, right?" Now it's my turn to bury my face into his neck, giggling.

"Momma." The girls run back into the room together, Vivienne finally dressed. "We go." Her chubby baby arms wrap around my neck while Francis goes to see Matthew. "Don't be sad, we come back." She puts her head on Matthew's shoulder.

We kiss them both goodbye along with Cooper, who walks in the room with the 'I'm forced to come back' look.

We get up from the playroom and walk upstairs, ignoring the flour footsteps that are all over the house.

"You tired, babe?" Matthew asks while in our bedroom.

Family pictures are scattered all over the place. Matthew's idea, not mine. Actually there are frames everywhere. It's his thing that I made peace with. If he likes a picture it's in a frame. There are three big picture frames in our room, of each child's first ultrasound.

"I could use a shower," I tell him, pulling my shirt over my head, standing here in front of him with my yoga pants and white plain bra. Gone are the days of sexing it up. Now don't get me wrong. I still have a whole drawer full of lacy, frilly things. I just don't wear them on a normal basis. Luckily running after three kids has kept the weight off of me, but my body is different. My hips are fuller, my breasts less perky, and guess what, I love my body. Well, not as much as Matthew does, but just about.

"I could use a shower also." He winks at me, walking past me to the bathroom where he opens the glass shower door. Once the rain shower starts working he pulls his shorts down, showing me all of him. It's been seven years we've been together and he still takes my breath away. His body is on point with all the training he does. "You see something you like, babe?" His hands go straight to his thick cock that's already ready to party.

I peel my pants off, unsnapping my bra, letting it fall from my shoulders. "You're okay to look at," I say, walking past him into the shower, the water the perfect temperature.

Another thing my neurotic husband did was install the perfect water gauge. I let the water fall over my shoulders, putting my neck forward. I don't hear the door open and Matthew step in, but I feel him on my back, his hands cupping my breasts, rolling my nipples. I moan out, my hands going to the back where I fist him in my hands, stroking his cock. He leans over, kissing my neck while his hands travel down with the stream of water, his fingers running over my landing strip right before they roll over my clit and his fingers enter me. My head now falls back on his shoulder, my fist moving at the same speed as his fingers in me.

"Missed you, babe." I turn my head to meet his lips, our kiss like coming home every single time. His tongue twirls with mine, our mouths hungry. The hand that isn't stroking him leans back to pull his hair.

His fingers come out of me. His lips leave mine. "Gotta taste you," he says, pushing me to the bench in the back of the shower. "Sit down and open for me," he orders.

I sit on the bench, my back to the cold tiles giving me goose bumps all over my body. I put my feet on the seat ledge, bending my legs to the side.

Matthew gets on his knees in front of me, his hands cupping my breasts again, rolling the nipples, then leaning forward and taking one in his mouth, then biting down on it, the zing going straight to my core. He repeats the same thing to the other nipple. "Matthew." My head rolls on the wall. My back arches away from the wall.

"My girl wants to come?" He kisses down my stomach. "How do you want to come?" he asks, kissing my inner left thigh. "On my finger?" He kisses the right thigh now. "On my tongue?" He kisses me right above my clit. "Or my cock?" he says, taking two fingers and opening me up. "Hmmm." Is the last thing he says before he sucks my clit into his mouth, then trails his tongue to the bottom where his tongue slides into me. His fingers join his tongue, my hips thrusting upward to get him deeper into me.

My eyes watch his finger and tongue play with me, sliding in and out, rubbing me in all the right places. "I'm going to come," I tell him, grabbing his head, pushing it into my pussy, and I ride his face up and down, my fingers now rubbing my clit frantically back and forth. I'm about to let go when his tongue comes out of my pussy. His face rips away. He pulls me to stand up. I moan my displeasure the whole time.

"You get to come on my cock," he says, sitting on the bench. "Come get it."

His cock is in his hand, pushing it up. I walk to him, my feet going outside of his. I put one foot on the bench next to his hips, with the other on the other side. I take his cock in my hand, rubbing it through my folds, placing it at my entrance, and sliding down on him so fucking slow I feel every ridge that he has, every single vein all the way to the end, all the way till his balls hit my ass. My hands go to the back of his knees while I use my legs to go up and down on him, the angle making him hit my G-spot right away.

"Look at your pussy take my cock," he says, watching us, watching my pussy swallow all of his cock. The sight makes my pussy quiver. "Look at this clit." His finger goes into his mouth, wetting it and then rubbing it in circles while I ride him. He takes my clit in between his two fingers, squeezing the shit out of it, the pain making me rise up and then slam back down. My legs burn, my arms start to shake, and his cock grows bigger in me. "Atta girl. Come on my cock," he says, leaning forward, taking a nipple in his mouth while he bites down.

It's too much and with that final move I moan and come all over his cock. I come and come and come. My pussy spasms all over him. My eyes close and I feel his cock grow bigger and his hands on my hips now slam me down on him and he comes in me. My mouth covers his, swallowing his roar. When his hands roam from my hips up my back I know he is finished. Taking my mouth from his, I lean forward, our chests heaving against each other.

"Never gets old," he says, kissing the top of my wet head. "I could be old with only one hip and I would always find a way to make love to you."

I smile to myself. I wouldn't have it any other way.

When I finally slide into bed, he looks over at me, seeing me with a top on. "You know the rules. Kids aren't here, we are naked."

I roll my eyes at him and take off the shirt, throwing it on my table.

"And the panties, babe."

I shake my head, taking them off and putting them on top of my shirt.

"How long are you home for?" I ask him, settling on my pillow while he watches SportsCenter.

"It's a break, so five glorious days. I told Allison if she called me during these five days for any business I would block her from attending Christmas." Another thing that has changed is that Allison is now the team's Public Relations person. Mindy took another job at the same time that Allison graduated. It was a win-win for everyone. Well, except Matthew, who has to see his beautiful sister being hit on by his teammates. I'm not even going to get into the amount of things she signed him up to volunteer for and when he wanted to yell at her, she would use her my big brother is the best speech and he would do it.

"Well, this is interesting," the sportscaster says, "we got more Max Horton drama," the reporter starts saying.

I sit up in bed, watching the television while Matthew chuckles beside me.

"Allison is going to rip him a new asshole. I can't wait to watch this."

The reporter continues, "It seems that the bad boy of NHL has eloped. And the word on the ice is that the new bride is none other than Allison Grant." My mouth flies open while Matthew immediately sits up, grabbing his phone. "Allison is none other than Matthew Grant's sister, as well as Cooper Stone's stepdaughter." He stops talking for a second.

"You will remember that Max was charged as an accomplice to the rape charge that came six years ago. Of course those charges were dropped and he was cleared of all charges against him."

He turns off the television, getting out of bed while I watch him dial Allison and it must go straight to voice mail. "Aly, you get this message, you call me." He hangs up and then starts dialing another number. "You better fucking hope that what I heard is a fucking rumor." He hangs up, looking at me.

"I guess now would be a bad time to tell you I'm pregnant again?" I smile at him, hoping that this news brings him down before the vein in his head actually explodes.

THE END

SOMETHING SO IRRESISTIBLE
COMING JAN 2018

## ABOUT THE AUTHOR

When her nose isn't buried in a book, or her fingers flying across a keyboard writing, she's in the kitchen creating gourmet meals. You can find her, in four inch heels no less, in the car chauffeuring kids, or possibly with her husband scheduling his business trips. It's a good thing her characters do what she says, because even her Labrador doesn't listen to her...

# ACKNOWLEDGMENTS

Every single time I keep thinking it's going to be easy. It takes a village to help and I don't want to leave anyone out.

**My family**: To my children, Matteo, Michael, and Erica, Thank you for letting me do this. You encouraged me, you pushed me, you support me, and I am utterly and forever grateful for all of that. Well when you weren't complaining you want real home cooked food, which was often. Thank you for going on this journey with me.

**My Husband**: You share me with this hobby that has taken over our lives. Thank you for holding my hand and for coming up with words when I'm stuck. I love you more than words can say.

**Crystal**: My hooker. What don't you do for me? Everyone needs someone like you in their corner and I am so blessed than you chose to be in mine. I can't begin to thank you for the support, love and encouragement along the way.

**Rachel:** You are my blurb bitch. Each time you do it without even reading this book and you rocked it. I'm really happy I bulldozed my way into your life.

**Lori:** I don't know what I would do without you in my life. You take over and I don't even have to ask or worry because I know everything will be fine, because you're a rock star!

**Beta girls:** Teressa, Natasha M, Lori, Sian, Yolanda, and Carmen, Yamina. You girls made me not give up. You loved each and every single word and wrote and begged and pleaded for more.

**Madison Maniacs:** This group is my go to, my safe place. You push me and get excited for me and I can't wait to watch us grow even bigger!

**Mia:** I'm so happy that Nanny threw out Archer's Voice and I needed to tell you because that snowballed to a friendship that is without a doubt the best ever!

**Neda:** You answer my question no matter how stupid they sound. Thank you for being you, thank you for everything!

**Emily:** Thank you for holding my hand and not giving up.

**BLOGGERS**. THANK YOU FOR TAKING A CHANCE ON ME. EVEN WHEN I HAD NO COVER, NO BLURB, NO NOTHING! FOR SHARING MY BOOK, MY TEASERS, MY COVER, EVERYTHING. IT COULDN'T BE DONE WITHOUT YOU!

**My Girls:** Sabrina, Melanie, Marie-Eve, Lydia, Shelly, Stephanie, Marisa. Your support during this whole ride has been amazing. I can honestly say without a doubt that I have the best Squad of life!!!!

**And Lastly and most importantly to YOU the reader,** Without you none of this would be real. So thank you for reading!

Made in the USA
Middletown, DE
04 November 2021

51671126R00119